THE LISTENING TREE

KATHRYN RANDALL

ALL THINGS THAT MATTER PRESS

*To Frances –
Best of luck with
your writing! I enjoyed
meeting you!
Kathy*

THE LISTENING TREE
Copyright © 2021 by Kathryn Randall

ISBN: 978-1-7377671-2-1
Library of Congress Control Number: 2021946704

Cover (c) All Things That Matter Press

To my grandchildren—Alexandria, Tucker, Markus, Molly, and Aden. You have been my inspiration.

And to all young people: Find your special place in nature. Protect it with all your heart.

Acknowledgments

I am so thankful to all the people that helped make this book possible. All Things That Matter Press has been amazing and my editor, Deb Harris, is phenomenal.

Thanks to:

Kathie Giorgio from All Writer's Workshop and all the members of my Tuesday night critique group for their insightful and helpful feedback.

Angela Rydell of Writer's Inlet and our novel-writing workshop members for their advice and guidance.

Mary Raebel for always being available for coffee and bouncing ideas around.

All the hard-working scientists and biologists providing the world with research on climate change and how nature works.

A special thanks to my daughters, Jennifer and Kristin, and their spouses, Andi and Andy. Your love and support helped me stay the course on this long journey to publication.

And to my grandchildren, whose excitement at their Mamaw writing a book made me smile and warmed my heart.

Last but certainly not least, to my husband Charlie, who put up with my stacks of papers, post-a-notes, storyboards, and musings about the plot and character development. You have supported me for years as I've pursued this path of writing. Thank you and I love you.

CHAPTER ONE
RUTH 1896

Ruth followed a raindrop down the glass of the big bay window with her finger, wondering about what Nana just told her. They'd finished reading the new book by H.G. Wells, *The Time Machine*, yesterday. Nana was obviously confusing the book with real life.

"The raindrops, Ruth. They have wonderful powers. Why, they can bend time for humans," Nana said. She rocked in her chair, wrinkled arms folded across her chest like crinkled ribbons, glancing back and forth between the rain and her granddaughter. Outside, the constant rain sent rivulets of mud racing down the cobblestone streets of Sweetwater.

Ruth turned away from the window. "Oh, don't be so silly, Nana. It's just rain." She patted the old woman's arm. "There's no such thing as traveling through time." Nana told her so many tales. Some true, some the workings of her vast imagination.

Nana clutched Ruth's hand, squeezing hard. "Do you understand me?" Her eyes gazed into Ruth's, searching for something. "The Listening Tree needs help. You must travel through time in the raindrops."

"What are you saying, Nana?" Ruth stared at the large drops gliding down the window. "That humans can travel through time in raindrops?" What did raindrops and time have to do with her Listening Tree? The trolley rattled past the house, splashing water almost to the porch. Ruth jumped. Nana's cane crashed to the floor.

Nana, her eyes closed tightly, whispered, "The trees know." *The trees know?*

Nana turned her head slightly, her eyelids fluttering. "Get my poetry book. Quickly, Ruth, quickly." She slumped further into the chair. Her body seemed to wither with each difficult breath.

In a panic, Ruth ran to the bedroom. She grabbed the small book of poetry they often read together from the dresser and raced back to the parlor.

Nana sat in the same position, limp and shriveled, making Ruth think of a seedling that hadn't been watered for days. Ruth laid the book in her grandmother's lap, gently resting the frail hands on it.

"Here it is, Nana. What do you want me to do?"

Nana's voice was so faint Ruth had to lean over her to hear. "The back page."

Ruth stared at the book. Nana never allowed her to look through it. She always opened it to the page they were to read.

Ruth slid the book out from under Nana's hands and turned it over. Wedged between the last page and the back cover, she discovered a folded piece of parchment paper, wrinkled and brown. On it was written:

E and F
Psithurism and Petrichor 1845

She picked up the paper carefully and tried to unfold it. A drawing became visible, but before she could study it, the paper fell apart, crumbling into pieces that drifted slowly to the floor. She picked the biggest pieces up and tried to put them together. "What did it say, Nana?"

"Go to the Listening Tree," Nana whispered. "It knows. Go soon." She slumped forward, perfectly still.

"Nana?" Ruth waited for a moment, then slowly reached out, touching Nana's hand. The coolness of it startled her and she reached up, laying the back of her hand on Nana's cheek. She shivered, whispering, "Nana?"

Ruth felt a heaviness grow inside her chest, a sob so big she couldn't contain it. It burst from her with a powerful force. Like the thunder and rain from the clouds outside the window. Had Nana been telling the truth?

"I will go, Nana, I will."

CHAPTER TWO
RUTH 1896

Three days later, Ruth sat on her bed, tucked in under the attic eaves, listening to the rain striking the tin roof. Rain fell all night and all day, without stopping, sometimes with such intensity she thought the house would fall on top of her. She couldn't get Nana's funeral yesterday out of her mind, so she kept herself busy all day. She'd just finished gathering the eggs from the henhouse and racing down the flooded street to her best friend Willie's father's store for milk and flour. Her wet clothes lay in a pile by the attic door. She'd put on her only dry dress and pinafore, brushed her wet hair and braided it, and now wanted only a few moments of rest before going downstairs.

Ruth took her poetry book from the small dresser beside her bed, caressing the smooth cover. Nana'd given it to her several years ago, an exact duplicate of her own book. Ruth held the book up to her nose, breathing in its sweet fragrance. The covering was unlike any fabric Ruth knew—it never got wet or dirty, even in the harshest of weather. Nana said the magic of her poetry and thoughts written inside made the book indestructible.

Ruth opened the book to the pressed leaf she kept there. Two years ago, when she was eleven, she'd spied the beautiful oak leaf hanging from a low branch on a massive tree she'd named The Listening Tree. It was her safe place, in the forest up the hill from her home, where she confessed her greatest fears and secret thoughts. About her life. About her love of words.

Ruth took out fragments of Nana's mysterious note. She'd put them in her book the day Nana passed away. She moved them around on her bed, trying to piece them together. Psithurism and Petrichor. She recognized them as Greek words, but what did they mean? And what was this drawing? She had to get to the Listening Tree today. "Go soon," Nana had said. "The trees know."

Ruth sighed as tears crept down her cheeks. She picked up the pressed leaf and ran her fingers along the edges, being careful to have a soft touch. Nana, with whom she shared everything, was gone, but she still had the Listening Tree. She closed her eyes and whispered, "You will help me figure it out, won't you?"

Suddenly, the edges of the leaf warmed. She yanked her fingers away, touching them to her cheek. The leaf wasn't on fire. She didn't have a fever. *Odd*, she thought, wiping the tears from her face. She put the leaf and paper pieces back in the book, then stuffed it into the pocket of her pinafore.

Ruth walked down the two sets of stairs to the bottom floor of the house. She peered around the doorway into the kitchen. Her mother, who'd spent the last three days in bed, now sat at the kitchen table, staring straight ahead while the kettle whistled faintly on the woodstove behind her. The dying sounds of an almost empty teapot filled the silent room. Ruth walked to the stove, grabbing the kettle by the handle with a dish towel. Resting a hand on her mother's shoulder, she waited for a response. There was none. Her mother was not of this world at that moment, lost somewhere in a place of her own making. For as long as Ruth could remember, her mother had had spells like this. Her "dark times", she called them. But in the last year, ever since Ruth's brother died at birth, they occurred more frequently.

Ruth's heart felt heavy with sorrow for her mother. All of her children, except Ruth, had passed away shortly after birth. And now her own mother, Nana, was gone, too.

Ruth touched her mother gently on the arm and spoke in a quiet voice. "Mother, you've turned the kettle on. I'll pour you a cup of tea."

Her mother turned. Ruth brushed her mother's unkempt hair away from her face. Her eyes shimmered with wetness. Her mother was the most beautiful woman in the world to Ruth. Even now, in one of her dark times, when she wore the same dress for days and left her hair unbrushed and matted. Ruth knew why her mother spent days hidden in her room. She knew why her father spent so much time at the bars after work. They'd lost so many children and life was so difficult.

But what about me? I'm here. Deep inside, she longed for a different life.

She patted the poetry book in her pocket. "You are a word girl," Nana had said. "You collect words like Darwin collects specimens." Ruth imagined herself traveling the world, writing about the beautiful places in nature she read about, places like the Listening Tree. *I am going to be a writer!* Her mother sat, staring as if Ruth was invisible. She shoved a wave of anger down deep inside. *Someday, you'll see me, Mother, and you'll be proud.* Perhaps solving the mysterious message from Nana would make that possible.

Ruth poured the tea and set the teapot back on the stove. She watched the steam above her mother's cup float away and disappear into the air. Just then, the kitchen door flew open. Startled, Ruth grabbed

4

the book in her pocket as her father stumbled into the room.

"Lizzie, where's my dinner?" Her father's voice boomed through the kitchen. He swayed on his feet, every inch of him covered with black dust from the coal mine. He leaned against the cupboard near the doorway and threw his metal lunch bucket on the table with a loud clatter. It fell to the floor with a clang. Ruth's mother jumped.

"Stop it, Father!" Ruth stood behind her mother, her hands gripping her mother's shoulders. "Stay away. I'll tell you when dinner is ready."

"*You'll* tell me? You'll tell *me*? I'll show you who will tell who," her father roared, lurching around the table towards her.

"You're drunk again. Leave us alone," Ruth shouted.

Her father staggered, clutching the table for support. He slumped into the nearest chair, moaning as he put his head on the table and passed out.

Ruth helped her mother stand. "Come, Mother. I will help you to bed." She led her up the stairs. "Father will sleep there for a bit. Like he always does." She tucked her mother into bed. "I'll be back," she said, kissing her on the forehead. "I'll help then."

"Ruth." Her mother stared up at her and, in a soft, pleading voice, whispered, "You must go." She closed her eyes, pulling the blanket up to her face.

Ruth stood for a moment. In a strange way, she felt as if her mother knew what Nana had told her about the Tree. She rushed down the stairs, past her sleeping father, and flew out the back door, running as fast as she could away from the house. Away from her life. She raced across the back yard, past their dilapidated carriage shed, and scrambled over the wooden fence that separated the forest from their garden. At the top of the hill, she sprinted down the path that led to the Listening Tree.

The sight of it filled her with comfort. The rain stopped. The late afternoon sun filtered through the large canopy, glistening off waterdrops on its reddish-brown leaves, warming her as she sat down at its base, pressing her back into the bark.

"Now that Nana's gone, you're all I have," she whispered up into the branches. "Oh, how I wish Nana could have lived forever." The branches above her swayed gently, even though she felt no breeze. A leaf drifted down and landed on her lap.

Ruth picked it up. Every so often, she found a leaf like this, one with a tiny path eaten through it. This one looked different, though. She studied it, tracing the path with her finger.

"Why, I think it spells something," she exclaimed, staring at the leaf. Could it have something to do with Nana's dying words?

Words are seeds, it said. She traced the path with her fingers again.

She wasn't imagining it.

She stood up and took out her poetry book, placing the new leaf inside. She walked back a few steps to look at the Tree. "What does all this mean?"

A soft red light radiated from inside her poetry book, and warmth spread through her hands. Ruth gasped as everything around her began to swirl and spin. The sweet, fresh smell of the air after a rainfall became overwhelming and the gentle sound of rustling leaves filled her ears, even though there was no breeze.

A sense of peace overcame her, even as she looked down to see her body breaking into tiny dust-like particles. She watched as the black specks of herself swirled about as if blown by the wind. They lingered in the air for a moment, and then, bit by bit, she vanished into a large root in the ground.

CHAPTER THREE
MICHAEL 1966

Michael threw another bag of grain onto the truck as his father and his older brother Matt went back into the feed mill. He leaned against the side of the truck, thinking about the lecture his father gave him at breakfast. Again. Every day, he heard the same reasons why he should quit school and work on the farm. He didn't remember Matt getting lectures like that when he turned thirteen.

Rain began to fall in sprinkles, making dirty trails of wet dust running down the truck. Michael couldn't wait to go to the forest when they got back to the farm.

"Get over here, Mike, would ya?" Matt yelled from the loading dock. "Where's your head, anyway? Pretending you're Captain Kirk kissing those alien chicks? Or maybe you're at that tree of yours?" Matt pursed his lips and blew Michael a kiss.

"Shut up." Michael walked over, grabbing the bag of grain from him. "Here comes Dad."

John Martin jumped off the dock, throwing a grain bag on the truck bed. He brushed the dust from his overalls and slapped his hands together.

He sucked on the blade of hay between his lips, giving Michael and his brother a wink and a grin. "That's the last bag. Your mother'll go crazy when she sees all this dust. The woman lives on a farm, for God's sake, right, boys?" Michael's father hoisted himself up behind the steering wheel.

"Right on, Dad. Mom's too uptight about the kitchen floor." Michael rolled his eyes at the thought of his mother standing in the kitchen doorway, broom in hand, glaring angrily at them as they entered from the barn. He crammed himself up against the truck door, away from his brother, who straddled the stick shift in the middle of the seat.

"Right on? What does that mean? Right on what? Right on Route 16? Just speak normal English, boy." He reached over to pat Michael's ball cap. "We talked about that this morning." He threw the truck into gear. "Let's get back to the farm before the rain starts. I don't want the grain getting wet."

"Hey, why don't you beam us to the farm, Mike? Use some of that *Star Trek* science." Matt laughed, elbowing Michael.

"When I boldly go where no man has gone before—and I will—I won't be taking you. Bummer, huh?" Michael looked out the window. Dust swirled beside the truck as they sped down the dirt road. Dark clouds crept across the sky. It looked like a planet where the Starship Enterprise landed in one episode. Michael wanted to captain a spaceship, travel to different worlds, different times. Far away from his father wanting him to quit school to work on the farm.

He inhaled the scent of fresh cut hay as they passed field after field. Only one aroma was better: the smell of the forest. He longed to be at his favorite spot, beneath the huge oak tree in the woods near the farm. The Listening Tree. The name was carved into the bark on one side of it, along with the date 1896. Michael had no clue who'd carved it all those years ago, but the name fit. The Tree listened to him every time he got frustrated or sad or needed a place to rest.

Michael curled his hand around the woodcarving in his pocket. He rubbed his fingers over the alphabet etched into the small tree whittled from a branch of the oak. He'd read better one day. He'd study and become a starship captain. Not quit school to be a farmer. It would just take him longer, that's all. He wanted to tell all the people that called him dumb if they couldn't tell a "b" from a "d", they'd have trouble reading, too.

Yesterday, he'd been standing in the hallway at school when he heard the familiar, "Heh, Dimwit!"

His throat had dried up instantly. He couldn't swallow. Down the hallway strode Robert. Robert's dad worked in the local coal mine. The mine wanted to expand and take the forest behind Michael's family farm.

"Heh, Dimwit, I said." Robert stood in front of him. "The mine is going to cut the forest behind your farm, starting next month. My dad says we're going to be rolling in the dough soon."

Michael took deep breaths, his T-shirt heaving up and down with each one. They would never cut down the Listening Tree. Never.

"And my dad said your dad wants you to quit school and work on the farm." Robert twirled his fingers beside his head. "Might as well, because nothing is goin' on in there, big boy."

Thinking about it now, Michael's head pounded. He couldn't believe his dad talked to other people about him quitting school. He wished he could transport himself to the Tree and get away from everyone.

"Mike, help Matt unload the grain." His father's voice brought him out of his thoughts as they pulled up the driveway to the barn.

When the last bag was stacked, he yelled, "I'll be back, Dad," and raced out of the barn.

"It's gonna rain again soon," his father shouted. "Get back before that. You know how your mother gets about mud in the house."

Michael stopped and turned. "Sure, Dad."

"And don't forget, we're gonna talk about your future tonight, son."

"Sure, Dad." He shook his head and waved as he bolted down the driveway, across the dirt road in front of the barn, and through the field. He jumped over the old stone fence between the field and the forest, racing on the path to the Listening Tree. Racing away from his life.

He rounded the turn and bent over, breathing heavily. The Listening Tree stood in front of him, late afternoon sun penetrating through its branches. He plopped down at its base and laid his head against the trunk.

"Man, I wish Dad would stop trying to get me to quit school." He took out his carving. "I'll show him. I'll be captain of a starship someday." He glanced up as a plane flew overhead. "Or at least I'll be a pilot." Leaves swished above him, swaying gently even though no breeze blew.

Michael walked a few steps away from the tree and tripped over something. Reaching down, he picked up a twisted and gnarled branch that had no bark. It must have just fallen because he knew it wasn't there when he arrived just minutes before. Turning it over, he saw a tiny trail carved in it. Probably made by a wood borer. Wood borer larvae grew by chewing their way through wood. He examined the trail. Now, that was strange. It looked like the trail formed letters.

Grabbing a stick, he scratched the letters into the dirt by the tree, and stood back, holding his carving. H-E-L-P spells help, he knew that word. U-S spells us. Help us.

Startled, he looked around, searching the forest. He looked up at the Listening Tree. Help who?

A soft red light radiated from inside his carving, and warmth spread suddenly through his hands. Michael gasped as everything around him began to swirl and spin. The sweet, fresh smell of the air after a rainfall became overwhelming and the gentle sound of rustling leaves filled his ears, even though there was no breeze.

A sense of peace overcame him, even as he looked down to see his body breaking into tiny dust-like particles. He watched as the black specks of himself swirled about as if blown by the wind. They lingered in the air for a moment, and then, bit by bit, he vanished into a large root in the ground.

CHAPTER FOUR
ARABETH 2035

"The last day of school for the year is officially over. Good luck with your summer science projects, and don't forget to enjoy your vacation." Ms. Countryman's voice sounded throughout the halls of Sweetwater Middle School. The word vacation had barely left her lips before the hallways filled with students clamoring clumsily to get their jam-packed lockers emptied.

Arabeth stood at a bench in the school greenhouse. She poked a hole in the soil of the small pot in front of her and gently set a delicate seedling into it. Adding it to the row of newly planted pots for her summer genetics project, she whispered, "See you tomorrow." Her plants needed tending every day, even on weekends and vacations.

Arabeth raced out of the greenhouse to catch the bus. She punched her home GPS coordinates into the Bus App on her Skincom as she dashed to the stop in front of the school. She couldn't wait to get to the Listening Tree. Sporadic raindrops fell as she ran. A storm was coming.

Would Mom and Dad make her stay home instead of going to the Tree? They were both climate scientists, always outdoors, and yet they were so protective of her. They knew she loved being in the rain, and that she was totally responsible. She couldn't figure them out sometimes. Did they act that way because she was adopted?

Arabeth stomped up the bus steps. She hated being adopted. She plopped into an empty seat at the back of the bus and took a deep breath. Her seventh grade science teacher, Mr. Grundle, known to all the students as Fuzzy Grumbles for his wild hair and grouchiness, ended the final day with a bang when his last experiment backfired, sending him ducking between the lab desks in the front row. Everyone rushed out of class, totally freaked out. As if the last day of school wasn't exciting enough, right?

Arabeth stared out the bus window. She watched the rain sliding down the glass, starting out as individual beads of water, then joining together as the wind blew them into each other. One giant raindrop made up of many tiny ones. Cohesion and adhesion at work. Thinking logically made her feel calmer.

She rubbed her necklace. On it hung an acorn from her and Paz, her best friend's, special place in nature, the tree they called The Listening Tree. They'd discovered the tree when they were in second grade, and found the name carved into the bark. Twice. One was dated 1896 and the other 1966. Who had carved the name? Was it the same person twice? The name fit the tree perfectly. The tree did listen. To all her secret fears and thoughts. She and Paz had made a pact four years ago, when they were nine, to protect the Listening Tree forever, with their lives if necessary. She'd heard her parents talking in bed last night and hadn't slept at all, thinking about their pact.

"What are we going to do?" she thought she heard her mother say. "It may be too late to save the Sweetwater Preserve."

Arabeth strained to hear her father's reply, but his voice was too low and muffled from the wall between their bedrooms.

Was the Listening Tree in danger?

The bus bumped along. She grabbed the genetics book from the library out of her backpack and began flipping through the pages. Chromosomes, genes, and traits all made sense to her. Did her dark brown eyes come from her mother or her father? She wanted to know so much about her parents. She would find them one day, her real family.

Right now, she needed to focus on her summer science experiment. An awesome project would help her reach her goal: world renowned geneticist Dr. Arabeth Wilkins. Arabeth smiled. Taking the bus gave her more time to think about it than riding her bike.

"Well, there's my favorite science girl. What brings you on the bus?"

Arabeth jumped as a boy dropped down into the seat beside her.

Zarek Millstone, the annoying boy who sat next to her in science class. Gross.

"My bike's broke," she muttered, eyeing an empty seat two rows up that suddenly looked inviting. "Can you let me out?" She tried to push her way around him.

"Hey, what're you doing for your science project?" Zarek slouched, resting his knees on the back of the seat in front of him, blocking her way. "Mine's going to be on genetics." He glanced at the book in her hand. "Looks like yours is, too. Maybe we can help each other? I mean, I just don't get RNA transcription. Can you explain it to me sometime?"

Arabeth's shoulders fell. She didn't want to spend the entire ride home answering more of Zarek's endless questions. Why was he always following her around, bothering her? She should have stayed at the greenhouse and waited for her parents to pick her up. Her seedlings wouldn't have asked her anything at all.

"I love genetics, don't you?" Zarek scratched his head. "Hey, can you roll your tongue? That's a genetic trait, right?" He turned toward her, rolling his tongue into a tight U shape. "I'll have to see if my father can do that. Not that he'd even have time to do it if I ask."

Her Skincom dinged, signaling her stop was coming up. "That'd work," she said "Besides, it takes two seconds to roll your tongue. I'm sure your dad has that amount of time, right?"

"You'd think." Zarek shrugged, looking away.

Arabeth didn't know what to say. "My stop's here. Gotta go." She shoved Zarek towards the edge of the seat.

"Well, guess I'll see ya around," he shouted out the window as she jumped off the bus.

"Sure," said Arabeth, breaking into a run. She ran across the road, past the old mine entrance, overgrown with invasive vines and bushes, and through the field to the forest.

When she saw the Listening Tree, she finally felt like she could breathe calmly. The late afternoon sun, shining through the branches, cast rays of light and shadow on the ground nearby. Arabeth sat with her back against the tree, resting her arms on her knees, her head on her hands.

She thought about Zarek. She knew not everybody loved science as much as she did. Maybe that was why he was always asking her questions. And what did his father do that kept him so busy? Rumors had flown around Sweetwater when the Millstones arrived, about Zarek's father's strange behaviors and businesses. No one knew what he did.

She stared up into the branches over her head, thinking that maybe she should be nicer to him, even though he irritated her. The branches swayed, rustling the leaves. But there was no breeze.

Suddenly, her parents' whispered conversation from the night before ran through her head. Was the Listening Tree in danger? She patted the trunk behind her, knowing she would protect it.

A ray of light filtered through the canopy and fell on an odd-shaped acorn a few feet away from her. She walked over and picked it up, turning it over and over. It had sprouted, but the stem and leaves coiled and looped in a strange pattern. She put it on the ground, attempting to straighten out the stem. But it wouldn't stay uncoiled. Each time, it twisted back into the same shape.

Arabeth thought she saw words in the coiled shape. She read it several times to make sure she wasn't seeing things that weren't there. *Bring the past to the future*, it clearly said.

Arabeth took a few steps back, absentmindedly rubbing her acorn necklace. She looked up at the Listening Tree. "What does it mean?"

A soft red light radiated from inside her necklace, and warmth spread suddenly through her hand. She gasped as everything around her began to swirl and spin. The sweet, fresh smell of the air after a rainfall became overwhelming and the gentle sound of rustling leaves filled her ears, even though there still was no breeze.

A sense of peace overcame her, even as she looked down to see her body breaking into tiny dust-like particles. She watched as the black specks of herself swirled about as if blown by the wind. They lingered in the air for a moment, and then, bit by bit, she vanished into a large root in the ground.

CHAPTER FIVE
IN THE DESERT

Ruth tumbled through a dark space, twirling as if in a giant tornado, feeling like she was disintegrating into a million pieces that filled the universe. She tried to scream, but all that came out was a strange garbled sound. Last summer, she'd tried to shout to her friend Willie as they swam in the pond, playing Marco Polo underwater. Dark water surrounded her, but she felt happy as she floated near Willie. They laughed when they surfaced. But there was nothing to laugh about now.

After what seemed like forever, she felt a pressure everywhere, as if giant hands were gathering every piece of her, molding her back together. The pressure became so intense, she thought she'd die—if she wasn't already dead. She concentrated on the smell of fresh rain and the sound of leaves gently rustling in the wind to calm herself.

Then, as if popping out of a bubble, she fell through the darkness onto something hard, landing on her hands and knees, her poetry book still in her hand. She sputtered and coughed until her sides ached.

"What happened?" Ruth squeezed her eyes tightly as panic filled her chest. She moaned as her hands and knees pressed painfully on what felt like tiny pieces of rock where she knelt. Raising her head inch by inch, afraid of what she might see, Ruth forced herself to open her eyes slowly as she stood, grimacing in pain, brushing off tiny pieces of rock embedded in her knees.

Sand and rock stretched for as far as she could see. No houses or cobblestone streets. Ruth saw several run-down buildings off in the distance. And a large broken sign.

M lst n   I d st es

What did the sign say? The temperature was so hot that the air around her moved in shimmering waves of heat, like ripples of water in the ocean. The place looked like it hadn't rained in months. Or even years. Nothing looked alive. No greenery, no people, no animals. She put down her poetry book and rubbed her hands over her pinafore, hair, and arms. She was still in the same body, with the same clothes. So this couldn't be Heaven, could it?

She noticed a shadow cast on the ground by something behind her. Ruth whirled around. She had to look, though every part of her body quivered with fear at what she might see. She felt the same way at times when her father came home drunk and angry. She feared what he would do then and she feared what she would see now. She told herself she had to deal with it, just like she had to deal with him.

A tree stood behind her in a square of dirt. The soil, dry and caked, looked as hard as stone. A faint breeze blew, and as she bent over to touch the dirt, tiny particles of dust swirled around her fingers. The dust accumulated around the base of the tree, filled the crevices in the bark. The air smelled stale and hot, not like the air around the trees at home.

Ruth searched the tree, looking for signs of life or anything threatening. One main trunk rose about twenty feet upwards. Broken branches, some looking like petrified wood, stuck out starting about five feet up the trunk. The tree looked like a giant old woman with wrinkled, skinny arms. For a moment, she was reminded of her grandmother.

She gasped. Wherever she was, was she here alone? Where was her family? Would she be able to get back home to them? A verse from a poem by Lewis Carroll flew drifted through her mind.

The pictures with their ruddy light,
Are changed to dust and ashes light,
And I am left alone with night

A shiver traveled through her. Here and there, greenish-brown leaves grew from some of the smaller branches. The edges of the leaves were brown and curled up from lack of water. There was no sign of life anywhere. *How did I get here?*

Something about the dead tree stirred an emotion inside her. She stepped up to it, touching the bark with her fingertips. Looking up at the branches, she was filled with an overwhelming sadness. Thoughts of her nana made her sad. Possibly never seeing her family again did, too. Ruth stared at the partially dead leaves hanging from the tree. Something about this tree also made her sad.

She stretched up to touch a leaf on one of the lower branches. Ruth pulled it gently from the branch, placing it tenderly in her palm. Dry and thin, it felt like it would crumple apart at her touch. Where had she seen this shape before? She imagined the withered leaf plump from rain, bursting with color. Suddenly, she knew. This leaf matched the leaf in her poetry book. Setting it down on the crusty dirt, she picked up her book.

Marks from her fingernails were embedded in its cover, but the book no longer glowed or felt warm. She opened the book to make sure the leaf she'd placed inside was still there. It was, and it looked like the ones on the dead tree in front of her.

A tear slipped from the corner of her eye, and she choked back a sob. The leaf was something familiar in this strange, hot, and lifeless place. What would happen to her mother if she never went home? A twinge of guilt gripped her for wishing for a new life. Ruth touched the leaf in the book. It might be the only thing she had left of her life as it was before.

"Well, at least, I have you with me," she whispered. For a second, she thought the dead tree quivered ever so slightly, even though the breeze had stopped. The smell of rain wafted over her.

"You have who with you?" a voice said. Ruth shrieked, turning to find herself face to face with a boy peering around the dead tree. Trying to keep her hands steady, she thrust the poetry book in front of her as if it were a sword. "Who are you?"

The boy took a step out from behind the tree towards her.

"Stay away from me!" Ruth waved the book back and forth as she slowly backed away.

The boy moved out from behind the tree, pointing something at Ruth. It looked like some type of carving. "Hey, I won't touch you if you don't touch me." He shifted from one foot to another, holding the carving out in one hand while touching his hair and his face with his other. Ruth wondered if this was some strange attack ritual. Was he human?

She held the book in front of her. "I'm not afraid to use this book on you if you come at me, whoever or whatever you are."

He patted his arms, chest, and legs. "Two arms, two legs. Guess I'm all here." He took another step away from the tree.

Ruth backed up, waving the book at him.

He sliced the carving through the air. "Look, this carving is pretty sharp. I'll defend myself if I have to."

Ruth squinted in an attempt to appear meaner than she felt as she looked the boy over. He wore strange-looking blue pants covered with dust, and a torn, dirty white shirt. He stood at least a foot taller than her. She looked up at him and said, in her most menacing tone of voice, "I'm not going to hit you. Did you bring me here? And if so, pray tell me how and why."

"Me? I don't pray." He frowned and glanced around. "I don't know why I'm here, either." He looked at her and shrugged. "Whoever you are, why are you dressed like you came out of my history book?" Instantly, his eyes widened and flashed with excitement. "This is too far out." He lowered the carving and slapped his head. "Holy Batmobile. Did you? I mean, did you come out of my history book?"

"Of course not," Ruth said, frowning. What was a bat mobile?

Whoever this person or thing was, his actions didn't seem to be very threatening. She thought he actually looked quite comical.

"Look, I'll put my book away." She slid the poetry book into her pinafore pocket. "And you put your carving away." She placed her hands on her hips. "This is my only dress. It's what I wear every day," she explained, holding her chin up in the air. She looked him up and down. "I won't mention how strange—and filthy—your attire is. Or how big you are. Why, you're the biggest boy I have ever seen. Perhaps you're from a different planet and have taken me there?"

The boy put his carving in his pocket and laughed. "Me? An alien?" He looked up at the sky, a bright cerulean blue without a cloud in sight. "Where have I seen a place like this before? Cloudless sky, dry heat, no rain." Suddenly, he jumped up and down, clapping his hands together. He let out a loud whoop, clasping his head in his hands and smiling. Ruth almost laughed at the sight of him.

"So groovy! I get it now. That's what I thought! I've transported somewhere. It's true! *Star Trek* is true!" He shouted up into the air, "Laugh's on you, Matt!"

"Star trek? What are you talking about? Who treks to the stars? Who's Matt?" Ruth shook her head. Her ears rang, her head throbbed, and she felt nauseous with uncertainty. Who was this boy or creature in front of her? Where had he come from? *Where on Earth, or anywhere else, am I?*

Suddenly, the tree quivered and shook. Ruth and the boy backed away as the bark on the tree glistened, and the smell of fresh rain filled the air. A girl stumbled out through the tree's bark as if someone had shoved her from behind.

She plopped onto the ground, but jumped up instantly, looking around. "I don't know what's happened," she said, her eyes widening when she saw them. "I thought I heard someone say aliens." Ruth saw her grab at something around her neck as she looked behind her.

"Did I just pop out of this tree?" She squinted at the necklace in her hand, glanced back at the tree, and then at Ruth and the boy. "Aliens? I don't think so. You both look as human as I am."

The three of them stood staring at each other for a few moments before anyone moved or spoke. The sun blazed overhead. The girl took off her hat, revealing curly blue hair that fell to her shoulders. She wiped the sweat from her face with her sleeve and looked at a device on her wrist.

"Um, did you know you have blue hair?" The boy pointed at her. He looked intently at her wrist. "Far out, what is that?" He stared at her. "Oh, man, do you have a transporter? On your wrist? Cool!" He frowned. "I didn't think *Star Trek* was real. But, man, maybe it is! Are you from the Starship Enterprise?"

The new girl studied them. "Starship Enterprise?" She laughed. "Of course not. That's a fictional TV show from long ago." Crossing her arms in front of her, she said, "And what's wrong with blue hair?"

"I've just never seen a girl with blue hair. I thought maybe transporting turned it blue," he said. "Did I beam to this place?" He looked around, scratching his head. "I'm confused. I mean, where are we? Am I on a TV set? Are you an actress? Or is this for real?" He looked at them, raising his forehead and shrugging. "Just like Captain Kirk does on *Star Trek* when he transports, I broke into a gazillion pieces. And then I found myself here. Did you?"

"I did," said Ruth, watching the new girl clutching her necklace again. "I felt like I was dissolving into millions of pieces that flew through space and then suddenly were pushed back together by something. Or someone. If that's what you mean by transporting?" Ruth shivered. "I could smell rain and hear leaves rustling. That kept me from being scared to death. Then I was here. Alone." She pointed at the boy. "That is, until you showed up." She pointed to the tree. "I guess we all came out of that tree?"

"Yeah, man, I think so, too," said the boy, turning to the new girl. "Are you one of those hippie girls from California? You sure look like one. Only I didn't know they had blue hair."

"Hippie girls? California? No." She looked at Ruth. "I experienced the same thing. It felt frightening, but the smell and the sound," she dropped the hard grip she had on her necklace, "made it less scary." Extending her fist, she said, "I'm Arabeth."

Ruth took a step backwards. "My name is Ruth, but I'm not sure what you mean with your fist." Arabeth seemed sensible and safe. Perhaps she judged her wrong.

"Just trying to be friendly. Fist bumping is a greeting." Arabeth looked puzzled. "We bump our fists together. To show friendship."

"I've never heard of it," said Ruth, but she extended hers, catching a glimpse of Arabeth's necklace. It was an acorn. Just like the one on her Listening Tree at home. She couldn't be an alien.

The boy stepped forward. "Well, then, I'm Michael. Groovy to meet you, Ruth." He bumped his fist against hers. "And you, too, Arabeth."

"Okay, Michael." Arabeth pulled her hand away, rubbing her fingers.

Michael smiled. "Sorry. My hands are pretty strong, I guess. Dad says it's from baling hay on our farm and wood carving. I just finished carving a blue-winged teal for this year's Sweetwater Carving contest." He looked at her wrist. "What *is* that thing? I've never seen one before." Michael scowled. "I'm so confused. It's really bugging me, trying to figure out what's going on."

Ruth thought for a minute. Arabeth said the show, *Star Trek*, was a TV show from the past. But what was a TV? She felt like Michael. Confused. What was going on?

Suddenly, a line from *The Time Machine* flew through her mind. *We all have our time machines, don't we? Those that take us back are memories ... And those that carry us forward, are dreams.* Perhaps they'd traveled through time. She shivered at the possibility.

"What year is it?" she asked Michael.

"1966, of course." He looked perplexed. "Why?"

Nana told Ruth many stories about "bending time", as she called it. And the last thing she mentioned was raindrops and time. "It's 1896 for me," she said softly. Could Nana have been telling the truth?

"1896? That explains your dress, not knowing TV, why you didn't know about fist bumping," Arabeth exclaimed, jolting Ruth from her thoughts.

Ruth smoothed out her pinafore. "It's what everyone wears." She looked at Michael. "You said something about Sweetwater? Why, that's the name of *my* town. Sweetwater is a mining town, though, not a farming town."

Arabeth exclaimed, "I'm from a place named Sweetwater, too. But it's not a farming area or a coal mine. It's a biodiversity preserve." She ran her fingers through her hair. "And the year is 2035."

"What's a biodiversity preserve?" asked Michael, his face scrunched into a frown.

Arabeth stared at him. "You really don't know, do you?" She looked at Ruth, who shook her head. "You really are from different times." Arabeth paused. "Well, it's a place where we protect all the different species living in an area." She took a few steps in a circle as she spoke. "Landscapes change over time, you know? And Sweetwater was a mining town that got flooded. And then some of it became farmland." She stopped pacing and stood staring at the dead tree. "And now, it's a preserve."

"I think I'll nickname you Spock." Michael looked at Arabeth. "You explain things just like him."

Ruth felt overwhelmed. "2035? That's over a hundred years into the future. And there are lots of towns with the same name." They were all from the same town? Could this really be happening? "I guess we all popped out of this tree. It's very perplexing. Like something out of an H.G. Wells book."

Ruth looked from the dead tree to Michael and Arabeth. There *was* something connecting all of them. Strange as it seemed, she knew it was more than just the same town. All of a sudden, her nana's last words flew into her mind. *Raindrops can bend time.* And that *the trees know.* What had she meant? Had it been a warning about this very thing?

CHAPTER SIX
SOMEONE NEW APPEARS

Arabeth gazed up at the tree while Ruth walked quietly around it, carrying her poetry book open to the page with her leaf from home and the leaf she plucked earlier. Michael fiddled with his carving. He sat down, propping himself against the tree.

"I have a tree at home, in Sweetwater," he said, looking like he was far away in a different place. "I like to go there and lean against it. People make fun of me about it. But I feel good there." He sighed. "Somebody else must have liked the same tree, too. Because I found a name, The Listening Tree, carved into it." He jumped up, pointing at Ruth. "And the date 1896."

Ruth gasped, struggling to catch her breath as he spoke. "Do tell, Michael. My friend Willie and I carved that exact phrase into an oak tree in the forest behind our house. With the date 1896."

"And my friend Paz and I go to a tree with that carved in it also. It's got two dates, though. 1896 and 1966." Arabeth looked at Michael.

"Holy cow! That would be me. I carved that earlier this year." He walked around the tree, shaking his head.

Arabeth twirled her hair, thinking. "So, here's what we know so far. We have several things in common. We seem to come from the same town, but in different time periods. In that town, we all seem to know the same tree, and now we all were somehow transported to this place by something or someone. Through this tree." She put her hand on the bark.

Ruth looked at Arabeth's necklace, then over at Michael, twirling his carving. Glancing down at her leaf, she said, "Here is something, perhaps. I have a leaf I've pressed from the Listening Tree. I keep it in this poetry book. I see you have a carving, Michael, and you have an acorn necklace, Arabeth. Are they both from the Listening Tree?"

"Yep," said Michael as Arabeth nodded.

"So, we all have something from that tree. What does that have to do with traveling through this tree?" Arabeth asked, staring up at it.

Ruth held out her open poetry book to Arabeth. "Look. This is a leaf I picked when I first landed here. It looks the same as my leaf."

Arabeth took the book and studied the two leaves carefully. "You're right. These are both leaves from the same species of tree, *Quercus alba*, the White Oak." She walked to the tree in front of them.

Michael shook his head. "How do you know all this stuff, Arabeth?"

Ruth whispered, "The wonder is that we see these trees and not wonder more."

Michael and Arabeth looked at her questioningly.

"Ralph Waldo Emerson said that. It is a bit odd that this tree is the same species as all of ours."

They walked around the tree, clearing a thick layer of dust off of it in some places. "Quick. Look here!" Michael waved them around to his side. He brushed an area of the bark clean. It exposed a carving into the tree that said The Listening Tree 1896 and, below that date, 1966. "That's my writing," he stammered. "I carved that last month." He shook his head in disbelief. "So, this *is* the Listening Tree. But what happened to it? And how did it get here?"

"I don't think it went anywhere," said Ruth.

"What do you mean?" Michael patted the dry, brittle bark and looked up at the dead branches above him.

Ruth didn't know how to explain what she thought. She didn't know if they'd believe it, or if she even believed what she was about to say, but she took a dreep breath and voiced her conclusion. "I think we went through time. Through the Listening Tree."

Arabeth laughed. "Scientists have been trying to prove time travel is possible for years. No one ever came up with the idea of traveling through time in a tree." She stopped laughing and added haltingly, "But we're all here from different times. There has to be an explanation."

Ruth told them what her nana said before she died, and what happened to her leaf and herself as she disappeared.

Arabeth looked perplexed. "Sounds like we all had the same experience, but with a different object." She held up her acorn necklace.

Ruth patted her poetry book. "Yes, which makes sense. Each one of us has a special object from the Tree, something that reminds us of how special the Tree is to each of us. What if the Listening Tree has feelings for us, too? What if—I know it sounds ridiculous—but what if the Tree needs us and somehow brought us here?" She pointed. "My nana said the trees know."

A look of dismay came over Arabeth's face. "My parents. I heard them last night, talking about how it might be too late to save the preserve."

Michael asked, "Is the Listening Tree on the preserve in your time?"

"Yes. The whole area has been made into a preserve."

The dust from the dried dirt around the tree swirled at their feet in a sudden gust of wind. Arabeth wiped the small beads of sweat from her forehead as she glanced at their surroundings. Waves of heat flickered in the air around them. "Do you think we're in the future beyond 2035? If my parents are right, something must be going to happen in my time, but what could it be? What could make the future so destructive to our Tree?"

The tree began to quiver and shake. Its bark glistened and the smell of fresh rain filled the air. Ruth grabbed Michael by the arm as they jumped back.

An old man stumbled out of the tree, as if someone inside had pushed him. He landed on the dusty dirt in front of them. His white hair stuck out from his head.

"Oh, dear," he mumbled, pushing himself off the ground, brushing the dust from his pant legs, and straightening up—inch by inch, it seemed to the young people. Dust speckled his white lab coat and clung to his greyish-white beard that reached to his shirt collar. He took off his lopsided glasses and wiped his eyes, sending tiny particles of dirt flying out from bushy eyebrows comprised of wiry grey hairs jetting out in all directions. "I see you are all here," he said, pointing at each of them. "Ruth, Michael, and Arabeth. Sorry it took me so long to get here. I'm a bit discombobulated, so give me a minute."

"You know our names?" said Ruth, her eyes wide.

"Did you bring us here?" asked Michael.

Arabeth opened her mouth, then closed it again. After a few seconds, she whispered, "Mr. Grundle?"

CHAPTER SEVEN
MR. GRUNDLE

"Mister Grundle? Is it really you?" Arabeth repeated as she took a couple steps closer to the wild-looking man in front of them.

"It's me, Arabeth, but let's dispense with the formalities, shall we? Just call me Fuzzy like in school." He smirked, setting his glasses back on his nose. As he moved them up into their proper position, his eyes seemed to grow three sizes larger, so thick were the lenses. "Should get that laser surgery, I guess, and dispense with these antiquated glasses."

Ruth could see Arabeth's shoulders relax and a broad grin sweep across her face. "Fuzzy!" She ran over and gave him a big hug. "Oh, it's great to see someone I know. I hope you can explain all this."

Fuzzy patted Arabeth's shoulder, turning to extend a dusty hand to Ruth.

"Francis Ferdinand Grundle, known as Fuzzy Grumbles to my students who, of course, adore me." He winked at Arabeth. "Nice to meet you in person, Ruth Weaver from Sweetwater, 1896."

Ruth frowned. Should she know this person?

He reached into his massive mane of hair, pulled out a pencil and scratched his head with it. "Oh, balderdash. I forgot to explain. I'm Arabeth's science teacher." He looked as if he wanted to say something else as he twirled the pencil in his hand. But then he shook his head. "Let's just say that's one thing I do, among many."

Ruth stared, unable to make words come out of her mouth. She'd seen pictures of men who looked like him. In books she and Nana read. Scientists who worked in strange, dark, mysterious labs far away from her simple life in a coal mining town.

Her brain whirled with questions as she inched her hand towards his. He clasped it gently. It was not the hard handshake she expected from a man with the nickname Fuzzy Grumbles. As their hands touched, she felt the presence of her nana nearby. *How strange*, she thought. Glancing up at him, she saw his eyes flash and he smiled warmly at her, as if he knew what she was thinking.

Fuzzy lightly squeezed her hand and reached for Michael's. "Michael Martin, from Sweetwater 1966."

Michael shook hands rapidly. "Don't know how you know me, but heh there. You look like my dad when he comes in after plowing the field when it's windy."

Fuzzy pulled his hand away, rubbing his fingers. "Yes, well, I've been in a bit of a hurry." He chewed on his pencil, seeming to be lost in thought. "Oh, potassium! We must get on with the business at hand." He paused, looking down at his wrist. Ruth saw a device that looked just like the one Arabeth wore.

Michael let out a whooping, "Yes! I knew it! You both have those wrist phasers!"

Fuzzy raised his eyebrows. "Good guess, but it's not a phaser, Michael. It's a watch that's also a phone that's also a computer. In 2035, it's called a Skincom." He patted Michael on the shoulder.

Ruth desperately wanted to make sense of what was happening. "You said we need to get to the business at hand. What exactly *is* that business, if you please? But first, can you tell us what happened to us and where we are?"

"Is this dead tree the Listening Tree we all know?" asked Arabeth. "Are we in the future?" She looked at Ruth, shrugging. "Ruth seems to think we might be."

"And did we really transport?" asked Michael.

Fuzzy shook his head. "I do have much to explain, don't I?"

They nodded.

He walked a few steps away from them, wiping sweat from his forehead. "It feels hot enough to be inside a Bunsen burner in my lab." He pulled on his beard. "How to begin? Let's start with your question, Arabeth. This," he said as he waved his arm in a circle, "is 2035."

"2035?" Arabeth looked around. "But how can that be?" She stared at the dead-looking tree. "This doesn't look like Sweetwater at all."

Fuzzy sighed. "We're not in Sweetwater. This tree was grown from an acorn of the Listening Tree. I planted it in one of the hottest places on Earth several years ago. As an experiment."

Michael frowned. "But it has our initials on it."

"I had one of my lab assistants carve them in. So in case I had to summon you here, you could identify it."

"But why?" asked Ruth. "Why bring us all here in 2035, especially Arabeth?"

He paused. "To show you what could happen to Sweetwater by 2050. The extreme heat and lack of rain here are similar to what Sweetwater will be like by then, if climate change progresses as scientists predict. This is the fate of the Listening Tree. In fact, the fate of the entire planet."

"The Listening Tree will look like this fifteen years from now?"

asked Arabeth, her voice low and quiet. "That's not much time at all."

Fuzzy pushed his glasses back, lowering his head. "You're right, Arabeth. The Trees need our help. Before it's too late."

Ruth was puzzled. "Our help? What can we do?"

He walked to the tree and placed his hand on it, his face softening. "I'm not just Arabeth's science teacher in 2035. I am a Rainwalker. As are all of you."

Michael frowned. "Rainwalkers? What do you mean?"

Fuzzy pulled at his beard. "Here's the brief version. I'll give you more later. Some humans, like all of us here, have a wonderful connection with trees. We contain some of the same genetic material they do and, as a result, can do some pretty amazing things. We make up the Society of Rainwalkers, and trees, being the longest living beings on Earth, are the Society's gatekeepers."

Ruth thought of a quote from Henry David Thoreau that Nana always said. "Talk of mysteries! Think of our life in nature," she whispered.

Fuzzy turned, gazing at her. "Ah, Thoreau. I knew a woman who loved his writing." He scratched his beard some more, a faraway look on his face.

Michael threw up his arms. "We just started genetics in science class. Genes and stuff, right?" He chuckled. "I'm related to a tree? That's just too funky."

Ruth thought Fuzzy seemed kind enough. Almost grandfatherly, in a way. But this was all so strange. "What do you mean by rainwalking?" Ruth shook her head. "I don't understand how I—we—got here."

Fuzzy straightened his glasses, sighing, seeming to search for words. "Water has been recycling around Earth since it formed. Rainwalkers are able to use the water that enters trees through raindrops to travel through time. It's a skill revealed on your thirteenth birthday, which all of you had in the past few weeks." Fuzzy's face took on a serious look.

Ruth stared at the strange man. Raindrops, trees, bending or traveling through time. The same things her nana'd said.

Arabeth frowned. "So you're saying that all of us are members of this Rainwalkers society? And we can move through time in trees? What we just did is travel through," she paused, pacing back and forth in front of them, "I guess the root system of the Listening Tree, in each of our time periods."

"That's right, Arabeth." Fuzzy smiled and rubbed his beard. "We entered the Listening Tree through the water in the roots, traveled through the xylem and the phloem, and ended up here."

"Flown?" asked Michael. "You mean, we've just flown really fast into this—" he looked around, "into the Listening Tree?"

"Oh, silicon! Not flown, phloem, Michael. It's one of the types of tissue in a tree. Phloem carries food to all parts of the tree. We, as Rainwalkers, enter trees through the xylem, which carries water from the roots."

Fuzzy bent over, patting the ground around them for a moment as if searching for something underneath the caked rock-like soil. He motioned for them to come closer.

"Now, each of you has something special from the Listening Tree. An object that you either found or made." He took out a wooden key from his pocket. "Like this. As Ruth surmised, these amulets have great power." He pointed to the wavy mound of dirt near the base of the tree. "In order to rainwalk, we must be aligned along one of the roots. Like right here. And have our amulets."

Fuzzy pushed his glasses back, lowering his head. "The trees need our help. Until now, the Rainwalkers have remained a secret. But our leader, the Mother Guardian, protector of the oldest living tree, has summoned all thirteen-year-olds to an emergency meeting." He glanced at his Skincom. "Oh, half-life! Time flies so fast. We must go. We'll be late." He held up his key.

"But, please, wait a minute," Ruth said, crossing her arms. "We didn't get to ask what our role in all this is." She took a deep breath. "And it's a bit rattling that we haven't had a chance to decide if we even want to go." She'd wished for a new life, an adventure. Now she wanted to know what she was getting into before embarking on it.

A look of tenderness crossed Fuzzy's face. "You are absolutely right, Ruth. The Society, over the centuries, has identified Mother Trees around the world. The Listening Tree is one. From its acorns sprouted the first generation of trees in the forest that surrounds it. As a Mother Tree, she looks after and communicates with all the trees around her, telling them of approaching danger and when they need to help each other. Her preservation is vital to the forest."

"Do you mean like the Banyan Tree in mythology? The eternal tree?" Ruth asked. She remembered reading about that in a book she found at Nana's house.

Fuzzy nodded. His voice quivered. "The Society has provided each Mother Tree with a human Guardian, someone who is genetically connected to that particular tree, which, in the case of the Listening Tree, is me." He looked at each one of them in turn. "You are all connected, too. Please. We need your help. Please trust me. After the meeting, you can decide if you want to be a part of this."

Ruth thought he looked sincere, and she did feel connected to the Listening Tree. And he did make her think of her nana, for some strange reason. But she wondered what the others thought. "Arabeth knows you, so I guess if she trusts you, I can, too."

Arabeth rubbed her forehead. "All this is so sudden. Genetically connected to trees? Rainwalking? Will this meeting answer my questions? And tell us what help we can possibly be?"

Fuzzy nodded.

Michael looked at them both, then said to Fuzzy, "I'm in if they are. This is all so cool, anyway."

Fuzzy stood on the root, waving them over. "Wonderful! Stand right here, please. But we need to hurry." He pointed to his Skincom. "Let's make like photons and travel light."

Arabeth sighed. "Fuzzy, I don't think Ruth or Michael know the term photon."

Michael cocked his head, looking toward the dilapidated sign in the distance. "Do you hear that?" He raised a finger to his lips. They became quiet. A strange *whoosh, whoosh* could be heard coming from that direction.

Two dark specks sped towards them. The specks turned out to be people, rushing across the rough ground on small horizontal objects. They weaved right and left as if riding on waves. Ruth squinted, shielding her eyes from the glaring sun with her hand. Were they riding on boards? The objects hovered about a foot above the ground as they sped towards them. How could that be? Was she delirious from the heat?

Fuzzy shouted, "We took too long. They're coming fast. Get behind me!" He ran out in front of them. "Stay behind me, stay near the Tree." Ruth grabbed onto the back of his lab coat, peering around his side.

"Ruth, get back, get behind the Tree." Fuzzy shook her off, pointing to the Tree where Michael and Arabeth crouched. She scrambled on the ground backwards as the people sped straight at them. One aimed an object at Fuzzy that looked like a short, fat version of one of her father's guns.

The rider caught Fuzzy by his sleeve, pushing the gun-like object into his arm while the board hovered stationary for a few seconds.

"No!" screamed Michael as he rushed forward. Michael snatched Fuzzy, throwing him to the ground. He turned, trying to catch the nearest board rider, but they both sped toward the dilapidated sign, leaving a trail of dust.

Fuzzy crumbled into a heap on the ground. Michael bent down, brushing dust from Fuzzy's face. "Fuzzy? Can you hear me?" There was no response.

Ruth and Arabeth ran over and knelt beside Fuzzy.

"What do we do?" asked Arabeth, touching him on the shoulder.

"Fuzzy wouldn't hurt anyone. Who were those people?"

Ruth looked at Michael who was staring in the direction of the speeding boards. "That was a brave thing to do, Michael. I mean, we have no idea who they are or what they're capable of doing."

Michael shook his head. "I had to do something. Did you see him? He risked himself. For us. For the Tree." He straightened his shoulders. "I only did what a future starship captain does."

Ruth shot him a quick smile and then began to examine Fuzzy's lab coat. "There's a spot here. Look." The lab coat sleeve had a small hole punched through it. "Did they stick something into him? Why would they do that?" Ruth stared in the direction of the sign. There was no sign of the two men. A dark feeling welled up inside her. She shivered. She shook Fuzzy gently. "Fuzzy. Please. Wake up."

Fuzzy grimaced, rolled over onto his side, and grabbed his arm. He opened his eyes and pushed himself slowly to a sitting position. "What just happened?" His words slurred as he moaned.

Arabeth knelt in front of him. "Two men on what looked like hoverboards rushed at us."

"Hoverboard?" asked Michael.

"It's a personal transportation device that allows you ride on a thin film of air."

Ruth held out her hand, trying to make a shape with her fingers. "They had an object shaped like this." She pointed to his arm where he held it. "They did something to you, right there."

Fuzzy moved his hand, and Arabeth helped him slip his arm, inch by inch, out of the lab coat. She rolled up his shirt sleeve. A tiny puncture wound became visible in his arm. "Lookth like they drugged me." His eyes closed and his head fell forward. "Get to the meeting. You muth get to the meeting," he whispered before slumping over.

CHAPTER EIGHT
THE HABOOB

Michael stood up, brushing dust from his pant legs. "Get to the meeting? How are we going to get him to the meeting? We don't even know where it is."

Arabeth bit her lip. "This is nuts. He's the only one who knows where we're going, and why. And now he's been attacked and possibly drugged by some strange men. I mean, where did they come from?" She looked off into the horizon. "There's nothing here but this tree and those dilapidated buildings." She wiped beads of perspiration from her forehead. "Is it getting warmer?" She lifted her hair off her neck. "We have to get out of here. The sun is so blasted hot."

Ruth dropped to the ground nearby, her heart racing. Who would do this to Fuzzy? "You're right. I don't want to stay here, either." She loosened the top button of her dress. "The heat makes my head pound." She dabbed drops of sweat from her cheeks with her sleeve. "Fuzzy was taking us on a rainwalk to a meeting of all thirteen-year-old Rainwalkers. Are they trying to stop him? How did they know he was here? Are they Rainwalkers, too?"

Arabeth scrunched up her mouth. "No idea. It's confusing. Why wouldn't they want him or us to go?" She rubbed at the pinpoint hole in his sleeve. "And why stab him with a needle?" She shook her head. "Something's wrong. We need to get to that meeting."

Ruth nodded. "What if we try to carry him with us? We can use our amulets. And he has one."

"But where are we going?" Michael asked. "He said the Mother Guardian, whoever that is, requested a meeting. But he never told us where."

Ruth jumped up. "But he did tell us. He said the Mother Guardian is protector of the oldest living tree on Earth. If we know that tree, perhaps we can rainwalk there."

Arabeth smiled as she got to her feet. "It's the Bristlecone Pine. We learned about it in science last year. When Fuzzy first came to our school. It's over five thousand years old."

Ruth grinned at her. "Hooray. Now we have a destination. All we have to do is get Fuzzy over to the Tree, put his amulet in his hand, and rainwalk out of here." She coughed, hoping to clear the dryness from her throat. "At least, I think that will work. My, the wind has picked up. Look." Small funnels of dust, forming quickly and swirling like little tops for a few seconds, began appearing here and there, disintegrating as fast as they appeared. "Little tornadoes are popping up everywhere."

Michael pointed. "Yeah, and what about over there? In the distance." Beyond the broken buildings, near the horizon, yellowish-brown clouds were developing. "That's weird. I've never seen clouds that close to land. Up in the sky, sure. But white or gray, not light brown like those." The ground clouds began to swell, billowing up higher and higher.

Ruth watched them for a few seconds. "They look far away." The brownish clouds appeared to be rolling along the ground as they rose into the air and fell back to Earth. "Are they moving? Toward us?" she gasped.

Arabeth shielded her eyes with her hand. "They are! I know what that is. It's a dust storm. A haboob."

The wind unexpectedly intensified around them, sending dirt and sand into the air. Michael rubbed his eyes. "All this dust." He tipped his head to one side, shaking it. "Maybe there's some in my ears, too. I didn't hear a kaboom, Arabeth, like you said, just a dull roaring sound."

Arabeth paced in front of them, watching the clouds. "A haboob, not a kaboom. A dust or sand storm that develops in dry conditions when the atmosphere is extremely windy. These storms are already appearing in places they never did before, just like scientists predicted would happen with climate change. And they're stronger and more dangerous." She pointed at the swirling clouds in the distance, frowning. "A haboob can grow and move very fast. We'd better figure out how to get going."

The clouds had grown larger and they were closer. Ruth wanted to leave right away. "If Michael can get Fuzzy to a sitting position and pick him up by the chest, perhaps you and I can help carry him to the Tree by grabbing his legs. We sit with him along a root, like Fuzzy said, and put his amulet in his hand while we hold ours."

"Do you think that will work?" asked Michael, spitting out dust.

"I don't know," said Ruth. "Earlier, I wasn't even sure if I wanted to go to the meeting. But now I think we have to try *something*. Those men attacked him for a reason. We need to find out what that is. And maybe the answer's at the meeting."

"But how do we rainwalk to a specific location like the Bristlecone Pine?" questioned Arabeth.

Ruth shrugged. "I have no idea."

Michael threw his hands up in the air and frowned.

Ruth fidgeted with her poetry book as she thought. She opened it to her leaf, her amulet. Could they use them to rainwalk to other trees as long as they went through the Listening Tree? Beside it was the leaf she found at the Tree that morning. She noticed the words in the insect trail again. "Look! I found this at the Tree this morning. It says 'Words are seeds'. Maybe it means if we think about the place we want to go to, like the Bristlecone Pine, it's like planting a seed. The thought will grow and take us to the place we want to be."

"You might be on to something," said Arabeth. Her eyes rested on Ruth's poetry book. "What a crazy thing. The poetry lover gets the words are seeds clue in a leaf." She held out her fist to Ruth who bumped it gingerly.

A sudden gust of wind nearby sent a small funnel of dust churning and swirling towards them. It engulfed them in seconds. Ruth bent over, struggling to stay upright, as she pulled her pinafore up over her mouth and hid her face in her elbow. The dust felt like tiny needles pricking her skin as it hit. She sputtered and coughed. As quick as it came, the funnel passed over them. Instantly, the air felt like a heavy wool blanket was thrown over top of her.

Michael, bent over Fuzzy, raised his head, coughing and wiping his eyes. "Holy haboob!" He blushed, glancing at Ruth and Arabeth. Sputtering, he shook Fuzzy. "Wake up. Please." But Fuzzy didn't move.

Arabeth, wiping the dust from her mouth, moved toward Fuzzy. "Haboobs can kill with their powerful winds and dust particles that hit like bullets." She grabbed one of Fuzzy's legs. "Let's go. You know, those men could come back, too."

Michael sat Fuzzy up, trying to wake him. Fuzzy moaned, but his eyes remained closed, and his head lolled forward. Michael held him from behind as the girls picked up his legs.

"We don't have far to go," said Ruth, breathing heavily. They worked their way to the closest root of the tree and sat Fuzzy on it as the air thickened even more and the wind blew harder.

"He's not going to stay," said Michael as Fuzzy slowly fell over, rolling off the root. "I'll have to hold him in front of me." He aligned himself along the root, propping Fuzzy between his legs and hugging him from behind. "Hurry. He's pretty heavy to hold up."

Ruth sat behind Michael and Arabeth sat down in front of Fuzzy. "He can't think about the Bristlecone Pine himself. We better make sure we're touching him so he rainwalks to the same place we do. Hold his foot," said Ruth, looking around Michael at Arabeth. She placed Fuzzy's key gently in his hand, wrapping her fingers around his to make sure he didn't drop it. A comforting warmth swept over her, like she felt in the presence of her nana. She gripped her poetry book tightly with her other hand as the wind roared suddenly.

"We've got to go. *Now*," shouted Arabeth.

The haboob, a brown wall as high as a mountain, rapidly swept across the land toward them.

Ruth shouted, "Think Bristlecone Pine."

CHAPTER NINE
THE BRISTLECONE PINE

Ruth fought back a wave of panic. Not only was she fearful of rainwalking, but what if Fuzzy didn't make it? Gusts full of tiny dust particles hit her cheeks, burning and cutting like minute shards of glass. She lost sight of Michael's back right in front of her. Tightening her grip on Fuzzy's hand, she focused her thoughts on the Bristlecone Pine.

She squeezed her eyes shut and leaned over to shelter her face. *The Bristlecone Pine.* She repeated it over in her mind as a force began to pull on her toes, as if the ground grew fingers made of rock, wrapped them around her feet, and was pulling her under. The smell of fresh rain and the sound of rustling leaves filled the air, even though neither was possible in this storm. She screamed but heard only a garbled sound as if she was underwater. Just like before.

This time, Ruth was more aware of what happened than during her first experience rainwalking. She felt stretched, particle by particle, until she was infinitely long and only as wide as a speck of dust as she was pulled through the soil into a tiny space. She raced through a liquid of some kind, surrounded as before by darkness. A quote Nana had read to her by Henry David Thoreau flashed through her mind. *From the right point of view, every storm and every drop in it is a rainbow.* Would there be a rainbow at the end of this? Images of her nana and the Listening Tree in her time floated across her mind, like frames in a picture show. She heard Nana say *The Trees know, the raindrops bend time.* She saw herself sitting at the base of the Listening Tree, its beautiful crown of leaves shading her, the wind blowing its subtle fragrance over her, the strength of its trunk supporting her, pulling all her fears and pain away. A feeling of warmth and safety wrapped around her like a blanket. Then the images abruptly turned dark, with a raging storm bending the Tree dramatically, wind howling around her, water rushing, rising rapidly around her and the Tree. She was drowning and part of the Tree was crashing to the ground. Was that the future of the Tree Fuzzy had talked about? She had to help. She reminded herself to focus on the Bristlecone Pine for now.

Ruth sped through a structure that smelled like wet soil, then passed into another tube-like opening, a bit wider, that smelled like sawdust at a lumber mill. In the next one, she felt herself flip around to travel headfirst, smelling something sweet. Each smell made her feel less panicked. With an abrupt jolt, she began to speed rapidly upward, upward, at a terrifying pace, through the liquid. Where were the others? She tried calling their names, hearing her own voice soft and far away. Faintly, she heard Michael and Arabeth calling back. Without warning, she screeched to an unexpected halt, landing with a thud alongside the others.

She opened her eyes. Fuzzy, Michael, and Arabeth had made it. Tears streamed down her face. But was this the Bristlecone Pine?

Fuzzy moaned beside her as he tried to sit up, rubbing his arm.

The stunned feeling from the hard landing wore off, and she found herself in the middle of an enormous room, stretching as far as she could see in every direction. It reminded her of the giant amphitheater in a book about ancient Greece she read with Nana. A hazy orange-yellow glow filled the space.

"Ruth." Michael shook her arm and pointed. "We're on some kind of stage."

Indeed we are, she thought as she looked around. Hundreds of young people sat in rows of seats, arranged in concentric circles that rose above her until they were mere dots in the distance. The front rows were filled with kids wearing togas, like in ancient Greece. Further up sat kids dressed in blue pants like Michael's, and further up, she could barely make out people with clothing like Arabeth's. It was like looking out at the history of the world from past to present. And most of them looked to be about the same age. Just as Fuzzy said: thirteen-year-old Rainwalkers.

The noisy room quieted as the crowd noticed Ruth and the others on the stage.

Ruth swallowed hard. "It's dry. Like my attic bedroom gets in the summertime." She took a long breath. "There's dust in the air here, too."

Michael gently shook Fuzzy. "Yeah, like our barn when we're putting in the hay." He nudged Fuzzy, who groaned.

Arabeth scooched over to sit near her. "I can't believe it, right?" She touched Ruth's elbow as she whispered, "The meeting is inside the five thousand-year-old tree itself. That would explain the dryness."

Michael frowned. "You mean, we're all inside the Bristlecone Pine? Not just traveling through it, but small enough to be inside it for a while? That's too outta sight!"

"Oh, bunkum." Fuzzy pushed himself up into a sitting position and adjusted his glasses. He glanced from side to side. "We're at the meeting." He pulled on his thick white beard and raised his bushy eyebrows. "What happened? I've forgotten." He looked down at his arm. Michael started to answer, but the crowd began pointing to the stage and shouting.

Ruth thought everyone was pointing at them, but then she noticed a large chair on the stage. Had it been there the whole time? The chair, made from dark brown wood with a swirling red design engraved on the seat back, was the most magnificent thing she'd ever seen. And the design, where had she seen it before? On the paper from Nana!

As she reached into her pocket to look, the smell of fresh rain and forest began to fill the air. A murmur spread throughout the room as the air above the chair glistened and undulated. A woman appeared, sitting in the chair. Her skin, the color and smoothness of ivory, was accented by brilliant red cheeks. Her hair, a combination of delicate branches or twigs, fragile green moss, and decorated with leaves of all shapes and colors, fell to her waist, flowing around her and moving slightly as if in a gentle breeze.

She wore a dress that looked to Ruth like it was made from birch tree bark, a white paper-thin bark, speckled with black, pliable and soft, snf adorned with lichens, mosses, leaves, and seeds.

"Welcome. I am the Mother Guardian, leader of the Society of Rainwalkers," she said in a voice that sounded like musical notes drifting through the air of the giant amphitheater. Everyone stopped talking. "I believe we are all here. Francis Ferdinand Grundle, you always make an entrance."

A look of concern crept across her face. She walked over, bending down to Fuzzy. "Francis. Are you well?" She touched his shoulder. Fuzzy groaned, shook his head, and tried to stand.

He looked out at the crowd, grabbing on to Ruth and Arabeth while Michael held him up from behind. "Oh, balderdash. I remember now. We encountered a bit of trouble getting here." Then his knees shook and he started to collapse. Michael grabbed him under the arms.

"Let's get him to the chair," said Mother Guardian. Fuzzy slumped into it as she spoke to the crowd. "Please, everyone, I know this is confusing. Give me a moment to talk with Francis."

The Mother Guardian and Fuzzy whispered for a few seconds, their heads close together. Ruth saw the Mother Guardian's back stiffen as Fuzzy spoke.

A boy sitting in the front row stared at Ruth. His eyes were wide and his hands gripped his seat as he watched the stage. So many strange things were happening. She took a deep breath and flashed him a brief smile as if to say it will be all right. But she wasn't sure.

The Mother Guardian motioned for Ruth, Michael, and Arabeth to sit near the chair as she walked to the center of the stage.

"Francis and I did not plan for the meeting to begin this way. You have all met with the Guardian of your tree and learned about the Society of Rainwalkers. We asked you here from all the known corners of our world because a crisis threatens our planet." She paused, looking over the crowded room, from one side to the other. "The Earth needs the help and strength of every thirteen-year-old Rainwalker." Murmurs spread throughout the room, and the Mother Guardian raised both her hands. "Listen, please.

"The Trees have called upon the Rainwalkers for help." Her voice softened and saddened. "Time is of the essence. That's why we have called this meeting."

Fuzzy nodded.

"We live in precarious times for Earth. Our beloved home, and all the creatures in it, are on the brink of global disaster. Rising temperatures and sea levels and changing patterns of weather have already resulted in treacherous storms around the world."

Michael whispered, "The haboob we just came from."

Everyone sat silent as she waved her arm through the air. "And they will only intensify as time goes on."

Swirling images appeared near the Mother Guardian. Images of trees bending and breaking while powerful winds blew and rain fell. Rain like Ruth had never seen, falling as if from a waterfall in the sky. Images of people fleeing tornadoes of massive size that destroyed everything in their path. Skies swirling with dark clouds, creating winds that tossed gigantic ships made of metal about on the ocean like wooden toys in a bathtub. A strange flying machine thrown about in the sky, crashing into the ground and breaking into pieces. Strange places, full of tall buildings and crowded with people, places she thought might be cities, washed away by floods and giant waves from the ocean.

As the pictures swirled, Michael asked, "How is she doing that out of thin air?"

"Look, it's a hologram. They're common in my time," Arabeth said, running her fingers nervously through her hair. "How to explain it? A hologram looks real, it can move, but it's just an image, a kind of picture. Like a film or movie, but you can send it through space without a screen. It doesn't really exist in front of you."

"Like the moving picture Edison made of a sneeze?" asked Ruth.

"Exactly," said Arabeth. "I can make them with my Skincom."

Michael's eyes widened.

In a voice that rang throughout the room, the Mother Guardian said, "This is what we face if nothing is done." With a sweep of her arm, the images were gone as fast as they'd appeared.

The Mother Guardian continued. "Our rainwalking skills, as you have found out, allow us to travel through time, in the water of the Mother Tree we are connected to. For example, Ruth, Michael, and Arabeth, here on the stage, are connected to The Listening Tree in Sweetwater. Francis is its Guardian."

The audience buzzed. The boy in the front row spoke to the kids on either side of him. Ruth heard him say Olive Tree and Crete. He was connected to a Mother Tree in Greece.

The Mother Guardian raised her hand, and everyone became silent. "The Trees have asked us to travel back in time to each of our Mother Trees. Back in time to major events caused by a human decision that have weakened each tree."

She turned to Ruth. "Three major events happened to the Listening Tree, one in each of your time periods. 1896," and she touched Ruth on the shoulder, "1966," she touched Michael, "and now in 2035." She tapped Arabeth. "Each of these events occurred because of a poor decision made by humans."

She swept her arms outward. "For each of you out there, it is the same. Events have happened throughout time that weakened your Mother Trees. The Trees have asked us to travel back in time to each of these events and try to change them. Lessen their impact on our Mother Trees, making them stronger and more able to withstand what is happening today. When the Trees survive, so does every living thing on the Earth."

A voice shouted from high up in the amphitheater. "But we can't go back and change history, can we?"

The Mother Guardian shielded her eyes with one hand as she peered in the direction of the voice. "True, but physics shows we can attempt to create new parallel universes, where the Trees will be stronger."

She continued, "From this meeting, you will travel through time and attempt to fix these disastrous events at each of our Mother Trees. When each event is lessened, a new universe will be created, one that will add strength and resilience to our Mother Trees.

"Each new universe will join with the others, until we reach our present time, making our Trees stronger." Her eyes moistened. "Otherwise, it will be too late for all of us by 2050. The climate will have changed so dramatically it will be impossible to bring the planet back."

"2050? Only fifteen years from now." Arabeth whispered. She stared at the stage floor, shaking her head.

Fuzzy struggled to lift himself from the chair just as a loud beeping sound filled the room. Ruth thought the sound came from Fuzzy.

He lifted up his arm, his eyebrows twitching rapidly as he looked at his Skincom. He punched at it, but the sound continued. "What's going on?"

Suddenly, a hologram appeared behind him. A loud voice come from it. Startled, the Mother Guardian jumped.

"Francis, at last, we meet again." A man with hair the color of the night sky stared out at them from the hologram. A sharp, pointy nose projected over long, delicate-looking threadlike lips. His beady little eyes of the deepest blue Ruth could imagine shifted side to side.

Fuzzy groaned and covered his mouth with his hand. "No." Ruth thought she heard him utter the name Martin.

"Yes, Francis, it's me. I made this hologram to tell you that soon I will have the ability to rainwalk just like you. All I needed was a sample of Rainwalker blood. And now I have that. And I intend to find the seed banks as well."

Michael whispered, "Seed banks?" His face turned white. "What are they and who is he?"

"I will follow you, Francis. Not just in the present, but back through time. To get all the genetic material I need for my creations." He nodded. "I know you want to save the Earth from climate change. I know you are at a meeting of all you Rainwalkers to try to figure out how to accomplish that. Something about creating parallel universes, right?" He laughed, a deep raucous laugh. "Well, good luck with that crazy idea. Meanwhile, my organization will be doing everything possible to thwart those efforts because it is already too late. You are wasting your time."

He gestured wildly. "Climate change will create new, harsher environments and my genetic creations will be ready to populate them." He pointed to a table nearby. "This is a prototype of my latest idea. A combination of plant DNA. The man-eating lily pad. It is capable of digesting flesh like the Venus fly trap, but grows to the size of a lily pad."

His face moved closer to the screen. "Now you see why I need the seed banks, Francis? To unlock the genetic potential of all those plants!"

He stopped abruptly, reached into the pocket of his long lab coat, and pulled out a small, dark object. "I've got my amulet ready, Ferdinand. Now all I need is the rainwalking serum, which will be ready soon. Good luck at your meeting and watch your back." He laughed and the hologram disappeared.

CHAPTER TEN
RETURN TO 1896

Ruth looked around, her mind racing to make sense of what had happened. Fuzzy sat, stunned. The amphitheater audience burst into loud noise.

Michael, wide-eyed, pointed to where the man had been. "Who was that? He knows Fuzzy." His finger shook as his voice quivered. "That was another hologram, right?"

Arabeth said, "Yes. Maybe those two men—"

Before she could complete her sentence, the Mother Guardian spoke, her hands on the back of the chair. "Please stay calm. Don't be afraid."

She glanced down at Fuzzy, who said in a weak voice. "He must have hacked into my Skincom and sent a hologram. That was meant for me to see, not all of you. Now, let's get on with the meeting."

The Mother Guardian took several steps across the stage, pausing to look at Ruth, Michael, and Arabeth. "If the Trees ever needed you, it is now. Please, help them. Help us."

The crowd erupted loudly.

Fuzzy's voice strained as he inched himself up from the chair. "Please, one at a time." The Mother Guardian held him as he braced against the chair's arm, motioning to the crowd for silence.

The boy in the front row shouted, "Why us? Why only thirteen-year-olds?"

Fuzzy took an unsteady step away from the chair. "I'll be fine," he said to the Mother Guardian. She let go of his arm but remained standing beside him. "Thirteen is the age when Rainwalker power is revealed." He stroked his beard, wobbling back and forth on his feet. "And when it is the strongest. As we age, rainwalking becomes more difficult and takes a toll on our bodies." He glanced at Ruth, his face softening. "You are the best chance we have to help the Trees and save our world." He looked down at the boy in the front row. "Remember, the guardian of your tree will help you as much as possible."

Michael turned to Ruth. "Is he just tired because he's too old to be rainwalking?" His mouth turned up in a slight grin despite his shaky voice. "You know, my dad made me join the Future Farmers of America because we're the next generation of farmers. Who knew I'd be in the next generation of Rainwalkers? Maybe we can call ourselves the Future Association of Rainwalkers Out to Help. Or FAR OUT for short."

Ruth smiled back, wondering why she had the urge to hug him.

Arabeth said, "Are you always making jokes, Michael?" She frowned. "My best friend Paz and I made a pact to protect the Listening Tree. With our lives, if necessary. But I never expected it to really happen."

Ruth wondered if she'd be willing to sacrifice her own life for the Tree as the room grew oppressively hot. "It's so warm." She coughed. "Is there more dust all of a sudden?" The stage quivered slightly. Out in the amphitheater, the dust intensified, obstructing the upper rows from sight. The entire room trembled and swayed. Everyone grabbed onto their seats and began shouting.

"Holy shakes! What's happening now?" Michael scrambled to his knees, then stood, rocking back and forth with the small tremors. He staggered over to hold Fuzzy's arm as the older man struggled to remain standing.

Ruth rubbed dust out of her eyes. She heard a loud beep coming from nearby.

Arabeth looked down at her Skincom. "I'm getting an earthquake warning." The room shook from a powerful vibration. "The Bristlecone Pine sits on a fault line. Scientist predicted a big quake," she added in a quavering voice, "could happen any day now."

Fuzzy, holding on to Michael's arm, shouted as his Skincom beeped. "I'm getting a warning, too." The floor shook. "This tree is ancient. It may not make it through this."

The Mother Guardian turned to the crowded room as small pieces of wood dropped from the ceiling around them.

"Please rainwalk to your Mother Tree. Try to lessen the damage to them throughout time. Do what you can to save them and build a new timeline." Her voice trembled as she held on to Fuzzy and the back of the chair. "We may not succeed, but we must try."

A large chunk of wood plunged to the floor nearby as the amphitheater oscillated back and forth.

Fuzzy shouted, "Come, Ruth, Arabeth. Get near Michael and me. Hold your amulets. Words are seeds, remember. Think The Listening Tree in 1896." A violent tremor shook the room. Fuzzy fell forward. "Oh, quivering quake!"

Michael grabbed him before he hit the floor. "Someone help me with him, please."

Ruth, gripping her poetry book in one hand, helped Arabeth and Michael hold Fuzzy up. A strong shock rattled the room, knocking the

Mother Guardian off balance, throwing her backwards onto the seat of the chair. Her eyes met Ruth's as more wood and dust filled the air. "You can save us, Ruth," the Mother Guardian whispered. She looked out across the crowd. "All of you. Listen to the Trees. Save our world."

A loud cracking sound filled the air. The stage fractured in half, creating a gaping hole. The Bristlecone Pine was breaking apart. The chair teetered on the edge and then, as if in slow motion, fell backward into the opening, carrying the Mother Guardian with it. Ruth tried to grab her, but she was too far away.

She screamed as the Mother Guardian tumbled into the blackness of the opening. *Where did she go?*

You can save us, the Mother Guardian had told her. She remembered a quote from Emily Dickinson that Nana loved. *Hope is the thing with feathers that perches in the soul—and sings the tunes without the words—and never stops at all.* She must get to the Listening Tree. Blocking out the sights and sounds of what was happening around her, Ruth filled her mind with thoughts of The Listening Tree in 1896.

Once again, she felt pulled into a thin line and transported through the darkness, the swooshing sound of water surrounding her as she traveled. She heard Arabeth repeating, "The Tree 1896" and Michael, "Beam me to the Tree 1896." Then, Fuzzy's voice, louder than theirs. "Rainwalkers. Hurry. You must help The Listening Tree by October 14, 1896. The manmade—" His voice stopped as strange muffled sounds filled her ears. Faintly, she heard, "Balderdash!" Then nothing except Michael and Arabeth screaming his name.

Moments later, she tumbled onto the ground. She leaped up, turning to search for the Listening Tree and her friends. Arabeth stood nearby, holding her head as she stared up at the massive tree in front of them.

"We made it?" Arabeth gasped, reaching out to touch the bark. "The Listening Tree? In 1896?"

Ruth nodded.

"But where's Michael? And Fuzzy?"

Michael walked around from behind the Tree, brushing leaves from his pants. "I couldn't make out what Fuzzy said." He glanced around, looking concerned. "I don't think he's here."

"He told us to do something by a date. Something about a manmade. But he never finished." Ruth felt herself panic. Without Fuzzy, they had no idea what to do next. "It sounded to me like he was struggling with someone. Or something."

Arabeth slumped against the Tree. "Someone got to him before he could make it." She slid down to the ground. "What about the Bristlecone Pine? I don't think it survived. My Skincom beeped while we were rainwalking, which I was really surprised it could do. There was a massive fire from downed power grids after the quake." She ran her hand through her hair. "The entire area is extremely dry from the heat and lack of rain." She covered her mouth with her hand. "And the Mother Guardian, all the other rainwalkers? Did they make it out?" She looked up at them. "What do we do now?" She put her head in her hands. "Where is Fuzzy? There are too many unknowns."

Ruth sat down, putting her hand on Arabeth's shoulder. She wasn't sure what to do, how to comfort her. Arabeth had seemed to be so confident up to this point.

Michael paced, rubbing his hands together. Stopping in front of them, he said, "I don't like the future, do you? I mean, climate change and crazy new organisms? Hey, do you think that guy in the hologram works with those two men?" He took a deep breath. "I've been thinking about what Captain Kirk once said." He put his hands on his hips and raised his chin. Ruth thought he seemed taller. "He said things are only unknown to us because they're hidden. Or because we don't yet understand them. So, the three of us need to find what's hidden and understand it. To save Fuzzy and the Trees." He smacked his head. "Holy quotes! I've only been around you a few hours, Ruth, and I'm starting to sound like you."

Ruth jumped to her feet. "You said exactly what I didn't know how to say."

Michael smiled, blushing all the way down to the top of his T-shirt.

Arabeth also got to her feet, wiping her eyes with the back of her hand. "You're right, Michael." She patted the Tree. "How magnificent she is in 1896. She's smaller in 2035 and, think about it, she could be destroyed by 2050." She twirled her acorn necklace. "Sorry about earlier. I hate not being able to explain things. And right now, there are so many things I can't explain." Her voice shook. "And, on top of that, Fuzzy's like a grandfather to me, you know? I hate not knowing where he is. Or if he's all right."

Ruth had only known Fuzzy for a few hours. "He *is* very grandfatherly, Arabeth. We'll find him."

Arabeth nodded, then smiled at Michael and squared her shoulders. "We scientists deal with the unknown all the time. So let's start with that guy in the hologram. He and Fuzzy know each other. The more I think about it, I think he has something to do with those two men."

Arabeth paced around the Tree. "He said he had a blood sample, remember? To make the serum for rainwalking." She stopped, tapping her head. "I've got it. The two men took a blood sample from Fuzzy and somehow got it to that man in the hologram. What if he has a laboratory in those dilapidated buildings off on the horizon in the desert?

Ruth rubbed her cheek. "But how do they know each other? Fuzzy muttered the name Martin when he saw the hologram. I think."

The leaves above them swayed up and down.

Michael glanced skyward. "That's odd. There's no breeze."

Ruth looked up into the massive crown of red and orange leaves rustling back and forth. "The Mother Guardian told us to listen to the Trees. Maybe The Tree is telling us we are on the right track, Arabeth."

She inhaled the musty, earthy aroma of the forest as a chickadee sang in the branch above her. A squirrel scampered by, carrying an acorn in its mouth. "The Listening Tree and the Society of Rainwalkers are depending on us to help save the Earth. We've got to find Fuzzy to tell us what to do to create a new timeline."

Michael asked, "And who that guy was. And what seed banks are." He scratched his head. "What date did he say we had to save the Tree by in order to create a new timeline?"

"October 14, 1896," Arabeth replied, her voice drifting off.

A wave of nausea swept over Ruth. "We only have two days. And this day is almost over."

CHAPTER ELEVEN
WILLIE

Two days? Where will we start? Ruth turned toward the forest behind them. "Listen." She pointed into the darkness where leaves crunched under the weight of footsteps. A small twig snapped. "Fuzzy? Is that you?"

A boy peeked out at her from behind a tree.

"Willie!" Ruth's heart fluttered and she ran forward.

"Ruth!" He bounded to her, and they embraced. The smell of cooking spices, coffee, and a wood burning stove overwhelmed her. Home. She was back in her own time. A tear slid down her cheek.

Willie wiped it away with his right hand, his left sleeve dangling empty by his side. "What in tarnation's going on?" He took a step back, raising his eyebrows. "I had a notion you might want company after your nana's funeral, so I headed up here." He looked around as he spoke. "I thought I heard voices, but it's just you." Then his eyes opened wide as he saw Michael and Arabeth. "Good Lord. There *were* other voices." He grabbed Ruth by the arm, stepping behind her. "Who *are* these people?"

"Oh, my, Willie. I don't know where to start."

Michael took a couple steps toward him. "I'm Michael, and this," he said, pointing, "is Arabeth."

"Hey," said Arabeth.

Willie stared at Arabeth, still holding tightly to Ruth's arm. "Hello?"

Ruth led Willie toward the Listening Tree. "So much has happened. Let's sit down and we'll explain it all to you." The three of them sat at the base of the Tree, filling Willie in on the developments of the past few hours, and the unknown crisis threatening them.

Willie gasped when they explained rainwalking. "Wow. So H.G. Wells is right. There *is* a time machine. And it's right here!" He reached around and patted the Tree gently. "I guess you know a lot," he whispered. "Perhaps we should be listening to you instead of you listening to us."

The Listening Tree towered above them, its immense canopy sheltering them like a colorful orange and red tent. Early evening sunlight filtered through its branches, dancing around them as its leaves swayed gently.

Arabeth put her hand up in the air, reaching for the branches above her. "The Tree in 1896—it's more awesome than I ever imagined." She turned to Willie. "We have to help keep it strong."

"That's Fuzzy's point in sending us on this mission," said Michael. "If we can stop whatever it is that we're meant to stop, the Tree will be bigger and stronger for the rest of its life."

Ruth nodded, explaining to Willie. "The Tree will help us. We don't know how, but Fuzzy told us that." She patted her pinafore pocket holding her poetry book and the paper from Nana. "And so did Nana. The day she passed away, she told me the Trees know."

Arabeth jumped up. "Two days to figure this out isn't much time." She looked at Willie. "Can you help us?"

"I'd do anything for Ruthie." Willie patted the empty sleeve of his shirt with his right hand. "If it wasn't for her, I would have died right here in the woods."

"Holy catastrophe," exclaimed Michael. He stared at Ruth. "How did you save Willie's life?"

"Anyone would do what I did," Ruth said quietly. "I found Willie injured here a few years ago."

"My arm got stuck between those boulders." Willie winced as he pointed behind the tree. "It hurt real bad. I tried to pull it out, but it just stuck more. Then Ruth came along."

"I didn't know what to do." Ruth looked at the Tree. "Then, I remembered Nana told me about the medicinal powers of oak trees. The bark and leaves help clean and stop bleeding, so I gathered up some leaves in my pinafore. I soaked them in the nearby creek and mashed them together. Then I packed Willie's arm with them and ran to get help."

Willie's eyes filled with tears. "Doc Brown says she saved my life." He fiddled with his empty sleeve. "They had to take my arm. But Ruthie saved my life with the oak leaves." He pulled out a whistle from inside his shirt. "Father gave me this whistle to wear after that."

"I'm not a hero," said Ruth adamantly. "It wasn't until a breeze came out of nowhere and blew leaves down around us that I remembered about using them." She stared at the Listening Tree, remembering that day. "That day proves what Nana said. The Trees know."

"What do you mean?" asked Michael.

Ruth twirled one of her braids. "I just thought of this." She leaned forward, looking at each of them. "Perhaps the Listening Tree sent a message to those oaks near the boulders to make the leaves fall so I'd remember about using them."

"The Wood Wide Web," murmured Arabeth.

"The what?" Willie squinted and shrugged his shoulders. "I haven't the faintest idea what you're talking about."

Ruth and Michael chimed in, "Neither do we."

Arabeth sat up straight as she explained. She sounded so much like a teacher Ruth thought a chalkboard would appear behind her. "There's mounting scientific evidence that Mother Trees like the Listening Tree communicate with other trees in the forest. They warn them of insect attacks and help send water and chemicals to trees that need help." She thought for a moment. "What if they can sense our dangers and help us as well?

"The Mother Guardian said listen to the Trees," Ruth whispered.

"And Fuzzy did say that Rainwalkers and Trees are related," said Michael.

A gust of wind blew through the Listening Tree. Its branches swayed back and forth over their heads; the rustle of its leaves and a sweet smell filled the air. Four leaves fell, drifting slowly through the air, one leaf landing gently on each of their shoulders.

"Cool," muttered Michael as he stared up at the Tree. He turned to Ruth. "Maybe the Tree did help, but you're still a hero. I can't stand the sight of blood."

"Speaking of being hurt, what about those guys on hoverboards who tried to grab us?" asked Arabeth. "I bet they're connected to the man at the Bristlecone Pine. That knows Fuzzy? The one you think is named Martin?"

Ruth shivered. "I've been wondering that myself." Fuzzy's garbled voice at the end of the last rainwalk echoed in her head. "Fuzzy hasn't shown up yet. Perhaps they captured him."

"I bet they came from those dilapidated buildings in the desert. What if that guy's lab was there? Remember the broken sign? Could that be where they're holding him?" Arabeth trembled.

"Maybe the sign is busted because he moved his entire organization to a different location," exclaimed Michael. "Or maybe a different time. Or even underground. Like the Bat Cave."

"Bat Cave?" asked Willie.

"It's a film they watch in the future," said Ruth, grinning at Michael. "Michael likes it as much as I like Emily Dickinson."

"It's on TV, not a movie," Michael said. "You don't know about TV, do you?"

Willie shook his head. "All I know is TB, and no one wants that. Besides, you don't watch TB, you get sick with it."

Ruth walked over to the base of the Tree and sat down, hugging her knees, resting her head on her hands. "The Time Traveler in *The Time Machine* went to a new world and had to find clues about how it worked. We have to work in reverse. We're in *our* world and have to figure out how to save it to create a new one."

"And find Fuzzy." Arabeth plopped down beside her. "What do we do first?"

Michael stared up at the Tree. "Okay, big gal, what's the answer? Give us a clue, why don't you?" He held his arms up in the air. "Come on, huh?"

They waited, but nothing happened.

Michael lowered his arms. "Now she decides not to help us." He frowned. "You know, on *Star Trek,* the ship's computer talks to them. Why doesn't the Tree just talk to us?"

Ruth shrugged. "I have no idea, Michael. But I don't think we can sit around and wait."

Should we go into town? Talk to people in town and find out if they know of anything dangerous about to happen? Ruth stared at Michael as she thought.

"We need to get Michael and you some different clothes." She glanced at Arabeth's head. "And cover up your hair. If we have to go into town, people will be suspicious."

"Or frightened," Willie said with a chuckle.

"I can get you some clothes," said Ruth, "but I don't know what to do about Michael."

"My father's clothes might work," said Willie. "He's downstairs in his store right now. Mother is visiting Auntie so I can sneak upstairs." He looked Michael over. "You're a bit bigger than him, though."

"It will have to do." Ruth smoothed out her pinafore. "There's Arabeth's hair, too." She stared at the wiry blue curls. "Nana's scarves. I'll show you how to tie one around your head."

A loud clap of thunder startled them. Michael looked up at the sky. "Those clouds are getting pretty dark."

"We'd better get going," said Ruth. "Willie, you run home and get your dad's clothing. I'll be back with some for Arabeth. Once we get changed, we can figure out what to do next."

Willie took a few steps. "I'll be back soon." He turned around. "Promise me you won't disappear again." He looked at Ruth questioningly.

"I won't," she replied, shooting him a warm smile. Willie raced out of sight in seconds.

Ruth brushed off her dress as she rose. "When I last saw Father, he was passed out in the kitchen. I hope he's still there. I can sneak by to get the clothes. Fuzzy did say that time stops for those in our own time while we're gone, right?"

"That's true." Arabeth frowned. "But we've been back here for a while. He could be awake by now."

"I didn't think about that," said Ruth. *Would he remember our argument?*

The Tree quivered and all the branches on one side shook violently.

"Odd. That's the same direction Willie went," said Michael.

Ruth stared into the forest. "Listen. I heard something."

A man's voice shouted from that direction. "Where is that tree?"

A shiver swept through Ruth. "That's my father."

Michael looked around. "We've gotta hide."

Ruth pointed behind the tree. "Go there. Run to the boulders. There's an opening between them. It's big enough to hold both of you. I'll deal with Father."

Michael stood still. "He's awful loud. And sounds mean." He shifted from foot to foot.

"Michael, I'll be all right." Ruth waved them toward the boulders. "Go, quick!"

They disappeared into the woods just as Ruth turned to find her father standing in front of her.

"What's going on?" he yelled, slurring his words, shaking his finger at her, and holding a rusted saw in his other hand.

"Father, I came up here to think about Nana." She had no explanation for why he had his old saw with him.

"Think about Nana?" shouted her father. "You gonna write one of your poems?" He blew hard out his lips. "Phh. I work all day in the mines. I come home and your mother just sits staring. And you, you do nothing but run around with that boy from town. Up here to this tree all the time." He swayed from side to side, his bloodshot eyes blazing as if on fire. "And fooling around with writing. Useless stuff. Now get back to the house and tend to dinner. I'm gonna cut down this tree right now. I've had enough of this nonsense." He rocked side to side as he approached the tree, swinging the saw.

Ruth couldn't believe what he'd said. Anger boiled up inside her like water in the kettle on the woodstove. "No, Father! You will *not* cut down our tree." Ruth rushed at him, grabbing at his hand. "You're still drunk. You'll hurt yourself."

He yanked his arm away from her, throwing her off balance. Ruth felt herself fall backwards, landing hard on the ground at the base of the Tree. Her father stared down at her, the saw hanging by his side. "I'll be back. When you're not here."

She slid herself back against the Tree and closed her eyes, tears streaming down her face.

48

CHAPTER TWELVE
THE DAM

"Ruth!" She heard Willie shouting her name, and opened her eyes. He leaned over top of her. "What happened?"

Ruth rested her head against the Tree. "Oh, my. Where's Michael? Arabeth?"

"We're right here," said Michael as he and Arabeth rushed up. "Are you gonna be okay?" He touched her arm, turning away. "Your dad. We hid in the boulders. We couldn't see, but we heard."

Ruth sighed. "He brought a saw. To cut down the Tree. I fell when I stopped him."

Michael rubbed his hands through his hair. "What kind of father does that? Are you hurt?"

Ruth pushed herself up from the ground, rubbing her back. "I just jarred myself." She brushed leaves from her dress. "I'll be fine."

She had to explain to them. Each word felt like a brick as it left her mouth. "My father drinks. Quite a bit." She straightened up, picking leaves and dirt out of her braids. "Don't be concerned. I can handle him."

Michael sighed. "I don't know, Ruth." Then, quietly, he added, "You did stop him from cutting down the Tree, though. But you could've been hurt."

Willie, sitting nearby, nodded.

Ruth turned to Willie, wanting to get the conversation away from her father. "You're back with Michael's clothes already?"

Willie looked down at the ground. "On my way home, I heard someone coming through the woods behind me. Your father staggered up and told me you fell and to check on you. I never got the clothes. I came right back."

"Do you think that was the crisis we're supposed to prevent?" Michael asked. "Your father cutting down the Tree?"

Ruth shook her head. "No. I wish it was. Besides, my father couldn't do much damage to the Tree with that old saw and the condition he's in."

"I remembered something, Ruthie, that might be helpful," said

Willie.

"Do tell."

"I overheard two men talking at the store yesterday while I was stocking the shelves in the back. Mr. Greenfield, the engineer for the Sweetwater Reservoir Dam, seemed very upset." Willie picked up a stick and scratched at the ground. "About shortcuts the owners of the resort made to the dam design. 'Life-threatening changes,' he said."

Michael frowned. "Sweetwater Dam? There's no dam in Sweetwater. At least, not in 1966."

Ruth answered. "There is now, in 1896. The Sweetwater Reservoir Dam. It's on the top of a high hill, less than a mile from here." Ruth saw a strange look come over Arabeth's face. "What is it?"

"The dam. It breaks." Arabeth's words hung like heavy fog in the air. "I just remembered."

"What do you mean? How do you know that?" Ruth knew the answer as soon as the words left her mouth. "You're from the future. You know what happens." A cold shiver wracked through her body. "It's been raining here for days. Nana and I were watching it when she died. She worried the dam wouldn't hold all the water."

"I can't believe I didn't think of this sooner. I've been too busy thinking about unknowns, not what I *do* know," said Arabeth. "We studied it in our place-based environmental class. The dam was built by the Sweetwater Lake Entrepreneurs, a group of millionaires from a nearby city, as a retreat for their families. The size of the dam was increased in order to make a lake big enough to hold docks, boats, and large homes. Construction was rushed to get their 'resort' ready for summer use. The design for the bigger dam had flaws. And they used cheaper materials."

Ruth looked at the sketch Willie was making in the ground. "Is that the dam, Willie?"

"I'm trying to draw what the engineer did on a piece of paper." He pointed to a line. "Something about the crest and a thing called the spillway."

"What's a spillway?" Ruth realized she didn't know very much about the dam itself.

Arabeth scratched her head. "From what I remember, dams can only hold so much water. Before they get too full, they need a way to let some water out. That's the spillway. It runs downhill beside the dam. Water runs down this section when the dam becomes too full of water, like in a bad storm."

Michael smacked his head. "Duh, that's why it's called a spillway."

"But isn't a dam built to hold water?" asked Willie.

"If there's too much water in the dam, then the pressure on the walls of it can cause it to break," said Arabeth. "And you don't want water flowing over the top of it and washing the top away."

Ruth grabbed Arabeth's arm. "Do you remember what happens?" She thought about the Tree. About her family, sitting inside their house in Sweetwater, surrounded on all sides by hills. With a massive reservoir of water at the top of one of them—and a poorly designed one at that.

Arabeth snatched Willie's stick, drawing squiggly lines in the dirt away from the dam he drew. "Ten million gallons of water crash down from the mountainside in a matter of minutes, destroying part of the town and causing damage to the woods."

The Tree quivered and shook above them.

"Willie and me. Our houses are halfway up a hill. Is that high enough?" Ruth felt like she'd be sick. "What shortcuts were made?"

Arabeth sighed. "Researchers have never found the blueprints. Everything was destroyed in the flood. We have a few faded photographs. That's all."

Michael's face turned red. "I don't think I studied it. Or, if we did, I wasn't listening."

Ruth turned to Willie. "Did the engineer talk about the flaws?"

"I don't know. Father didn't say. But he heard the engineer talking about going over the blueprints with the owners tomorrow. Ten o'clock in the morning. At the resort office."

"I think we have our crisis to fix," said Ruth. "Stopping the dam creates the parallel universe and saves the Listening Tree."

Michael stood up, pacing. "We need to be outside that resort office at ten tomorrow morning so we can listen."

CHAPTER THIRTEEN
THE SHED

When Ruth opened her eyes the next morning, light filtered through her bedroom window. For a moment, everything seemed normal. Then she remembered the day before. Michael and Arabeth. Rainwalking and the Listening Tree. The dam and a parallel universe. She bolted upright. Michael and Arabeth were in the shed out back, sleeping. She'd thought about taking Michael and Arabeth to her nana's house for the night, but couldn't bear the idea that Nana was no longer there. Willie'd gone home but was coming back with clothes for Michael.

Ruth jumped out of bed, dressed, and ran downstairs. She made tea for her mother and packed her father's lunch. He grabbed it off the table and stomped out the door without mentioning the incident at the Tree. After he left, she grabbed the pillowcase of clothes she'd hid in the cupboard the night before, snatched the sausage and leftover bread off the table, and ran to the dilapidated shed in the back yard.

Ruth yanked upwards on the bolt on the back door of the shed. The door scraped the ground as it opened, flecks of whitewash falling off. Early morning sunlight filtered through cracks in the walls and ceiling, bathing the interior of the shed in thin lines of brightness. Small muddy places were scattered on the dirt floor where rain had leaked through holes in the roof. Broken furniture and odd pieces of wood leaned against the shed walls. She found Arabeth and Michael asleep behind a pile of furniture.

She nudged Michael on the shoulder. He bolted upright, swinging his arm at her. "I'm getting up, Matt! Leave me alone."

Ruth jumped back.

He rubbed his eyes. "Sorry, Ruth. I thought I was back home. Thought you were my brother for a second."

Arabeth sighed underneath her blankets, from which curly blue strands of hair shot out at all angles. "Could you guys be quiet for a few more minutes?"

"Look, a mound of talking hair." Michael laughed, rolling onto his side.

Arabeth sat up, patting at her hair. "Guess I better put a scarf on right away. Did you bring clothes?"

Ruth pulled a dress, pinafore, and scarf out of the pillowcase. "Here's the only scarf of Nana's I have." Arabeth took the clothes and changed behind a large stack of wooden planks. "Willie should be here soon with yours." Ruth said as she handed Michael half of the bread and sausage.

"I'm so hungry, I could eat a horse." Michael sat up, wolfing down the sausage in two bites.

"We have the same expression," said Ruth. She scrunched up her mouth. "By 1966, do people really eat horses?"

"No, silly," said Michael, stuffing a piece of bread into his mouth. "Man, am I hungry!"

Arabeth reappeared, wearing the dress and pinafore. She pulled the scarf around her head, tucked up a few loose strands and took the sausage Ruth handed her. "Sausage? My parents told me about this." She turned it over. "We don't eat meat anymore. There's not enough resources to sustain meat production, so we eat plant-based protein."

"Plant-based protein? What on earth is that?" Michael grimaced. "You eat grass butt instead of pork butt? Wood roast instead of chuck roast?" He smiled. "Or maybe you eat wood chuck roast? Get it?"

Ruth laughed as Arabeth rolled her eyes toward the ceiling. She brushed her hands on the dress. "Feels pretty strange to be wearing this." She pushed down on the bulging mound of hair under the scarf wrapped around her head, tucking a few more straggling pieces up underneath it. "Won't people think this is odd, this dress and scarf together?"

Ruth looked over the outfit. "Actually, no. Sweetwater has a train station and once a week a train comes through with many children on it. Some get off here and live with families in town. People will think you both are from the train."

"An orphan train?" asked Arabeth.

Ruth grimaced. "I guess you could call it that. I don't know if they're all orphans, though. I'm not even sure why they're here."

"Orphan trains ran across the country in the late 1890s. People couldn't afford to keep all their children so they'd send them to a different town, hoping a family would take them in. But, many times, they were just used as workers." Arabeth stopped. "How strange. I'm an orphan from 2035 disguised as if I'm from an orphan train in 1896."

The back door creaked open and Willie appeared, carrying a bundle and a glass bottle.

"Here's your clothes, Michael." He dropped the parcel beside Michael and yawned. "I couldn't sleep all night, thinking about today and the blueprints." He handed Arabeth the bottle. "I thought you might like some milk."

Arabeth took the bottle. "I'm excited, too. No one's ever seen the blueprints, remember?" She held the bottle up. "Is it soy or almond?"

Willie frowned. "Um, it's from a cow." He scratched his head.

"Don't tell me you can milk almonds in 2035?" laughed Michael.

"We don't have space or enough water to raise dairy, so we use soybeans or nuts."

Michael shook his head. "How do you get a milking machine on an almond? They're so tiny. And where does the milk, um, you know, come out?" He blushed. "Guess I'll find out when we get to 2035."

Ruth interrupted. "We better discuss what we're doing today. We have to save the Tree here first in order to even go to 1966."

"You're right, Ruth." Michael slipped behind a stack of wood, emerging a few minutes later wearing black pants that ended at the top of his socks. A white shirt stretched taut across his chest, with the cuffs a bit below the middle of his forearm. "Hey, thanks, Willie. But I'm certainly a lot bigger than you all."

Ruth giggled. "You'll fit right in, Michael. People will think you're wearing hand-me-downs from a brother." She turned to Willie. "What time did you say the meeting is today?"

"Ten o'clock."

"How far is the resort office?" Arabeth sat on the floor, her dress pulled over her knees, resting her elbows on them. She looked at her Skincom. "It's eight right now. If this is right in this time period."

Michael got up and walked to the shed door. He peered out. "I'd say eight is about right. According to the sun." He sauntered back, hands in his pockets. "How do I know that, you asked? Dad taught us how to tell time by using the sun while haying in the field."

"That's a great skill to have," said Ruth. "It'll be useful no matter what time period we're in." Her words earned her a grin from Michael.

"Back to the question of how far the resort office is," said Arabeth as she rose, dusting off her dress.

"It's not far," said Willie. "We have to go up the trail through the woods for about a mile."

They left the shed, running low across the back yard and into the woods. When they got to the Tree, they stopped. Ruth pointed towards the hillside a distance from them. "The resort office is there. At the top of the dam. You can see a bit of the roof."

"That red thing?" asked Michael.

"That's it," said Ruth. "It sits on a hill a little above the dam. We better hightail it up there in order to have time to find a place to hide."

Ruth and Willie led the way from the Tree to a path through the woods.

They'd walked along it for a few minutes when Michael asked, "Who uses this path, Ruth? We're going uphill pretty quickly, and it's not cleared out very well." He stepped on top of a large rock in the middle of the trail. "There's tons of rocks in it."

"People from town made this to get a view of the lake. Willie and I didn't make a path to the dam from the Tree because we didn't want people visiting the Tree too much."

Fifteen minutes later, after a steady climb upward, they arrived at a fork in the pathway.

Ruth stopped. "If we keep going straight, we'll come to the dam up ahead. This turn-off leads to the resort office." The red-roofed building they'd seen earlier was visible at the end of the turn-off. "We better sneak up alongside it, don't you think?"

They walked slowly along the edge of the turn-off. The back of the building was ahead of them. "The path goes around the side to the front. They built it that way so the front faces the dam and the lake. We should hide along the side?" Ruth said questioningly. They had no way of knowing if the men attending the meeting were already inside.

CHAPTER FOURTEEN
THE RESORT OFFICE

Suddenly, loud shouts filled the air from the direction of the resort office. Ruth jumped. "It sounds like someone fighting in there."

Willie grabbed her elbow. "Maybe it's the engineer and someone from the resort association arguing over the dam." He pulled at Ruth. "Come on, we need to get closer."

They crept to a small group of trees along the side of the building, crouching down in the bushes. Above them, angry voices drifted out through an open window

"I've told you over and over, sir. You've already lowered the dam by a foot and raised the spillway too high. It's not safe now. There shouldn't be a carriage road on the crest. It's too dangerous," the angry voice shouted. "It's covered with debris. With all this rain, water could collect there and wash the top of the dam away." There was a pause. "Good Lord, man, there's millions of gallons of water behind it."

Another voice, deep and threatening, responded. "Look, we hired you to build a dam to our specifications."

"Listen, sir. The dam is dangerous. We used substandard materials in the construction of it to cut costs as you wanted." The voice choked and softened. "It's been raining for days; rain like we've never seen. New leaks are already appearing." Silence. Then, the same voice continued. "Thousands of people live in the valley below the dam. Not to mention the forest and the resources there, all at risk should it break. I can't stand by and watch this happen. People need to know the danger they are in."

"You will say nothing!" Loud sounds of feet shuffling, things being pushed, and heavy breathing flowed out the small window several feet above them.

"What's happening in there?" Michael got down on his hands and knees, motioning to Willie. "Arabeth, help him get up on my back. Willie, see if you can peek in the window."

Willie climbed up onto Michael's back. Just as his head reached the level of the window, scuffling, shouting, and a loud thump could be heard.

Willie stared down at them, a look of horror in his eyes. "I can't look. Something just happened to someone." He jumped down. "Oh, dear."

A door slammed, and footsteps could be heard, racing away from the building, out the front.

Arabeth crept toward the front of the office and peeked around the corner. "A man in a black suit with a top hat is running down the road," she whispered back to them.

Ruth snuck up beside her. The man was already out of sight. "It had to be one of the entrepreneurs. No one in town can afford clothing like that." Ruth motioned for Willie and Michael to join them. "We have to see what happened, don't we? Maybe we can help."

Slowly, Ruth pushed open the door to the office. "Oh, my, oh goodness," she shouted, running into the building.

CHAPTER FIFTEEN
THE ENGINEER

The main room was in complete disarray, with tables overturned, chairs thrown askew, and papers scattered about the floor. In the center lay a man, a pool of blood beneath his head.

Ruth rushed over to him. "Oh, dear Lord. He's suffered a terrible blow." Michael covered his mouth and rushed outside. They heard him coughing and sputtering. Ruth gently put her head on the man's chest. "Oh, dear. He's not breathing. Oh, dear."

Willie inched toward the man. "It's Mr. Greenfield, the engineer. From Father's store." He swallowed hard, his voice quivering. "Is he dead?"

"I think he is," said Arabeth, kneeling beside the body. "It looks like he was hit on the head with something." She paused to look around on the floor, then shivered as she pointed to a paperweight lying a few feet away. "That might be the object that killed him." She slid back from the man, wrapping her arms around herself. "What do we do now?"

Ruth fought back tears as she heard Arabeth sob. "What we do is right. We've got a dead man and a dam that could break."

Michael slowly entered the building, his face a strange shade of green. "Sorry."

Arabeth looked up at him. "Are you all right? Take some deep breaths and try to relax. Don't look. Maybe try to find the blueprints for the dam? That will take your mind off the—" she paused "—the situation."

Michael walked around the room, looking everywhere but at the body. He shuffled through some papers on a desk, then began to rummage through a pile underneath it. "Hey, look at this." He crawled out with a large cardboard tube. "I bet this might be them."

He moved to an empty table on the other side of the room, underneath a window, and pulled a long paper from inside the tube. "Don't think about the body. Don't think about the blood." He spread the paper out, looking back at Ruth. "Can you hold the sides of this paper down?"

Ruth stepped over some papers and moved a chair out of the way.

"They must have had a terrible fight to mess up this room like this." She held the opposite edges of the paper, flattening it on the table. The diagram certainly looked like a dam. "I think this is it, Michael."

Arabeth and Willie joined them at the table. Arabeth put her finger on a paragraph at the top of the drawing. "It's the blueprints, all right. It gives the dimensions for the height and width of the dam, plus a list of materials needed for the construction."

Willie added, pointing to each in turn, "And here's the crest. And over here is the spillway."

Michael fiddled with the cardboard tube, tapping it lightly, upside down, on the table as he looked at the diagram.

"Do you mind?" asked Arabeth, a note of irritation in her voice.

"Sorry." He shrugged and held the tube up to his eye as he said softly, "Um, I have trouble reading." He stuck his finger into the tube. "Hey, what's this?" He pulled out a small paper and put it on the table. "What's it say?" he asked Ruth quietly.

Ruth couldn't imagine what it would be like to have difficulty reading, and she could tell he was embarrassed about it. "A List of Modifications to Be Made at the Request of the Sweetwater Lake Resort Organization." She read slowly, pausing after each word.

Michael studied the new diagram. "Okay. These numbers don't match up. The dimensions are off. By more than a foot, even." He looked back and forth between the two papers. "Is this the list of materials?" he asked, pointing to the box on each side.

"Yes," said Arabeth.

"The words and numbers are different. So that means they used different materials and different amounts of them?"

"That's what the engineer said," mumbled Willie, turning to look at the body on the floor. "At Father's store."

Ruth wondered how they could possibly fix a dam that was already built to the wrong dimensions and with the wrong materials. It seemed impossible. Was that even what Fuzzy was referring to when he said to fix an event?

Willie tapped Ruth on the elbow, a look of urgency on his face. "I know we need to help with the dam, but what do we do right now? I mean, about the engineer? Do we tell someone?"

"I don't know." Ruth glanced over at the engineer. "I guess you and I could go to town and tell your father we were in the forest and heard shouting at the resort office. Someone will come and find him." She looked out the door. "But his killer is still out there. And we only have one day left before the dam breaks."

Arabeth held her Skincom over the blueprints. "Einstein, save image please."

"What are you doing?" asked Michael. "Who are you talking to?"

"I'm saving an image of the blueprints. We can call it up anytime in case we need it. Einstein is the name of the virtual assistant in my Skincom programming. That way we don't need to carry this tube with the blueprints in it around with us."

"Einstein is like the computer on the Enterprise." Michael shook his head and walked away. "Can Einstein help us figure out how to save the Listening Tree?"

Ruth stood, peering up at the darkening sky through the window above the desk.

"What's wrong, Ruth?" asked Michael.

"I'm thinking about what the engineer said, about all the people who live down in town, below the dam. When it breaks, which we know it will, what will happen to them?" Thoughts of her family filled her mind. A gusty wind blew, sending leaves swirling into the building, through the open window and the door. "We need to get to the Tree. We need her help."

CHAPTER SIXTEEN
THE LOCKET

They closed the door behind them and hurried toward the Tree. Ruth tried, but she couldn't keep the sight and feel of the dead engineer out of her mind as she ran. When they rounded the bend to the Tree, a squirrel ran across their path. After a few more steps, another rushed by. The squirrels raced through the woods beside Ruth, darting in and out of the bushes and trees.

"Why, the squirrels are certainly out today," said Ruth, watching the last one who ran in front of them. He sat at the base of a tree a few feet away, scrutinizing them and chattering incessantly. "They must be gathering acorns for winter." He chirped loudly. Within seconds, they were surrounded by noisy squirrels, racing in circles at their feet.

Ruth giggled. "Do you think he sent out a call for more? Look at all of them."

A squirrel stopped at her feet, sitting on its backside, rubbing its paws together. He stared at her, chattering loudly. With a forceful bark, he raced toward the boulders behind the trees, several others following. They stopped every few feet to look back at Ruth and scold.

Ruth turned to Michael. "I think they mean for us to follow them."

"Let's go," said Michael, scratching his head. "Maybe the Tree has told them something? We might not be the only ones she sends messages to."

When they reached the boulders, the squirrels scampered up to the top and scurried along the edges of the opening between them. They stopped, turned to look at Ruth, then jumped into the surrounding trees, filling the air with loud chittering.

Ruth stepped slowly into the opening, rubbing her hands along the boulders. "They want us to go in here." She closed her eyes. Her skin tingled. "There's something here. Some kind of clue. "

Michael stood at the opening. "But Arabeth and I were just here when your dad came up with the saw."

"I know, but there's something here. I can feel it." Ruth walked along the passageway between the boulders, with Arabeth and Michael following. They came out the other end into a small clearing surrounded by dense woods and brambles.

She turned and looked back through the passageway. *Why do the squirrels want us here?*

Faint rays of sunlight filtered through the grey clouds gathering overhead. Ruth caught a glimpse of a shiny object on the ground several feet back down the passageway. She hadn't noticed it while in the darkness between the boulders. "Come, look," she said, pointing down and walking toward the shimmering piece. She picked it up. "Let's get out where there's more light." She walked back into the clearing. "Why, it's a locket. How on Earth did it get here?" She turned it over, looking at the design engraved in the silver. "Odd, but this design looks familiar to me." She pushed upwards on a tiny clasp on the side. The locket opened to reveal two small pictures. "Oh, my," she gasped.

"What is it?" asked Arabeth, moving to look over her shoulder.

Ruth pointed at a small picture of a woman in the locket cover. "This is my nana," she whispered. "When she was younger, like marrying age. I've seen pictures of her like this."

The image on the right perplexed her. "I don't recognize this person." Her grandmother and a man sat close together, as if they were a couple. "I wonder if he's my grandfather. Something about him looks familiar." Ruth was puzzled. "But I've never met my grandfather, and we have no pictures of them together." The man had kind eyes and a wide smile. "Nana said she loved him deeply."

"Could he be her brother?" said Arabeth. "Let me see it." She held the locket up. "Strange. He looks familiar to me, too." She closed the locket, rubbing her finger over the top. "And this design, I think I've seen it before as well."

Ruth took the locket back. "How can he be familiar to you? You're from over hundred years into the future." She shook her head. "Nana had no brothers, not any that I know." She paced around, searching the ground. "It's very bizarre. How did it get here?"

The woods had become strangely silent. Ruth looked at the top of the boulders. "The squirrels are gone. This must be what they wanted us to find." She hung the locket around her neck, hiding it underneath her dress. "I think I'll wear it so we don't lose it. If it *is* a clue, I have no idea what it means."

Michael shrugged as Willie said, "I've been to your nana's a lot, Ruthie, and I've never seen that locket."

Arabeth bit her lip. "She could've had it in a jewelry box and never worn it. But that doesn't explain why it's up here and how I've seen that design before—which I know I have."

At the mention of Nana's house, Ruth felt a strong urge to go there. Perhaps the answer to the puzzle of the locket was there somewhere.

Willie suddenly put his fingers to his mouth, his eyes darting toward the opening between the boulders. Rustling sounds drifted down the passageway toward them from the opposite end. "Those noises. They're too heavy to be squirrels," Willie whispered.

Ruth stared down the passageway as she motioned for the others to hide behind the boulders. She could just see the Listening Tree at the other end. And two men standing beside it, facing away from her.

Ruth flattened herself against the rock, next to Arabeth. Her voice came out in a high-pitched whisper. "Remember the two men on hoverboards? In the desert?" She swallowed hard. "They're here. By the Tree."

"They're here? In 1896? Why?" asked Arabeth. "Is it that locket?"

"I don't know if I want to find out," said Michael as he and Willie hid behind the boulder on the other side of the passageway.

"What men? What are you talking about?" Willie whispered, looking around Michael.

Ruth didn't want to see those men again. "We'll explain that later. We don't want them to find us." She pointed to the woods across from them. A small gap, cut through the brush, was barely visible. "Willie, let's take the old path back into town. I want to look for something at Nana's."

Willie nodded and ran across the small clearing. "Follow me. It's really overgrown cuz no one uses it much anymore." He pushed aside the brambles on each side of the path as he entered. Arabeth and Michael followed close behind him. "You might get scratched up a bit."

Michael turned back. "You coming, Ruth?"

"I'm right behind you."

The brambles on either side of the path sprang back into place after each of them passed through, almost hiding the person in front. Ruth took several steps along the path but stopped as she heard a voice behind her. Were the men following them?

Turning around, she didn't see anyone. She waited for a moment, wondering if she should look again. She crouched on her knees, just inside the woods. Two men emerged from the passageway and stood in the clearing. The men on the hoverboards.

"It's got to be here," a rough, gravelly voice said. "Martin said to be sure we find it."

Ruth sucked in a breath. She'd heard Fuzzy call the man at the Bristlecone Pine Martin. The two men on hoverboards had to work for him. But what did they want? The locket?

"What if we don't?" a shrill voice wailed. "We'll be in big trouble, won't we? We will, won't we?"

"Shut up and get looking. We can't go back without it."

"I told you we shouldn't have brought that Fuzzy guy back here. He's responsible for this, you know. He dropped it. On purpose."

Ruth swallowed hard. *They have Fuzzy. Here in 1896. Where? Did he drop the locket? But where did he get it?*

The thick bushes and brambles blocked her view. She wanted to get a better look at their faces so she'd recognize them if they showed up again. She crept forward, hoping to find a bigger space between the branches for a clearer view. A bramble caught the hair on top of her head, yanking it painfully when she moved. Biting her lip to keep from crying out, she looked down, trying to get the thorns on the branch unstuck from her hair. She put her head down further, the prickly barbs scratching her fingers as she struggled to get her hair loose.

Suddenly, she was yanked upward by the shoulders.

She looked up into a man's face, his lips pursed and eyes squinting. "I know you. You were at that tree in 2035." His deep voice pounded in her head as if he'd hit her with a hammer. "Where is the locket?"

"Let me go," she shouted, squirming and twisting in his grasp.

"Stop wiggling," the man commanded. "It's no use." He tightened his grip on her arm as they stood in the clearing behind the boulders. "Get over here and help me," he yelled at the other man. Ruth saw him crawling on the ground near the boulders, searching.

"Ouch, you're hurting me," Ruth cried. "Who are you?"

"Don't ask questions," said the man with the squeaky voice, approaching her from the other side. "We're from the future. And we're about to change your future forever!" He grabbed her other arm, hustling her back toward the passageway. "Where's the locket?"

Ruth felt her neck getting red as she thought about the locket. It must be very important. Her head reeled with questions and fear. "Let me go," she yelled, trying to brace herself against the boulders.

They dragged her back through the passageway and out the other side.

Ruth looked up at the Tree. A vision flew across her mind of her and Willie sitting at the base of the Tree, their backs pressed against it, letting it absorb all their worries and pain. Oh, what she would give to have that power with her right now. *Please,* she begged, *please help me, Listening Tree. I have to stop them from getting the locket somehow.* Her poetry book began to glow and warm the pocket of her pinafore. It's the leaf. She had to get her arm free.

"Let go of me," she hissed, "and I'll show you where it is."

The man with the squeaky voice relaxed his grip on her arm. She brushed her hair out of her face. A familiar smell seemed to be emanating from her fingertips as she shoved her hand into her pocket. Where had she smelled that before?

She remembered! When a certain type of insect tried to eat the leaves of the Tree, the leaves emitted a particular fragrance. The insects, after taking a bite of a leaf, buzzed and squirmed as if ill, and then flew away. As if the Tree could suddenly make itself distasteful to them.

Was this a clue? Did she have the power to do that as well?

She brought her poetry book out from her pocket.

"Is it in there?" The larger man looked at the book. "Is that where you have the locket?"

Her fingertips felt warm and began to glow. "Is that what you think?" she asked.

He grabbed her arm and tried to pull the book out of her hand. "Don't get smart with me. Ouch!" he screamed. "Your fingers are on fire," he shouted, stepping away from her.

Ruth wiggled out of their grasp and thrust her arms out. She held the book in both hands, focusing all her energy into the tips of her fingers, feeling the Tree's strength and power flowing from the leaf inside the book throughout her body. She aimed the book at the men as a mist emerged from her fingertips and strong smell of ammonia and sulfur filled the air. The mist swirled around the men, enveloping them in a ghostly white fog. She saw them bend over, their bodies shaking and twisting as they coughed and sputtered.

"What in the universe?" choked the squeaky-voiced man. "What's happening?"

"Don't have a clue, but we're out of here," said the other, dropping to his knees. "Let her go. We'll—" he choked, spitting on the ground "—tell Dr. Millstone about this."

Ruth knelt on the ground, all her energy spent. She had to remember their faces and that name. Millstone.

The men stumbled past her, leaning up against the Tree. They each took out a tiny vial of red liquid and gulped quickly. Then they disappeared into the Tree.

CHAPTER SEVENTEEN
PHEROMONE POWER

"Ruth! Are you okay?" Michael raced out of the passageway, kneeling down beside her. "You were behind me and then all of a sudden you were gone."

"Are you all right?" said Arabeth, emerging from between the boulders as Willie rushed to Ruth's side, putting his hand on her shoulder. "What happened?"

"Those men. I heard them talking about looking for something." Ruth pushed herself up from the ground. "So I hid by the entrance to the path to listen. They grabbed me and brought me back out here."

"What did they say?" Michael asked. "It's the locket, isn't it? They want it."

Ruth put her poetry book back in her pocket. "They do. And they brought Fuzzy here, to 1896."

"He was here? Where is he now?" Michael looked around.

"They didn't say. They grabbed me and tried to get the locket." She held the locket in her hand. "To take to a man named Martin. That's the name I heard Fuzzy call the man at the Bristlecone Pine. And I think his last name is Millstone. They talked about telling a Doctor Millstone."

Arabeth looked startled. "Millstone? What? No, it can't be. It's a coincidence."

"What's a coincidence?" asked Michael, walking near the edge of the woods.

"Zarek, an annoying boy in my class. His last name is Millstone." Arabeth frowned at Ruth. "Next time, don't go off doing this by yourself. You could've been hurt."

Ruth shrugged. "You're right. They did scare me. But something very strange happened that made them leave."

"What do you mean?" Michael came back from looking into the woods. He sniffed "What's that smell? Like rotten eggs."

Ruth stood beside him, examining her hands, which were perfectly normal now. What had she done? "I really don't know," she whispered as she reached into her pocket and took out her poetry book with the leaf inside. "They wanted the locket." She glanced at Willie. "I thought about us, Willie, at the Listening Tree and how it always helps us solve our problems. I asked it to help me. And then my leaf started to glow and get warm, and I remembered the smell that radiates from the Tree when those insects hatch out. It keeps them from eating the leaves, remember?" She glanced at Willie, then back at her fingers.

Willie nodded. "Sure I do." He looked at her hand. "What's that got to do with your fingers?"

Ruth said in a quiet voice, "A powerful smell came out my fingertips. It made them sick and they ran off." She touched her fingertips to her cheeks. They were no longer warm. "It sounds extraordinary, but I felt like we were one, the Tree and I, that we made the smell together."

Arabeth took off her scarf and ruffled her hair. Michael looked at her. "What are you doing?"

"I have to think," Arabeth said. "This scarf gets in my way. In fact, this entire outfit bugs me." She pranced in a circle, talking. "So, what do we know? We know we have these amulets from the Listening Tree. We know they allow us to travel through time, through the water in the Listening Tree. But this," she pointed to Ruth's fingers, "is something new." She held out her acorn necklace. "What if the amulet gave you the power to make a pheromone against the two men and also the power to control its release it into the atmosphere?"

"A what?" asked Michael, chewing on his lip. "A fearamine? A fear a'mine is that I don't have a clue what's going on!" He plopped down. "Can you explain?" He looked at Arabeth with raised eyebrows.

"A pheromone is a chemical released by an organism that helps protect it or attract other organisms to it, depending on what the organism wants. So, if it wants to attract a mate, it releases a chemical that the opposite sex finds appealing. If it wants to protect itself, it releases a chemical that makes the intruder or predator sick or might even kill it."

Ruth put her hand over her mouth. Had she killed the men? "The Tree helped me to produce a pheromone that made them ill or ...." She dropped her hand. "I didn't want to kill them. Just stop them."

"I don't think you did," said Arabeth. "Kill them, I mean. They got away, right?"

Ruth told them about the two vials of red liquid, and their disappearance into the Tree.

"What? A red liquid?" Arabeth appeared lost in thought. "It must give them the ability to rainwalk. I mean, why else would they drink it right before they entered the Tree?"

Michael turned his hands over, wiggling his fingers. "Do you think we can all do that? Not drink red liquid, but make those things called fearamines? Like maybe I could make a fear—a smell that would attract I don't know who, but say, someone special to want to go out with me?" His face got red.

Arabeth smirked. "Jeez, Michael."

"Just asking." He rose to his feet. "How do you think you got this power, Ruth?"

"I felt like the Tree and I were connected through our feelings. She was afraid for me, too."

Arabeth muttered, "Empathy." She turned to Michael. "It's the ability to share the emotions of another."

Michael looked up at the Tree for a moment. "Trees have emotions?"

Ruth walked over to the Tree and put her hand on it. "We've all felt the connection to the Tree. And look how she's helped us in the past few days. She's obviously connected to us. Empathy is having a connection."

Michael smacked his head, grinning. "Okay, empathy, got it. I've had it with my prize Holstein, Uhura."

Ruth interrupted him. "Uhura? Where did you get that name?"

"From *Star Trek*, of course," he responded. "She's the most beautiful woman I've ever seen." His face got red again. "Anyway, when my Uhura gave birth, she had a terrible time. She couldn't get the calf out. She moaned something awful. I couldn't stand it. I stood in front of her, looking into her big brown eyes and … it sounds silly, but looking at her, it was like she was trying to tell me something. Like help me or something. So I rubbed her head, and I swear I felt her pain coming through my hands. Almost like we were giving birth together." He looked at them. "I know that's not possible. I mean, I'm a boy and she's a cow. I tried to tell my dad, but he thought I was crazy or something. It was pretty embarrassing."

Ruth said, "That's empathy, Michael." She patted his hand.

"Back to the trigger," said Arabeth, rolling her eyes. "I think when we're at the Tree, we can use a physical connection, like touching it or standing along a root, along with our amulet, to rainwalk, and move through time. And it also seems that when we need help, we can use our empathy connection along with our amulet to help us even more." She began to put her hair back up under the scarf. "We have even more questions now. One, does this connection to the Tree give us all a power? And are they the same or different?" Willie and Michael looked at their fingertips. "Two, how far away from the Tree can we use empathy? And three, if Fuzzy was here, where is he now and what's the significance of the locket in all of this?"

Gray clouds drifted through the sky and a gentle rain began to fall.

Ruth added, "We need to find the answers quickly. We're running out of time."

CHAPTER EIGHTEEN
GRANDFATHER

They huddled under the Tree's branches, protected from the rain. Ruth knew what they needed to do. "We should go to my nana's house." She wiped a tear off her cheek and took a deep breath. "I haven't been there since the funeral, but I know we need to look there for an answer." She held up the locket. "This is Nana's picture. We have to find out how Fuzzy got it. And why this locket looks familiar. I've never seen her wear it. And why is this important to us?"

Michael raised his eyebrows. "Do you believe in ghosts?"

"Ghosts?"

"Yeah, ghosts. What if your nana's spirit was up here, wearing that necklace, and dropped it?"

Arabeth frowned, shaking her head. "There's no scientific explanation for ghosts."

Michael looked at her sideways, throwing his arms in the air. "Not yet. But who knows what we'll find out in the future? I mean, the future beyond your time."

Arabeth shrugged. "Yeah, I guess, Michael. Think about it. Even in my time, we have no explanation for lots of stuff that's happening here. Like a human making pheromones with her fingers. I mean, who knew that could happen?"

"You're right," Michael said.

Arabeth stuck out her hand, "Can I see the locket?" She looked at the design on the front as Ruth gave it to her. "I don't get it. Why is this design familiar to me, too?" She pushed on the clasp.

"Be careful it doesn't get wet," Ruth said. "We can't ruin the pictures."

Arabeth slowly snapped the locket shut. "It's driving me crazy. I know I've seen this image before." Then she jumped up and down. "I know where!" She grabbed Ruth. "When you said 'be careful it doesn't get wet,' I thought about Fuzzy's science class. Let me show you all something."

She gave the locket back to Ruth and punched at her Skincom. An image of Fuzzy, standing at a lab desk in the front of a roomful of children, hovered above her wrist. Ruth and Willie stepped back, gasping.

"Holy hologram! Just like the one at the Bristlecone Pine, right?" Michael exclaimed.

"So right, Michael. I can store videos of past events and bring them up as hologram images."

They gathered around, watching the video of Fuzzy gesturing and speaking. "Don't let the potassium get wet, my budding scientists." He perched on a stool. From the corner, a boy walked up to him.

"That's Zarek. Zarek Millstone," Arabeth added as they watched. "Same last name as this evil Martin fellow." She shook her head. "It's got to be coincidence."

She pushed a button, and the hologram continued. Zarek stood by Fuzzy, asking, "Mr. Grundle, when are we going to sample our own DNA? My father wants to know."

Arabeth paused the Skincom. "That kid is so annoying. Always asking questions about DNA." Her eyes widened as she spoke. "Always asking about DNA? Guys, that's too coincidental. Something strange is going on." She started up the hologram again.

Fuzzy's face took on a serious look as he straightened the collar of his lab coat. He seemed to study Zarek for a long time before responding, "Soon, Zarek. Now, back to your lab experiment. You shouldn't leave the potassium out for long."

Arabeth pressed her Skincom, freezing the image, then enlarging it until Fuzzy loomed about a foot high off her wrist. "Look at his neck."

Peeking out from underneath the top of his white shirt was a silver necklace, only half of it visible.

Ruth drew in a breath, whispering, "The same design. Fuzzy's wearing a necklace just like this one." She turned the locket over. "But it has Nana's picture in it."

A squirrel chattered loudly above them.

"He dropped the locket so we'd find it." An acorn fell to the ground in front of Ruth. She glanced up to see the squirrel staring down at her. "And the squirrels brought us to it." She stared at the hologram. "What I'm thinking is very bizarre." Opening the locket, she showed them the picture. "The man in this picture, who we think is Nana's husband, is Fuzzy. Of course, he's younger. But it is him; don't you agree, Arabeth?"

Arabeth rubbed her head. "That makes sense as to why he looks familiar to me." She looked back and forth between the locket picture and the hologram. "He's younger, but it's him."

"But he'd be," Michael said, then paused, staring into space, "he'd be close to two hundred years old now. How can that be?"

Arabeth paced around the Tree. "Maybe he traveled back in time and met your nana, Ruth. The only other explanation I can come up with is that his cells don't deteriorate like regular human cells. What if they act more like plant cells? They don't age like animal cells do."

"What are you saying, Arabeth?" Michael said. "I don't get it."

"So, we've found out that plant cells contain a substance that keeps them from aging as fast as animal cells. And all Fuzzy had time to tell us was that we're connected to the Trees. That's why we can do what we can. But what if Rainwalkers have enough genetic material from plants to allow them to age slower? And live longer?" Then she gasped. "What if all of us have that ability?"

"But I've been thinking my nana had to be a Rainwalker. How else would she know about the Trees?" Ruth thought for a moment. "Unless she was just human, and somehow met Fuzzy." She put her hand on her chest. "Imagine. He must have traveled back in time and met my nana. Or been born at the same time, but he didn't age like her. How heartbreaking to watch a loved one get old while you stay younger."

Willie walked over to Ruth. "You're not going to age the same as me?" His face fell and he stared at the ground. Then he added, "In a week, I'll know if I am a Rainwalker."

"We're just guessing about all this anyway," Arabeth added.

Michael pointed at the boulders. "You're right again. We've got to find Fuzzy and talk to him. Get some answers. He wasn't with the two men when you saw them, Ruth?"

Ruth stared at the Tree. "No, he wasn't. He must have gotten away from them somehow. The two men disappeared into the tree after they drank that liquid."

"That's it!" Arabeth snapped her fingers. "Remember when they stuck Fuzzy with something? They took a sample of his blood. To extract his DNA and get the ability to rainwalk. And, possibly—and I'm basing this on what we've figured out since we've seen the locket and the picture—to acquire the ability to live longer."

Ruth's eyes widened as she remembered the meeting at the Bristlecone Pine. "And that Martin guy said something about all he needed was a blood sample."

Ruth's mind raced with questions. All at once, she remembered the time she and Nana sat in her parlor, reading a passage from Thoreau, one of Nana's favorite writers. It said something about what lies within each of us is greater than what lies ahead of us. *Why did I think of that particular saying right now?*

The answer was in Nana's house. She knew it. She held up the locket. "We need to go to Nana's house quickly. This locket is a clue to something more." She looked at Arabeth. "You know Fuzzy. What do you think?"

Arabeth agreed. "You're so right. He left this for us to find. I bet there's more to it than that he might be your grandfather."

Willie's voice quivered. "Ruth, what do we do about the engineer?" He shivered. "He's dead."

"Oh, my. You're right." There was only one thing they could do. "Willie, you and I will go to the store. We'll explain to your father that while we were in the woods, we heard shouting at the office building. Then we looked in and saw a man on the floor. We can even tell him you recognized the man as the engineer. Your father will leave immediately and take some men and Doc Wilson with him."

"He sure will. But what about Arabeth and Michael?"

Michael chimed in. "We can hide in the shed again until you get back. Then we all go to your nana's house?"

Ruth nodded. "Her house is next to mine. I thought you two could just go to Nana's, but if the neighbors see you go in, they might think you're robbers. Wait in the shed."

CHAPTER NINETEEN
NANA'S HOUSE

After Ruth and Willie told his father about the engineer, the men gathered around the woodstove left quickly, shouting about grabbing Doc Wilson at home on their way to the office building. Ruth and Willie hurried down the street toward Nana's house.

A bolt of lightning flashed through the sky, followed by a loud clap of thunder. Rain began to fall, splashing off the rivulets of water racing down the street. A trolley went by, splattering them with a wave of muddy, cold water.

"The streets are flooding," said Willie, jumping to the side. "Did you see how worried Father and the men looked?"

Ruth brushed the mud from the bottom of her dress. "I did." She stepped over a large puddle in her way. "I've not ever seen this much water in the streets." She glanced up. The sky loomed above them like a dark grey ceiling, so close she could almost reach out and touch it. The world was closing in on them. A shiver swept through her body, and she hugged herself, pulling her pinafore close around her for warmth and comfort. The silver necklace felt cold against her neck.

Willie stopped and grabbed her arm, his eyes wide and flashing. "Ruthie, look how much water we got since this morning."

She brushed his hair away from his face. "I know." She hugged him close. "Let's get Michael and Arabeth and get to Nana's."

They raced down the street, bending into the rain, focusing on the ground to avoid the growing puddles dotting it.

As she jumped over a stream of water, Ruth felt someone catch her shoulder.

"Ruth Weaver! Where's your father?" She jerked away, gasping for air, her hand covering the locket around her neck.

"No! You can't have it!" she shouted, twisting her arm.

"Ruth! What are you talking about?"

She gazed up through the rain into the eyes of Mr. Decker, foreman at the mine. It wasn't the two men, trying to get the locket. It was Mr. Decker, asking for Father.

"What in tarnation are you and Willie doing running around in this weather?" He frowned at them. "I need your father. We're organizing a group to go work on patching the dam." He turned to Willie. "We could certainly use your father as well, young man."

Willie, a look of panic on his face, turned to Ruth. "Umm, Father's busy." She nodded at him. "He's gone to the dam office building. Ruth and I heard shouting up there earlier." Willie shivered.

"We think someone might be hurt," Ruth added. "He took some men from the store, and Doc Wilson."

"Find your father, Ruth. Tell him we're having a meeting this evening. We need as many people as we can get. He can help us. I've got to get the word to the others." He released her arm and turned to Willie. "You children get home. You're catching cold out here." He dashed a few steps away from them, then looked up at the sky. "I've never seen rain like this. God help us."

Where was her father? "I'll try, Mr. Decker," she shouted to him as he ran away, raising his arm to wave back at her. She would think about that later. They had to get to Nana's house.

They rushed down the street, sneaking behind her house to the shed. Ruth opened the back door to find Michael and Arabeth standing just inside. The floor of the shed had become a massive mud puddle. "We're here. And we've found out some things. Come on, let's go to Nana's quickly," she said.

Ruth led them behind her house and up to the back door of Nana's house. She took a long gold key out of her pocket and opened the door.

As Ruth stepped into the kitchen, her heart shattered. The cups in the cupboard, used every day for tea, the mark on the kitchen table from a hot pan she'd rested on it, the smells of the dried herbs hanging from the ceiling that they collected every summer in the garden all reminded her of moments with Nana. She leaned against the counter by the door, trying not to cry. She'd never been in this house without Nana. She drew in a deep breath, closing her eyes. Nana would want her to be strong. To save the Tree.

Michael walked over to her. "Are you okay?"

The sound of rain falling on the roof filled the room. Grey light filtered through the sheer curtains at the kitchen window.

Ruth looked out the window. "I cannot believe she is gone." She watched the trees outside, their branches swinging back and forth in the wind. They looked like long arms, trying to get her attention, some waving at her, others reaching for the top of the house, trying to tap on the attic window. She turned to find Willie, Michael, and Arabeth watching her, waiting. She squared her shoulders, stepping away from the window. "Look at the tree branches. We need to go to the attic." Ruth had never been there before, but knew that was where they had to go.

Willie asked, "Don't you want to tell Arabeth and Michael about what Mr. Decker said? Before we go to the attic?"

Ruth wiped her eyes and nodded. "Thanks, Willie. Of course. I forgot. Mr. Decker, my father's foreman at the mine, told me to find my father. The townspeople are organizing to try to patch the leaks in the dam." The wind rattled the kitchen window. "People are getting frightened. We've never had weather like this before."

"That's true," said Willie. "And I heard the men at the store talking about the level of the water behind the dam. It's really high, almost to the top right now."

Arabeth paced around the kitchen table. "That's great news!"

Michael frowned. "That the water is to the top of the dam?"

"No, I mean about the townspeople. We need some help. I've been thinking that patching the leaks may be the only way to save the Tree from too much damage."

Ruth sighed. "And perhaps some lives of the townspeople."

Michael scratched his head, staring at the cupboards above the sink. He put his hand on his stomach, which rumbled quietly. "Ruth, before we go to the attic, do you think I could have an apple? Maybe two? I'm so hungry."

Ruth took down the bowl of fruit from the cupboard. "You're right." She got out a loaf of bread and some butter. "I guess we're probably all hungry."

Willie nodded, reaching into his pocket and pulling out some dried beef and a slab of cheese. "I snuck these from our kitchen earlier."

"Let's go up to the attic. We can eat up there while we look for— well, I'm not quite sure what." Ruth led the way out of the kitchen, through the parlor. Nana's rocker by the window made her think of the many afternoons spent there, reading. The citrusy fragrance of her favorite tea, bergamot, swept over her, and she could taste its tartness as she swallowed, trying not to think of those days.

Ruth started up the stairs, every step creaking as always. Her heart broke with each sound. When she got to the second floor, she continued down the hallway, stopping in front of a small door at the end.

She jiggled the large white porcelain knob back and forth. The door didn't budge. "I've never been in Nana's attic," she said, exasperated. "Why won't the door open?"

"Maybe you need a key," said Michael.

"I only have the one for the back door," said Ruth, holding up the long gold key from her pocket. She looked below the doorknob and all around it. "Besides, there's no place for a key."

Arabeth shrugged. "We don't use keys. It's all fingerprints or facial recognition."

"What do you mean? A door can know it's you and not me?" Michael stared into the wood of the door. "How do you give wood a brain to do that?" Then he stepped back, tapping his forehead. "Duh, a computer. Like in your Skincom. You put a computer in every door?"

"Well, not exactly," said Arabeth. "There's about eighty points on your face that define you. Like your cheekbones, your jaw, and a bunch of other ones. We program them into a computer so when you look into a screen on the door, it recognizes you. And then, voila, it unlocks."

Michael studied the wooden door. "There's no screen or anything on this door." He rubbed his hand over the frame on the side opposite the doorknob. Three flat metal hinges kept the door in place. Peering closely at the center one, he said, "Look here. Most doors have two hinges." Arabeth raised her eyebrows at him. "How do I know that? My farmhouse was built in 1850. We still use the original doors, and they have two hinges." He pointed to the top and bottom hinges. He touched the center hinge. "But this one is unusual. I bet it means something."

Arabeth moved beside him to look. "I wouldn't have noticed that."

Michael cocked his head and shrugged, grinning. "I can find stuff, and you can explain it."

Ruth tried to wiggle the hinge, but it didn't budge. She felt the bottom hinge. "The middle one isn't nearly as smooth as the other hinges." She grabbed Michael's hand. "Feel it."

He rubbed the hinge, back and forth. "Holy secrets! I think it's some kind of code."

Arabeth chuckled. "A code? On a hinge? You've been watching too many old TV shows."

"They're not old in my time," he responded without turning his head. "As Captain Kirk would say, 'I want the impossible checked out as well as the possible.'" He looked at Arabeth, who snorted. "Well, he said something like that."

"Let me feel it again." Ruth ran her right fingers over the hinge as she toyed with the locket hanging around her neck. Suddenly, she stopped.

She took off the locket and put it into Willie's hand. "Feel the design on the locket. And the bumps on the door hinge."

Willie rubbed the door hinge, then the locket. "They're the opposite of each other! The hinge marks are holes and the locket marks are bumps. "

"Let me see it," said Arabeth. She took the locket and nodded to Michael. "The locket fits into the hinge, Captain Kirk."

Michael pointed at her. "Right on, Arabeth!"

Ruth took the locket, lined up the design with the hinge, and pushed it in. A loud clicking sound filled the air, and the door groaned slowly open.

Narrow wooden steps rose in front of them, the walls on either side covered with stained and peeling wallpaper. A sliver of dim light from an attic window pierced the darkness at the top of the stairs. The smell of old wood and stale air drifted over them.

Ruth heard a creaking sound behind them. She raised her finger to her lips, pointing back down the hallway with her other hand towards the staircase from the parlor. Her heart beat loudly in her chest. Creak. She knew that sound. Someone was on the staircase, coming up from the parlor.

CHAPTER TWENTY
INTO THE ATTIC

Ruth motioned for the others to climb up the attic stairs. She checked to make sure she had the locket and pulled the door shut, leaving a narrow crack to peek out. Who would be in Nana's house?

Ruth sucked in her breath as she watched her mother walk into a room at the top of the stairs. *What is my mother doing here?* She hadn't seen her since she brought her tea this morning.

Ruth turned to Michael, who was on the step above her. "It's my mother. I must go see what she's doing," she whispered.

She left the attic door open just a crack and crept down the hallway to the room her mother entered. The door, partially closed, hid her from view. Ruth went down the staircase toward the parlor a few steps and walked back up so it appeared she'd just arrived at the house.

Ruth pushed the door to the room open. "Mother? Are you all right?"

Her mother stood gazing at a painting of the Listening Tree on the wall. "I thought I'd find you here." Ruth looked questioningly at her mother, who continued in a soft voice, "Your nana loved the Tree. When you were a toddler, we walked to it every day. The Tree made her feel closer to my father." She wiped her eyes. "You are like him, Ruth."

"You knew your father?" Ruth's mouth went dry. "You've never talked about him, Mother." *Would she tell me we were right? It was Fuzzy?*

Her mother's eyes wandered over Ruth, stopping at her neck. They widened as she stared at the locket, her hand covering her mouth. "You've seen him," she gasped.

Ruth took the locket off. Her hand trembled at the thought of what she was about to find out. "You recognized this locket."

"Yes." From her pinafore pocket, her mother held out the exact same locket. "Nana and he had matching lockets." She opened the locket. "Francis Ferdinand Grundle. This is him with your grandmother. Before I was born." She searched Ruth's face. "Do you know much about him?"

"I know he's from the future. And that he and I are Rainwalkers. Oh, Mother, are you? Was Nana?"

"Did he give you his locket, Ruth?"

"He didn't give it to me. I think he dropped it."

"Dropped it?" asked her mother, frowning.

"He's missing," Ruth said slowly. "I met him, then he disappeared. We think someone from the future may have kidnapped him."

Her mother took a deep breath, sinking down into a chair. "Missing? Kidnapped?" She opened the locket, running her finger over the images inside. "We've kept so much from you." She closed her eyes and grabbed the arms of the chair as if to keep herself from falling over. "The day your nana passed away, he came to see me, very distraught over her death. I hadn't seen him in years. He told me about the lockets and we found hers in a drawer. He said that he was in danger. And that if I saw you with his locket, I was to give you this note."

Before Ruth could say a word, her mother reached into the pocket of her apron. She took Ruth's hand, laid a piece of paper in it, and squeezed it shut. She touched Ruth on the cheek.

Ruth slowly opened her hand. The same type of parchment paper she'd found in the back of Nana's poetry book the day she died. She held the note up. Her name was written on it, along with a drawing of the same image on the front of the locket.

Ruth sat on the bed, putting the note in her lap. She didn't know what to think. "Why didn't you tell me about him? Why didn't Nana?" She put her hand over top of her mother's. "Tell me, Mother. I need to know. Everything."

Her mother slumped back in the chair. "Your nana met my father at the Tree when they were both thirteen. He walked right out of the Tree, she said." Her mother smiled weakly. "Even though he was a Rainwalker and she wasn't, they fell in love, secretly married, and had a child, me. When I turned thirteen, I showed no signs of the powers my father had. He visited us often when I was growing up. I married Samuel, and right before you were born, something occurred in my father's time that scared him."

"What happened, Mother? Did he stop coming to see you and Nana?"

"Your grandfather is a scientist from the future, working in a laboratory. All I know is that he discovered something important. And that a fellow scientist got angry with him when he wouldn't share it."

Ruth gasped. The man at the Bristlecone Pine said almost the same thing. Could he be the same person? Martin Millstone? "Do you know his name, Mother?"

Her mother shook her head. "No, but your grandfather became very frightened and protective. His visits with my mother became very secretive. I wasn't allowed to know where they met or what they did.

He wanted to protect me and you from something. Especially you, if you had the power to be a Rainwalker." She moved to the window. "The day your nana passed away, when he came to see me, he told me that Earth was in serious trouble, that he was in danger, and that he needed your help. I didn't know what to do."

Ruth thought about what she'd just heard. All her life, her mother had been afraid for her. Afraid of what would happen if she did have the powers of her grandfather. "You kept all this a secret? For thirteen years?"

"Yes, Ruth. I didn't handle it well, I'm afraid. I was afraid for you."

"The day of Nana's funeral, Father had been drinking, do you remember? You were so sad and tired you went to bed. Nana had told me about the Trees knowing and I told her I'd go to the Listening Tree. And you told me to go." She held up the note. "Grandfather came and gave you the note while I was at the store, didn't he?"

Her mother nodded. "I knew you'd go to the Listening Tree, where you always went when things got difficult. And, if you had the powers of a Rainwalker, you might find out that day. Father said you had a great destiny to fulfill." She pointed to the note in Ruth's hand. "Perhaps the note will explain it to you?"

"I don't know what this note is about, Mother, but the future of our world depends on what happens in our town right now. I have to help." She knelt beside her mother. "But I am not alone. I met two other Rainwalkers the same age as me. We're all connected to the Listening Tree, but from different times. Arabeth, from the year 2035, knows my grandfather, too. She calls him Fuzzy. He's her science teacher." She told her mother what had happened over the past two days. She left out the part about the locked attic and her friends hiding there.

Her mother handed her the locket from Nana. "Take this, too. Maybe it will help."

Ruth waved the note. "I'll figure out what to do, Mother. I know one thing. We must try to save the Tree. Fuzzy—I mean Grandfather— disappeared before he could tell us what we need to do, but we think we have to save the dam."

"The dam?"

"The dam is about to break and flood the town and damage the Listening Tree. Mister Decker is looking for Father. He wants him to help at the dam. Do you know where Father is?"

Her mother rose from the chair and stepped towards the door. "He's sleeping at home."

"Does Father know? About Fuzzy, about me?"

"He has met him but doesn't know about his powers. Or yours. He hasn't seen him since you were born."

Ruth put her hand on her mother's shoulder. "Please, Mother. Try to get Father to go help. Please."

"I know. I must try." She turned, wrapping her arms around her daughter, holding Ruth tightly as if trying to make them become one. "Be careful, Ruth. I love you and my father." She touched Ruth's cheek. "My brave daughter."

Ruth couldn't breathe. Her mother'd spent her entire life trying to protect her, another reason for her "dark days". But deep inside Ruth, a small angry flame burned. It seemed so unfair—all these years she'd had to be the strong one while her mother slept and her father drank themselves through their lives. She sighed as she heard the front door close behind her mother. Her mother loved her; at least she knew that now. Perhaps her father did, too.

Ruth grabbed a lantern off the bureau and rushed up to the attic, pulling the door shut behind her. Arabeth, Michael and Willie sat at the top of the stairs, chewing on beef jerky and apples. She explained what her mother told her and showed them the matching locket from her nana.

"Why didn't you tell your mother about the attic?" asked Willie.

"I almost did. But there must be an important reason why this is locked. I guess I thought we should figure that out first." She held up the note. "Maybe the answer is in here."

Dim evening light danced on the specks of dust in the attic air, casting flickering shadows on the walls. "We need more light. I brought a lantern from downstairs."

Willie pulled matches from his pocket. "And I've got matches." He handed them to Michael. "Can you light it?"

Michael laughed. "How deep is that pocket? You've got everything in there." He lit the lantern, raising it up to the level of his head.

Bookshelves lined the attic walls, from floor to ceiling, built into every available space, and packed with books until they bulged to the point of tipping over.

Michael whispered, "Far out! Look at all the books." He turned to Ruth, his eyes shining. "You read all of these?"

Ruth walked toward the closest shelf. "Oh, good Lord, no, Michael. Why, I had no idea this even existed." She reached out to touch one of the books. A thin layer of dust coated everything. She sneezed, sending it flying into the air in tiny poofs around her.

Michael moved the lantern to reveal the entire room, pointing. "Hey, a bench and a table down there." He walked to it and hung the lantern on a hook on the beam above the table.

Ruth coughed. "Oh, my, no one has been up here for a long time." She brushed off the bench and sat down. "We need to figure out this note." She opened the note.

Nb wvzi lfgs,
Gsv olxpvgh slow gsv gitgs.
Dliwh ziv hvvwh. Svol fh.
Yirmt gsv kzhg gl gsv ufgfiv.
Khrgsfirhn zmw kvgirxsli.

"It's in code," exclaimed Arabeth, dropping down on the bench beside her.

Ruth thought about what her mother had said about being in danger. "Fuzzy doesn't want others to find out what this says."

Michael leaned over the table from the opposite side. "I love codes." He took out his tree carving with the letters on it. "I know, it's zany. Guess it's cuz I see letters in words differently than others. I can help you solve it, Ruth."

She angled the paper so he had a better view. "I think we should start with a two or three letter word."

Michael pointed, "Well, this word, GSV, appears four times. The most common three letter word I know is 'the', spelled t-h-e."

"Great idea, Michael."

His mouth stretched into a broad grin. "We need to figure out the rest of the message using G for T, S for H, and V for E."

They bent over the paper, studying it. "I've got it," they exclaimed at the same time. "He wrote the alphabet—" Ruth said as Michael jumped in with, "Backwards." He read the translated letters out loud as Ruth corrected his B's and D's.

"How do you do that so fast?" asked Ruth.

"When I'm in the barn, mucking out the cows," Michael said sheepishly, "it gets pretty boring, so I goof around with the alphabet in my head. Like saying it backwards."

"Mucking out?" Arabeth scrunched her forehead. "What are you talking about?"

"Um, well, cleaning out their stalls. With a shovel and a wheelbarrow." He raised his eyebrows and arms. "What goes in must come out." He chuckled. "Can you dig it?"

Arabeth stood at the end of the table, staring up at him. "You're talking about manure?" She crinkled up her nose. "Yuck." She bent over, her pointer finger poised above the surface of the table. "Let's get back on track here, right? We should write the translation down so we can see it better. Can you say those letters again, Michael?" She traced them into the table dust as he read them.

The message read:
My dear Ruth,
The lockets hold the truth.

Words are seeds. Help us.

Bring the past to the future.

Psithurism and petrichor.

Ruth studied the message. "Psithurism and petrichor. They're on the paper Nana gave me the day she died. What do they mean?" She opened the locket. "And what truth do the lockets hold? The fact that we're related? Or something else?" She sat upright, took out her poetry book, gently removing a leaf and laying it on the table. "Look, I found this at the Listening Tree. The day we all met. See?" She pointed at a dark line weaving throughout the leaf. "Where something ate a trail inside it. Do you see words?"

Arabeth studied the leaf closely. "Well, an insect called a leaf miner makes a path like this as it eats its way through leaves." She held the leaf up to the light, exclaiming suddenly, "You're so right, Ruth. It seems to say 'Words are seeds.'"

A bolt of lightning streaked across the sky outside the attic window, followed by a deafening clap of thunder, startling everyone. Suddenly, the wind roared, shaking the tree branches, sending their leaves swirling at the rattling window. The scent of fresh rain wafted through the attic.

"The storm's getting worse," said Ruth. Several loose twigs grazed the window as rain began to fall in sheets.

Arabeth shot up from her seat at the table. "Okay, I just remembered. When I went to the Tree the day we met, I found a sprouted acorn." She twirled her acorn necklace as she spoke. "It had the strangest sprout on it, very long and curly. I thought I was seeing things." She pointed to the translated words on the table. "I swear I saw the words 'Bring the past to the future' in its coils."

Michael looked perplexed. "I found a stick at the tree that day. I thought it said 'Help us' in the bark." He pointed to the third line on the note. "Help us."

Ruth sighed as she put the leaf back in her book and crawled over the bench. "I need to go home and talk to Father." She patted Arabeth on the back. "We all need some sleep. I'll talk to Father quickly, then perhaps I can sneak out some food as well." She glanced around the attic. "We can sleep up here tonight. We have to figure this out soon. Only one day left."

Willie stood up. "I have an idea. I'll run home, see if Father has any news on the engineer and when the townspeople will work on the dam. I can grab some food, too."

Ruth nodded. "There should be a chest up here with some blankets in it, Michael. Maybe you and Arabeth can find them while we're gone?"

Arabeth removed her scarf, running her fingers through her hair. "Jeez, does that feel good or what? I could've taken this scarf off hours ago." She peered at the note. "Now I can think better. I'll think about what this means, and Michael can look for the blankets."

Michael looked at Ruth. "Okay. It'll take my mind off my stomach and you going home. Be careful."

She nodded. "I have to try to convince Father to help Mister Decker." She held up the locket around her neck. "I'll keep this one. You keep the one from Nana. Just in case something should happen, each pair of us will have one."

Ruth and Willie walked down the attic steps and opened the attic door. As they stepped into the hallway, the wind and rain from the storm rattled the house. Shadows flickered outside as lightning flashed. Tree branches bent back and forth as if ready to snap, gloomy silhouettes of the houses across the street wobbled like they were riding on ocean waves. She rubbed her arms, trying to calm the goosebumps that covered them, her hands shaking with anxiety. They had so much to figure out. She would be the strong Rainwalker her grandfather said she was.

CHAPTER TWENTY-ONE
FATHER

When they got to the front porch, she gave Willie a big hug. "Be careful. Tell your father you're spending the night at my house. And hurry back."

Willie nodded, racing down the steps, splashing through the water that now covered the street and spilled into house yards. Ruth watched him disappear into the mist and fog that lay thick in the air.

She ran to the back of her house. The rain slowed slightly, but her clothes were quickly dampened, sending cold shivers down her body. As she climbed the back steps to the kitchen door, she noticed light from the kitchen lantern. She paused at the door, thankful that the small roof over it kept the rain off her at least a bit. She needed to think of what to say to her father.

Suddenly, she felt as if someone was watching her. She peered out into the dark and the fog. There was no one there that she could see, and the only sound was voices coming from the kitchen. She gasped. Her mother and father were both in the kitchen. Arguing.

"Please, Samuel. Go and help with the dam. We have all that wood in the shed."

Her father sat at the kitchen table, glaring up at her mother who stood beside the stove. "Why should I? Those men building that reservoir are the same men who built the mine, and made all their money off our backs, Lizzie. Literally off our backs. Why should I help solve the problem they created?" He raised the bottle sitting on the table to his lips, draining its contents in one gulp. "What have they ever done for any of us? What did they do for me? Let me watch my father die in the mines setting a beam in an area that wasn't safe for mining?" He cradled his head in his hands. "That day, Lizzie, they deprived me of my father. And they ended my chances—*our* chances of ever getting out of this town!" He raised his head, wiped his eyes and looked around the kitchen. "Where's my other bottle?"

Her mother walked to the other side of the table. Ruth watched her in the lantern light as she brushed her hair back from her face, slowly smoothing it against her head. Even in the dim light, Ruth saw a spark in her mother's face and eyes, something she hadn't seen for years.

"It's been long enough, Samuel. Enough time drinking for you. And sleeping for me." She rested her hands on the chair in front of her and leaned towards him. "All these years being helpless and bitter. What have they gotten us?" She bent forwards until her face almost touched his. "We must help. If not for ourselves, for Ruth."

Her father slammed the table, startling her mother and sending Ruth jumping backwards down the steps, falling onto the muddy ground. She scrambled back up in time to see her mother grab her coat from its rack and disappear down the hallway. She heard the front door slam. *Mother left?*

She opened the kitchen door and went in, her breath stuck in her throat. Her father turned from searching through the cupboard beside the woodstove.

"Why are you here? Shouldn't you be in bed? Or up at that tree? Or is it too stormy for that?" He turned back to the cupboard.

"Father, I heard you and Mother."

He sat an empty bottle on the table, his mouth descending into a frown, his eyes blazing with anger. "You have no right, young lady, listening in. You have no idea what you heard."

Ruth took a deep breath. She'd confronted him before. Sometimes it went well, sometimes it did not.

"I didn't know your father died in the mines. I didn't know you wanted to leave this town." She paused. "Father, I want to leave, too. I want to make a different life. And a different future. But we are all in danger and we need to try to stop it. And maybe if we do, the entrepreneurs can be held accountable somehow. We have to try. Please, Father."

Ruth rubbed her eyes. Something was wrong with her eyesight. The kitchen and her father appeared as if she were looking at them through a kaleiodoscope. The image wavered for a moment. What was happening? Suddenly, everything was clear again.

Her father pushed his way past her towards the back door, raising his voice. "Who are you to tell me what to do? This is the life I've been dealt." And he raised the bottle in the air as he walked out the door.

She raced after him, tripping down the steps as he disappeared out into the yard. Anger flashed through her body like lightning bolts. She screamed into the wind, "And what kind of life have you and Mother dealt out to me, Father? I've decided not to accept it. It's up to me what kind of life I have. Just like it's up to you, Father." She saw him stop, standing in the rain and fog, for a few seconds. Then he took off toward the street. She collapsed onto the ground, burying her face in her hands, her body shaking with deep sobs.

CHAPTER TWENTY-TWO
MISSING

Suddenly, she felt a hand on her shoulder. "Ruth, are you all right?"

She looked up. "Michael?" She brushed her hair out of her eyes and stood, mud clinging to her dress and face. "What on Earth are you doing here?"

"I, um, followed you. To make sure you were okay in the storm. And with your father."

She looked at him, his clothes saturated with rain, his hair plastered to his head and face. "Have you been outside this entire time?" He nodded, shivering and rubbing his hands together.

"Oh, good Lord, Michael. Let's get inside." She grabbed his hand and pulled him up the steps into the kitchen.

Ruth ran to the living room, grabbing two afghans off the chairs, and rushed back to the kitchen. "Here, wrap yourself in this until we figure out what to do now." She threw one of the afghans over her shoulders, gathering it tight around her, struggling to keep from shaking. "Did you hear everything?"

Michael flung the afghan over his back and up onto his head like a cape. "Yeah, I kinda did, Ruth." He smiled. "I think you're pretty darn brave, to take on your father like that." He looked at the floor. "I wish I could do that with my dad."

She looked at him. "You already are, Michael. You never give up. You know what you want, and you do not listen to people who say you'll never be an astronaut."

He squinted, his mouth curling up in a grin. "We're never gonna let anyone stop us from our dreams, okay?" He stuck out his fist. "We can fist bump on it."

She bumped his fist. "We now have an official pact, Michael. Now, we need to find some food and clothes and to get back to the attic."

Ruth ran upstairs, gathering up another dress and pinafore for herself and Arabeth. They rummaged through the cabinet to find some bread, fruit, and dried beef, and grabbed more milk and cheese from the icebox.

They rushed down the street to Nana's house. When they got to the front door, they saw Willie coming down the street from the other direction, carrying a large bag over his shoulder.

Once in the parlor, Ruth said, "Did you find anything out, Willie?" She headed up the front stairway.

Willie started up the steps behind her. "I did. Father said the townspeople are meeting in the morning at the old Miller barn to get supplies and repair leaks."

"We should be there. You and I can join them, but Michael and Arabeth will have to hide outside until we figure out what to do about them."

They walked down the hallway towards the attic door. As they knocked for Arabeth to open it, Willie said, "We just tell Father we met them at the train station. They can be orphans from the train who volunteered to help us."

Michael laughed. "You said we look the part, Ruth," he said, glancing down at himself.

Willie held up the large bag. "I brought you more clothes." He knocked on the attic door again. "Arabeth, it's us." Silence from the attic.

Ruth took off the locket. "Maybe Arabeth fell asleep. We'll just let ourselves in, I guess." She put the locket onto the hinge and the door clicked and slowly opened.

Michael led the way up the steep steps, carrying the bag of food from Ruth's house. "I'm starving. We gotta eat. Right away." As he got to the top step, he shouted, "Arabeth, we're back. And we've got more food."

Ruth reached the top step right behind him and looked toward the table. The lantern blazed, light flickering on the bookshelves lining the attic walls. But she didn't see Arabeth sitting on the bench or standing nearby.

"Arabeth?" Ruth yelled as she walked to the table. Nothing seemed to be out of place. The deciphered letters of the note were still etched on the table's dusty surface. Her chest tightened. "She's not here." She swung around toward Michael and Willie. "Do you think she went out to look for us?"

Michael set the bag of food on the bench and scratched his head. "Why would she do that?" He paused. "Well, to be honest, she wasn't really happy about me following you. Not that she minded being up here alone. She just didn't want me to go after you." He looked down at the table. "Man, I hope she didn't follow me to your house. Wouldn't we have seen her when we left?"

Ruth gazed out the small attic window. "I would think, since we're right next door. Although it *is* very foggy."

Willie looked around the attic. "We're all pretty tired," he said, yawning. "Maybe she fell asleep up here somewhere?"

Michael shrugged his shoulders. "I mean, there are a lot of old things up here besides the books. Maybe she found some blankets and curled up behind something."

"Even so, surely she could hear us up here now," sighed Ruth, anxiety growing inside her by the second. "Arabeth! It's us." The attic window creaked in the wind as rain drummed on the roof, but there was no answer from Arabeth.

CHAPTER TWENTY-THREE
HIDDEN PASSAGEWAY

Michael wandered around the edges of the attic, peering behind chests and stacks of objects, investigating all the bookshelves. "Hey, look over here." He waved them over to the opposite side of the attic, pointing at the bookcase in front of him. "This is pretty strange. It's not lined up with the others."

A section of the bookcase swung outwards at an angle, revealing a space behind it.

"That is odd." Willie peered into the narrow opening. "Why would someone place a bookcase like this when the rest of them are all lined up?" He turned to Michael. "Can you bring the lantern here?"

Michael grabbed the lantern off the table, shining it into the opening. "I can't see all the way in." As he stood back, his eyes widened in the lantern light. "Far out. I don't remember this section being like this before. What would make it move?" He stuck his head into the opening, "Maybe it's a secret passageway and Arabeth found it somehow."

"Oh, Michael," said Ruth. "Your imagination runs wild sometimes." But she wondered if it might be true.

"Arabeth? Are you in there?" Michael called. There was no response. "If she's in there, she should be able to hear us. The space is pretty small."

Willie looked him up and down. "Perhaps for you. But I can fit in there, and Arabeth is about the same size as me." He stuck his head into the opening. "Arabeth? Are you in here? We're back."

After a few seconds, a muffled voice drifted up from the darkness, sounding like it was coming from beneath the floor. Willie turned around, wide-eyed. "Did you hear that? Is that her?"

"Willie? Michael? Ruth? Jeez, am I glad to hear your voices! I didn't know who was up there."

Ruth exclaimed, "Arabeth, where are you?"

"Just listen to me right now, okay? Look for a book on the nearest bookcase. It should have the word Petrichor in the title."

"Petrichor? That's one of the words in the note." Ruth immediately began searching through the nearby books.

"So right. When you find it, feel the book's spine. There's a place to put the locket in at the bottom." Arabeth's voice paused. "Try to hurry, okay? It's a bit tight in here. I climbed down a bunch of steps and ran into a wall in front of me. I can't see and I can't really turn around. I'd have to climb back up backwards in the dark. Just a hunch, but I hope something will happen to the wall in front of me when you find that book."

After a few moments of searching the shelves, Ruth exclaimed, "Here it is. The title is *Petrichor: The Perfume of the Forest.*" *What a strange title*, she thought as she ran her fingers along the spine. "There's an indentation here at the bottom." She inserted the locket in the opening.

Through the darkness, a snapping noise and a loud click sounded from Arabeth's direction. They heard her exclaim, "Oh, wow. Get down here. You're not going to believe this."

Ruth moved Willie and Michael aside to peer into the narrow opening. "Michael, can you give me the lantern? I'll go first. We need the light in front of us." She couldn't wait to ask Arabeth how she knew to look for a book with Petrichor in the title. And about the indentation in the spine. Petrichor was one of the Greek words on the coded note. Petrichor and Psithurism. And on the note her nana gave her the day she died.

Ruth took the lantern from Michael and squeezed into the tight gap between the bookshelves. Her shadow danced on the wall. She stopped after a couple steps. "Michael, can you fit?"

Michael groaned behind her. "It's pretty tight, but I'm in."

The three of them were cramped, one behind the other, in the narrow space behind the bookshelves. A musty smell filled the stale air surrounding them.

"Arabeth was right. There's no room to turn around." Michael grunted. "Now I know how my cows feel in their stanchions, waiting to be milked."

"I'm at the stairway," Ruth said, shining the lantern in front of her. "It's very steep. Be careful." She put her foot down, her toe touching the first step. She touched the wall with her free hand to steady herself. "Watch yourselves." Carefully, she climbed down to the next step.

Willie's voice echoed over Michael's shoulder. "How come you never found this, Ruth?"

Ruth sighed. "Nana never let me into the attic." Her voice stuck in her throat and her cheeks burned with heat even though a chill filled the air. Every hour, it seemed, she discovered something new about Nana. "I guess I didn't know about a lot of things." Why would Nana have kept so much from her? She blinked hot tears out of her eyes so she could concentrate on the steps and didn't fall forward.

The wall under Ruth's hand felt rough. She raised the lantern and gasped. "Look at the walls." An intricate forest mural was carved along the entire wall of the staircase, from floor to ceiling. Majestic trees, many with leaves and shapes she'd never seen before, decorated the whole length. Plants and animals were in the carving also: deer grazing and gracefully running, mushrooms growing from decaying logs, squirrels digging and storing acorns in the forest floor, moles scurrying through tunnels. Exotic forests, plants, and animals from faraway lands that she'd only seen illustrated in books were engraved in the wall as well. She looked closer. A complex underground root system extended from each tree, interconnected with each other like a giant web.

Michael reached over Ruth's shoulder, rubbing his hand over the carving. "A master carver did this. I've never seen anything like it."

Arabeth shouted up to them, "Guys, come on. You're not going to believe this."

After a few more moments spent admiring the wall, they crept further down the steps. The stairway made a slight turn, and, at the bottom, they found Arabeth standing in the doorway of a room. She whirled around and hugged them. "I'm so glad to see you all. I was freaking out on that tiny staircase." She pointed into the room. "But the book opened the door. Look!"

Ruth walked into a room like nothing she'd ever seen before. The clear walls appeared to be made of glass, holding back a dark material. A black ceiling twinkled with stars and moonlight. "Why, there's Orion," she whispered. How could she see the sky from down here, wherever they were? They had to be beneath Nana's house. Bending down, she touched the wooden floor to find it carved into roots. The smell of fresh rain in the forest filled the air.

Ruth whispered, "Petrichor. The perfume of the forest." The title of the book that opened the door. "It must be the meaning of the word."

Willie turned in circles as he stared at the ceiling. "How in tarnation does the ceiling light up like that?"

Michael put his arm on Willie's shoulder. "It sounds crazy, but I think this room has electricity."

Ruth exclaimed, "Nana had electricity?" Another secret. Why? She frowned. "Fuzzy and Nana kept all this secret for a reason. There has to be more explanation," she said. "I wish we could find him and get some answers. Things are getting complicated and we're running out of time."

Michael walked over to stand in front of one of the walls, his hands resting on the glass. "Look at this." In the dim night light, they watched as moles, worms, and other underground animals scurried by in their tunnels. Through the glass walls, they could see the entire room was surrounded by a vast system of roots.

"We must be in a room carved into the ground under your nana's house," whispered Arabeth.

Ruth turned to the center of the room where an oak tree grew in a patch of soil. It stood seven feet tall, full of leaves and acorns, some of which littered the ground beneath it.

Ruth walked over to the tree. "This certainly looks real. Do you think it is?"

Arabeth broke off a small twig from the tree. "There's green inside, meaning this is alive. But why it's here, I don't have a clue."

An acorn plopped to the ground in front of Ruth as a leaf fell slowly off a branch. She leaned in to look closer. "There's mushrooms growing on that branch on the ground. Things really are alive in here. But how? And why?"

Arabeth patted the glass wall near where she stood. "I think this room is some form of self-contained environment, a kind of biodome."

"Biodome? Another new word?" Michael threw up his hands. "Wait, let me guess what it means." He crossed his arms. "Biodome? You said Sweetwater is a biodiversity preserve in your time, right?"

Arabeth nodded.

Michael continued. "And bio means life, right?"

Arabeth nodded again.

"A life dome?" He looked puzzled.

Arabeth smiled. "What rhymes with dome?"

"Dome?" He looked around the room, his eyes landing on her wiry hair. "Comb?" He flashed her a sheepish grin, then smacked his head. "Home! That's it. Life home." Michael waved his arm. "So this container is the tree's home. It has everything in it to keep it alive."

Ruth walked around the room. The tree certainly looked healthy and vibrant in its underground room. "Do you think Nana and Fuzzy grew this from an acorn from our Listening Tree? Like the one he planted in the desert?"

Arabeth shrugged. "Maybe."

Willie frowned. "Why would your nana and Fuzzy go to all the trouble of building this secret place? And starting a tree in it?"

Ruth told them what her mother had said about Fuzzy having enemies. "Nana and Fuzzy hid everything so no one would find it, especially the people who were angry with him, like that Martin Millstone." She looked around the room. "All these secret clues make me think that no one was supposed to find it but us. Now."

Ruth straightened her pinafore, her hand resting on the poetry book in its pocket. "We need to know more. And quickly. There must be more clues to figure out in the note." The lines of the note raced through her mind. *Words are seeds. The lockets hold the truth. Help us. Bring the past to the future. Psithurism and Petrichor.*

Just then another acorn plopped to the ground. And something Ralph Waldo Emerson wrote popped into her mind.

She walked around the Tree. "Emerson said something in one of his writings about a thousand forests are in one acorn. What if the acorns are a clue?"

Michael knitted his eyebrows. "What are you talking about? Acorns as clues?"

Ruth pointed to Arabeth's necklace. "Acorns seem to be appearing often. Arabeth's acorn necklace, the acorn sprout that Arabeth found that said bring the past to the future, the acorns inside this room. This one must mean something."

Michael paced around, rubbing his forehead. "It's an oak tree, Ruth. They make acorns. Maybe it doesn't mean anything at all."

Ruth shook her head. "I know there's more to find out down here. Think about what we've had to go through to get this far. Fuzzy and Nana were protecting something down here from people upset with Fuzzy. They didn't want them to find this."

"But we don't even know what this is for or about," Willie said with a sweep of his arm.

Michael put his hand on his stomach. "Sorry, but, right now, all I can think about is food. I'm starving. Maybe I can run back up to the attic and get the food, and we can eat while we keep looking?" He nodded as if to answer yes for them.

Ruth said, "I suppose we all need to eat. Just be careful not to close the doorway out of here."

Ruth toyed with the locket at her neck. "Arabeth, how'd you know we should look for the Petrichor book?"

"I got worried when Michael followed you," Arabeth said, looking down. "So I sat down at the table, reading the note over and over, trying to figure out what it meant. Then I had a hunch.

"You know, the line words are seeds. Seeds start plants growing. And then I thought about those two unusual words, psithurism and petrichor. Maybe the two words start something? I started looking for them in book titles, and I found one. *Psithurism: The Voice of the Trees.* It must mean the sound of the wind through the trees. When I looked at the book spine, I saw an indentation that looked similar to the one on the hinge for the attic door. The note says the lockets hold the truth—"

Ruth interrupted her. "So, you thought maybe they would 'unlock' something related to the book."

Arabeth nodded. "So right! I stuck the locket into the indentation. When the bookcase moved and I saw the opening, I got so excited, I went right in. At the bottom of the stairway, I bumped into what I thought was a wall, but it felt cold, and smooth, like metal." She pointed to the door to the room. "I couldn't find any way to move it, so I thought maybe I had to look for the other book. The one with petrichor in the title."

Ruth jumped in. "Using different books to open each door. That way, if someone happens to get the bookcase open, they still can't get into this room."

"An extra layer of protection." Arabeth continued, "I was about to back up and get the other book when I heard creaking in the attic. And mumbled talking. I couldn't tell if it was you guys. I just stayed quiet down here, hoping if it wasn't you all that they wouldn't find the open bookcase."

Michael returned, eating a piece of bread and carrying the food bag. A dark shadow ran into the room behind him.

"Michael, what was that?" Willie asked, pointing.

"What?" he asked, whirling around, chewing. "What do you mean?"

A dark brown squirrel scampered over his shoes, dashing across the room.

Arabeth shouted, a squeak of surprise in her voice, as the squirrel stopped in front of her and sat back on its haunches. "Where did the squirrel come from?" He looked directly up at Arabeth, chattering loudly.

Willie covered his mouth with his hand, a stifled chuckle seeping through his fingers. Ruth couldn't help but grin at the sight. "Nana must have a hole in the roof. Sometimes squirrels get in our house through the roof."

Willie added, "But squirrels don't act like this normally." The squirrel barked loudly. "He sounds angry, doesn't he?" Noisy babbling filled the little room as the squirrel jumped from side to side in front of Arabeth's feet. "Gee, I wonder if that's the same one from up at the boulders. Remember, the one who threw acorns at us?"

The squirrel turned to Willie, chattering even louder. Then he looked back at Arabeth.

"Why, he has something in his paws," exclaimed Ruth. "Look, I think he wants you to have it, Arabeth."

Arabeth looked down. The squirrel held up a large acorn in front of its face. "Okay, okay, I'll take it." She cupped her hand and bent down in front of him. He plopped the acorn into it, ran around the tree, stopping every few feet to scream at her, then raced out of the room, his toenails scratching on the floor. Ruth heard him scampering up the staircase.

"Man, that was strange," said Michael between bites of bread.

Ruth looked over Arabeth's shoulder. "Another acorn. They mean something."

Arabeth bounced it up and down in her hand, then held it up close to her face. "It's just a regular acorn. Delivered to us by an odd little squirrel!" She took her acorn necklace in the other hand, comparing the two. "Nothing unusual about either of them."

"The squirrel was chewing you out about something, though," said Michael, reaching into the bag to pull out a large chunk of dried beef. He waved it in the direction of the biodome. "You know, the way he stopped every few feet to yell at you. I think he wants us to do something with that acorn." He bit off a piece of the beef, chewing it as he spoke. "This jerky is the best!" His eyes sparkled.

Ruth smiled at him. "It's a recipe my nana used, very different from what people were used to." She paused. "Maybe it was a recipe from my grandfather. From Fuzzy. From the future." Ruth watched him chew, then she clapped. "That's it! I know what we're supposed to do."

CHAPTER TWENTY-FOUR
NANA AND FUZZY

Ruth circled the tree. Michael followed her, still gnawing on the beef jerky. She reached out to touch his hand. "Michael, you eating made me think about what acorns are—besides the seed of an oak tree."

"They're food for lots of animals." Willie looked toward the open door. "Like our overly friendly squirrel."

Ruth added, "That's exactly what I was thinking. Acorns are food. But I don't think we're supposed to eat it." She smiled. "That's silly enough to make a stuffed bird laugh."

"What? A stuffed bird laugh? They can't," said Michael.

"That's just a saying we use when something is too silly to be true," said Willie, grabbing a piece of jerky out of the bag.

Arabeth held the squirrel's acorn up, shaking it as she walked around to join Ruth. "The squirrel was telling me to do something with this acorn in here. Do you—"

Michael interrupted her. "I told you that." He ripped another piece of jerky off with his teeth, raising his eyebrows at her.

Arabeth shot him a hard look. "I was about to say do you think we're supposed to plant it? In here somewhere? Acorns are dropped by oak trees and buried by squirrels to eat in the future." She shrugged. "I have no idea."

Ruth walked around the tree, thinking. Out of the corner of her eye, she noticed something glistening on the soil near the tree. She knelt down, brushing the dirt off of a round metal plate. "Come here, look. There's something stuck in the ground here."

The others stood around her as she tried to lift the metal plate out of the ground. "I can't budge it." She looked closer at the metal. "Why, there are symbols on it. Two acorns. Look."

Michael knelt beside her. "Sure are." He couldn't lift the metal plate either. "I think it's a lid over something buried in the ground." He dug around the edges. "It's covering a box or something." He sat back. "I'm so confused. What's the connection here?" He frowned, then smacked his forehead. "I got it! One time, Captain Kirk and his crew got stuck on a strange planet. They came to a cave, and the only way to open it was to rub these two symbols carved on a rock." He poked his finger toward the acorns on the lid.

"Perhaps that's it," said Ruth. "Try it, Arabeth."

Arabeth looked at her hand. "The squirrel brought me the acorn; I guess I should be the one, right?" She held the acorn in one hand, using her index finger to rub the tiny acorn symbols.

They waited in silence, staring at the lid.

"Well, it was worth a try, I guess," said Michael. "Looks like we'll have to think of something else."

"Wait, look," said Ruth. The lid rose slowly from the ground to reveal a small tube underneath.

Arabeth rolled the acorn in her hand. "Should I?" They all agreed. Ruth held her breath as Arabeth put the acorn in the tube.

The lid slowly closed as a cloudy white mist seeped out from around its edges. A musty smell filled the air.

"Interesting," said Arabeth. "I wonder what happens now?"

They watched the tree. Nothing seemed to be happening.

"What was that mist about?" asked Michael.

Willie sucked in his breath, kneeling down. "Look." He backed up.

Ruth's heart raced as she watched the ground near the tree spring to life. Tiny particles of soil bounced into the air as a slender green sprout burst out of the ground near the tube. It twisted and turned like a tiny worm, rapidly lengthening and sprouting two leaves, one on either side. "Oh, my. Do you think that is our acorn sprouting?"

Arabeth ran her fingers through her hair, pacing in front of the growing sprout. "It's like time-lapse photography."

"Time-lapse photography?" Michael asked, not turning from the sprout, which now had eight leaves, and stood almost two feet tall.

"Photography that is sped up to show in only minutes what takes a long time to happen." Arabeth stood by Michael. "It's developing crazy fast. It would take a year for an acorn to grow that much." Arabeth's voice rose with excitement. "We learned in Fuzzy's class that plant growth is controlled by hormones inside the plant called gibberellins. That mist probably contained a gibberellin developed to cause rapid growth and maturity. That's why we had to put it in that tube."

The sprout continued to twist and turn, growing steadily towards the tree. Its tip curled around the tree's trunk, disappearing out of view. Emerging from behind the tree, the sprout completely encircled the tree and stopped growing.

The air beside the tree rippled back and forth in waves. "What's going on?" Michael asked. "Holy shimmering!" His voice dropped to a whisper. "Remember that evil guy at the Bristlecone Pine? That we think is named Martin Millstone?" A shiver swept over his body. "That looks exactly the same." His finger shook as he pointed at the undulating space near the tree.

Arabeth watched as the shimmering began to coalesce into an image. "It's a hologram, for sure, triggered by the acorn."

Ruth watched the emerging image, suddenly aware of a strange sensation in her feet. She glanced down. "What's happening to the floor?"

Michael knelt down. "The root carving. It's popping out of the floor!"

The wooden floor beneath them began to rise where the tree roots were carved.

Ruth stepped in between two roots that appeared where she stood. "Why, they look just like the ones in the forest."

Beneath the majestic branches of the tree, two people, a man and a woman, began to appear. Ruth gasped. "Oh, my heavens." Nana! The person she loved more than anyone in the world. A warm feeling flooded over her but melted away when she rushed forward to embrace Nana, only to find her arms passing completely through her. She glanced around, embarrassed that she'd raced to hug someone who wasn't really there. She stepped back, covering her mouth with her hands. Nana stood in front of her, her arms by her side, making no effort to return the hug, and, even though she was smiling, she looked right through Ruth as if she wasn't even there. Ruth felt as if all the air was sucked out of her lungs, leaving her deflated and empty. She had to remember this Nana wasn't real.

"Hello," said the hologram woman, her voice soothing and quiet.

"Nana," Ruth whispered. *It's only an image,* she told herself, placing her hand on the pocket of her pinafore. Inside was the poetry book they'd spent so many afternoons sharing in Nana's parlor. Hours reading and discussing things no other person in Ruth's life cared to listen to and understand. Her secret thoughts shared only with two beings in her world: the Listening Tree in the forest and Nana in her parlor. Hadn't Nana trusted her and confided in her, too? But now she knew Nana had kept secrets from her. She felt her cheeks grow hot. The glow of heartfelt love from a few moments before, first replaced by emptiness, now became the heat of anger.

She squeezed the poetry book so hard she thought the pages would explode. "Why did you keep secrets from me?" She waited for a response, but there was none. The Nana in the hologram wasn't the Nana she knew: grey-haired, fragile, and weak. The woman standing before her looked like the Nana from pictures of long ago: younger, stronger, full of energy. Ruth stared at her as if she could will her to speak. But, sighing, she realized she couldn't. It was just an image of a younger Nana she never knew. A feeling of helplessness overcame her.

"I was just a baby," she whispered.

"What, Ruth? Are you okay?"

Ruth turned toward the voice. Michael stood nearby, staring at her.

She fiddled with her braids as she looked back towards the hologram. "I was just thinking about how young she looks, and when they might have made this hologram." The Nana she knew and loved was dead. She would never get answers from her. She sighed, telling herself to stop dwelling on that. There was too much at stake to keep wishing for Nana to come back to life.

"Greetings," said Fuzzy. His black hair, streaked with strands of gray, was pulled back into a ponytail—nothing like the wild white hair and crazy eyebrows she knew him by. And his eyeglasses were not like anything she'd ever seen. She took a deep breath. Fuzzy was from a different time, when glasses like that were worn. It was all so confusing.

Fuzzy reached for Nana's hand, pulling it gently to his chest. They looked at each other, then back toward the air near Ruth. She could see that they obviously loved each other very much. But then, Nana loved everyone. Even this man from a totally different time period. *What was it like for Nana and him, to fall in love, but be from such different times?* She realized she was looking at Michael. *Why? What's wrong with me?* Turning back to stare at Nana and Fuzzy, she suddenly understood something important: even though she'd only known Michael for a short time, he was important to her. She didn't want to think about what it would be like when their mission was over and he returned to his own time, 1966. What a difficult secret Nana kept for all those years. Ruth relaxed her grip on the poetry book slightly.

"Fuzzy, wow, he looks so young. I guess your nana does, too?" Arabeth asked.

"Oh, yes. And her voice. So strong," Ruth said, struggling to keep her own voice from cracking.

Michael turned to point at a spot above Ruth's head. "Why are they looking over our heads?"

Arabeth shrugged, moving towards the image. "My guess is that holograms were just being developed when they made this." She turned to Michael. "You remember the one we saw at the Bristlecone Pine, of Millstone?"

Michael nodded, shivering. "How could I forget!"

"Well, that hologram seemed more like the ones from my time, 2035. Much more realistic than this one." She pointed to Nana's face. "See how her eyes aren't focusing on us? That technology wasn't developed until the late 2020s. And the 3D quality of this one isn't that great, either. I'd guess this was an early version. Probably around 1990 or so."

"Three D?" Willie asked. His face was an eerie shade of white as he watched the flickering image.

"I got this one," said Michael, grinning at Arabeth. "It's like this: a drawing of a hay bale on a paper is flat. I can't pick the square up because it has no real shape. But I go to the barn and get a real hay bale, and I can hold it in my hands. It has three dimensions: length, width, and height. It's got shape, not just flat. That's 3D. Length, width, and height." He thumped on a tree root with his toe. "Like these. They were flat, but now they have shape."

Ruth moved closer to Willie. "What's wrong? You look terrible." She put her arm around his shoulders.

"I've ...," he muttered in a low trembling voice, "I've only seen one of these things before. Out of that object on Arabeth's wrist at the boulders." Ruth felt his body shaking beneath her arm. "These picture shows, or whatever they're called, are creepy."

Ruth patted him gently. "They are quite strange. I'm still shaken when I see one."

"Me, too," Michael added. "Didn't you see my finger shaking? I couldn't even point straight."

"I guess I'll get used to them," said Willie, frowning.

Michael looked sheepishly at them. "You could say these holograms give us the willies, Willie."

Willie grinned. "How do you know that saying? Aren't you from the future, too?"

"My brother says that all the time. Talking about hay bales made me think of him."

Arabeth swept her arms in a wide circle. "Come on, guys. Think about it. Fuzzy brought all of this technology, to build this room, with him to 1896." She paced in front of the tree, staring at Fuzzy and Nana. "But why?"

Fuzzy's voice startled them out of their conversation. "Welcome to the Listening Tree II and what we call the biodome." He looked over at Nana. "I know we have a lot to explain." They both nodded.

"Listening Tree II?" asked Ruth. She stepped up to the tree, resting her hands on its trunk. "Biodome? That's what you called it, Arabeth. But Listening Tree II?"

Fuzzy continued, "You are standing in an experiment. A room designed to sustain life in an artificial environment. Everything in here, the sun, the rain, the clouds, are all artificial. Except for the living things. Like this tree, sprouted from an acorn from the one thing all of you have in common: The Listening Tree in the forest near here." A grin spread over his face, and his eyes softened. "That's where I met Elizabeth." Nana smiled and squeezed his hand. "On my first rainwalk. She was sitting beneath it. I thought she came out of my history book." He laughed. "You see, I didn't realize I traveled through time then."

Ruth glanced over at Michael, who was shifting nervously from one foot to the other. Was he thinking what she was? He'd said the same thing to her when they met.

Nana glanced over at Fuzzy, making a circling motion with her hand. He nodded at her and cleared his throat. "But I digress, and we don't have time for that. I have used The Listening Tree II here for years, to rainwalk back and forth between Elizabeth's house and the rest of the world."

Arabeth glanced at Ruth. "Why didn't he just use the real Listening Tree?"

As if she heard them, Nana said, "Fuzzy had to create this room to have a secret place, hidden from a fellow research scientist he worked with in the mid-1990s. A dangerous man who wanted to use Fuzzy's research in genetics for his own benefit."

Ruth whispered, "It's Martin Millstone. The man at the Bristlecone Pine. It has to be."

Arabeth threw her arms up in the air. "I figured Fuzzy did something before teaching that had to do with genetics. That's why we talked so much about genetics in his science class." She frowned, rubbing her hands through her hair, then pointing at Fuzzy. "What was he working on? It had to be something pretty serious."

Ruth shook her head. "I'm having a hard time imagining all this. All these scientific discoveries that we have never even dreamed of."

Fuzzy's face took on a serious look. "We don't really have time to explain everything. Because you are seeing this hologram, it means that my lab partner has discovered how to travel through time. All my work, the work of the Rainwalkers, may be in jeopardy."

Michael stepped forward. "What work? What is he talking about?"

"We have been involved in a worldwide genetics project designed to save the world's plants from destruction by my corrupt lab partner. He wants to use the natural disasters caused by climate change to create his own world, inhabited by genetically modified creatures designed in his laboratory."

Willie blew through his lips. "What?" He sat down on the floor, resting his chin on his hands.

Fuzzy continued, "I've been saving seeds from around the world, throughout the different time periods, and bringing them here, to this house, using the Listening Tree II to rainwalk back and forth. Elizabeth has been hiding them for me. Millstone has discovered the genetic code for rainwalking and time travel, and if he finds the seeds, he will use them for his own evil purposes. You must ...."

The hologram crackled, and blurred, the images of Nana and Fuzzy distorting and flickering in and out of visibility.

"What did he say?" Ruth asked, her voice rising. "Did you hear it? What do we have to do? And what is happening to them?" *It's only an image,* she told herself over and over as she watched them fading in and out. "And he said Dr. Millstone was his lab partner."

Michael jumped up. "You were right, Ruth. Millstone from the Bristlecone Pine was Fuzzy's lab partner."

Arabeth rushed forward towards the hologram. "Something's gone wrong."

The images of Fuzzy and Nana flickered as Fuzzy appeared to be saying something but they couldn't make out what it was. Then, with a sputtering and soft popping sound, they were gone.

"Whoa." Michael sprang forward, waving his arms through the air where Nana and Fuzzy had stood just a moment before. "They're gone. We need to know where the seeds are." He stomped his foot on the ground. "And what to do with them. Come on. You can't dissolve now!"

Arabeth, staring down at the floor, muttered, "Um, the roots. They're disappearing back into the floor." She knelt down, touching the wood as it slowly sank to become a flat carving on the floor. "Interesting. A hologram that can trigger actual events in real time. Now, that's cutting-edge technology." She stood up. "Well, this is not good. Did anybody hear what he said at the end?"

Ruth, her hand clutching the poetry book in her pocket, stood beside Michael, almost in the exact spot where the hologram had appeared. "And the dam breaks tomorrow." Her mind replayed the last few seconds of the hologram. Had she heard what he said? She sighed. "I did not hear it. Did you, Willie?"

Willie's head shook frantically. "All I heard was a popping sound." He looked at Ruth. "I don't think I'll ever get used to these hollow thingies."

Michael grabbed an acorn from the dirt near the tree. "Let's put another one in. See if the hologram comes back."

Arabeth found the metal plate and rubbed the symbols, but it remained shut. "I guess it's closed for good now."

Ruth sank to the floor, rubbing her hands over the intricate roots carved into it. What were they to do? Looking around, she saw exhaustion and worry on everyone's faces. Her mind whirled like the spinning teetotum she and Nana used to determine who would read out loud to the other. She closed her eyes, recalling an afternoon from last year.

She and Nana sat in her parlor, reading Alice in Wonderland: Through the Looking Glass, a book they both loved. Nana's frail hand gave the teetotum a gentle whirl.

"You got a Y, Nana. It's Your Turn." Ruth heard her own voice as if it *were happening right now.*

Nana began to read. "It's a great huge game of chess that's being played — all over the world — if this is the world at all, you know."

Ruth remembered admiring how Nana's voice, weak and shaky from age and frailty, still portrayed Alice's excitement at looking over the checkerboard landscape spread out in front of her in the book.

Ruth took a deep breath, the aroma of bergamot tea washing over her just like it had that day. Opening her eyes, she glanced around, expecting to find Nana sitting in her rocking chair in the biodome. But she wasn't.

Ruth rested her hand on her own cheek, like Nana did with hers that day. "The world is not sensible and ordered, like a chess game, my dear," Nana had said. "Life is full of wonderful and dangerous twists and turns. You can't be a pawn in your own life."

Ruth had wondered what she meant. Now she knew.

"I understand why you kept secrets from me now," she whispered to the spot in front of her where the hologram was before it disappeared. "You were protecting the future. Do not worry, Nana and Grandfather Fuzzy, wherever you are. I won't let anything happen to the seeds." She looked up at the tree in front of her. "Or the Listening Tree."

CHAPTER TWENTY-FIVE
BOOKS

Ruth stepped back from the tree, glancing around at the others. The look on Michael's face told her she'd been speaking out loud. Her face heated with embarrassment.

She smoothed her pinafore with her hands. "I was thinking of something my nana said. I forgot where I was for a moment," she said, her voice barely audible.

Michael stepped beside her. "Hey, it's okay." He leaned close to her and muttered, "I've been thinking about my family at the whackiest times, too. Something happens and, bam, my dad or my brother or my mom will pop into my mind." He rubbed his forehead. "I couldn't wait to get away from them before this happened. And when I first got to see all these new inventions, like the holograms and stuff, I thought I'd never want to go back to my time. I mean, this stuff is so cool. Sometimes I guess I miss them more than I thought I would."

Arabeth circled around the tree. "It's tough to be away from family. Especially the way we all left. But we've got to keep trying to save the dam." She held up one finger. "Find out what happened to Fuzzy." Another finger went up. "And now figure out what's going on with these seeds." She stood, wiggling three fingers in the air.

Ruth smiled. "You're making a list again. You always keep us on track."

Arabeth tapped her cheek with her fingers and smirked. "Action. Not concentrating on being homesick for my own town or family." She spread her arms wide. "To think I'm experiencing how you guys live in 1896. I could never have done that if we weren't on this mission."

Willie stood rigid, gawking at the spot where the hologram disappeared.

"You're right here. With your family, Willie," said Arabeth. "And that doesn't make all this any less weird for you, right?"

Willie nodded. "You bet your old boots it doesn't." His eyes squeezed shut for a moment. "I knew Nana, too. She helped me learn to read. I'm going to miss her." A few seconds passed, then his eyes popped open. "And come to find out, Ruth has a grandfather from the future." His body relaxed as he slapped his hand on his thigh. "I feel I'm in a dream."

Michael's stomach rumbled loudly as he stood, looking at his dirty farm boots. "I'd like to bet these boots for some more of the food we brought back from Ruth's house." He looked longingly at the stairway back up to the attic. "Do you hear that? It's calling my name."

Arabeth smiled. "Actually, I'm pretty hungry myself." She glanced up at the ceiling. "It must be close to sunset." She looked at her Skincom. "I think this sky matches the real one outside. I mean, it seems like the right sky for the time of day it is."

The artificial sky above them had changed from bright blue to the color of blueberries with tinges of red and amber at the edges. The sun, a small orange ball, perched on the horizon. Dusk approached, and Ruth, trying not to focus on her nana, wondered what they should do now.

She looked over as Willie's stomach rumbled. "I guess we're all hungry. Let's go back up to the attic. We can eat while we look for seeds up there."

Everyone looked lost in thought as they ate. Ruth knew they were all thinking the same thing: tomorrow, they had to save the dam. Which meant tonight they must find the seeds. Ruth looked around the attic. If the seeds were hidden up here, where would they be? Rain began to pelt against the attic window, and a flash of lightning lit up the room, followed by a loud clap of thunder. She stood by the bookshelf near the secret door, reading the titles, not knowing what else to do. Nana and Fuzzy had so many books. All the ones she wanted to read. She ran her finger along their spines. Books by Thoreau, Jules Verne, H.G. Wells, and Mark Twain. Even one by Charles Darwin. She stopped at the last book on the shelf, pulling it out and turning it over. Ralph Waldo Emerson. She gently rubbed her hand over the cover and held the book up to her nose. The earthy, sweet smell of the leather reminded her of the days in Nana's parlor. She and Nana often read Emerson, their favorite writer. He had so many important things to say. She patted her pinafore pocket, her poetry book safely inside it. She closed her eyes, picturing the pages on which she wrote her favorite Emerson quotes.

Suddenly, Ruth whirled around to the others, waving the book at them. "It's the books! I just remembered something Emerson said. 'You can tell a man by the books he reads.'" She set the book on the table and pointed at the bookshelves around them. "Books! Don't you see?"

Arabeth folded her arms on the table and sighed. "Yeah, I see books. Everywhere. But so what?"

"The books were the key to opening the attic door to the biodome. Fuzzy, in the hologram, said the seeds were hidden somewhere here.

They don't have to be in the biodome." Ruth grinned. "And my leaf says words are seeds. Do you understand?"

Willie looked at Michael. He tilted his head to the side. "No, Ruth. I don't."

Michael nodded. "Guess you'll have to lay it on us."

Willie looked surprised. "Do you think if she lays a book on us, we'll understand?"

Michael laughed. "No, silly. It means tell us. I say it all the time to my dad. He hates it when I talk cool like that."

"Cool?" asked Willie.

Ruth jumped in. "Here's what I mean. Nana and Fuzzy loved books. What better place to hide seeds than in the books somehow?"

"Seeds? In books?" Arabeth cocked one eyebrow. "I see what you're getting at. Well, we've had some strange clues to solve. So, why not? Let's get looking. Time's running out."

Ruth picked up one of the books that triggered the biodome door opening and gave the other one to Michael. "These two books seem very important. I think we should look in them. Arabeth, look in the Emerson book I just set down."

Ruth opened the Petrichor book. She flipped through the first few pages, brown with age. It seemed like a normal book. Maybe she was wrong. She held the book up and shook it. Nothing fell out. Laying the book on the table, she opened it to the middle. "Oh, my. Look!" She turned the book towards them.

The middle of the book, hollowed out, contained several small silver containers, each covered by a lid.

"Wow," said Arabeth, opening her book to the middle. "This one has them, too."

"Do they come out?" Willie peered over her shoulder.

"Perhaps." Ruth noticed a small ring embedded flat into the lid. "This might be a tiny handle." She pulled the container out. "It worked."

"Mine came out the same way," said Michael.

In a few moments, a dozen small containers sat on the table.

Willie held one between his knees and tugged at the ring with his only hand. "The seeds must be in these." He pulled and twisted the small ring. "The lid won't come off."

Ruth rested her hands on the table, unable to open hers, either. "Oh, dear. There must be a secret way to open them."

Arabeth studied one of her boxes. "Secret? Why not. We're surrounded by secrets."

Ruth thought about the secrets they'd encountered so far. "What about a locket? We used them to open the attic door." She tried prying open the top with the locket without success. Ruth twirled her braid as she had another idea. "We used lockets, yes. But what other object did we need to solve these secrets?"

Willie tilted his head back, staring at the ceiling as Michael tampered with the box he held.

"Acorns," shouted Ruth impatiently, holding up both hands. "We've solved several things with them. We should look on the boxes for acorns."

She picked up the smallest container from her book. The small ring handle was the only decoration on the lid. The bottom was completely smooth. She turned the box to examine one of the sides. "Hooray," she exclaimed. "Look, an acorn engraved in the side of the box."

Michael took the box, holding it up to his face. "Yeah, you're right. It's really small." He studied the engraving. "They even made a tiny hole in the acorn. Like those bugs do that eat the inside." He gave the box back to Ruth. "Now, that's some fancy carving. No way could I carve something that tiny in wood."

Willie walked over to her side. "This one has an acorn, but I don't see a hole."

"Right there, it's tiny." Michael pointed to the acorn on Ruth's container.

Arabeth exclaimed, "There's a hole in this one as well."

They examined all the containers and found that each acorn had the same tiny hole.

"It does seem odd that an engraver would put something like that on the design." Ruth looked at Michael. "Do you think it means something?"

"Do you have anything sharp and small? Like a pin or something?" Michael asked. "Let's stick something in it and see what happens."

Ruth thought for a moment. "Nana has some hat pins in her room." She ran down the attic stairs, returning in a few minutes with several long pins, each decorated with a colorful bead on the top. She gave one to Michael.

He stuck the hat pin carefully into the small hole. Ruth heard a soft click. He wiggled the lid, lifting it off the box, a grin spreading across his face. "Ta-da!"

Soon the table was covered with open containers, each of which contained several envelope-shaped packets, milky white in color.

"What a strange material this is. It looks like silk, but it feels like paper." Ruth held one up to the light. "And so frosty, I can't see into it."

"Yep." Michael rubbed his hand over the material. "Got any ideas what this is, Arabeth? I've never seen anything like it. It must be from after 1966."

"My best guess would be material made from hagfish slime. It's stronger than steel, almost indestructible. Scientists are developing a new line of fabric for clothing from it. That will last almost forever."

Michael grimaced. "Yuck. Clothing from fish slime? Nothing like that on *Star Trek*. I guess the future is more bizarre than a TV show imagined."

"Ow," exclaimed Ruth. "Something inside this one is sharp. And it didn't poke a hole through the fabric." Her heart raced. "I think we've found the seeds." She turned the packet over. "Why, there are no seams. How did whatever is inside get in?"

"I have no idea," said Arabeth. "None of them have an opening."

"This one has a label. Anethum graveolus, Sweetwater, America, 1865." Ruth picked up another packet. "Taraxacum officinale, London, 1973."

Michael added, "Look at this one. Man, I'm not even gonna try to pronounce the first two words, but the place is Saint Pet-ers-burg in Rus-sia. And the date is 1997." Ruth saw his face turn red as he stumbled over the words.

Ruth flashed him a grin. "These have to be the seeds. That's why they're labeled."

Arabeth held a packet up. "The first two words are the scientific name. A unique name for each living thing. Don't worry about reading them, Michael. They're in Latin."

Michael plopped into a chair. "Too far out. Fuzzy traveled the world, collecting seeds. And through time, too." He shook his head. "It's cool we found them, but now what? Are there seeds in all these books?" He jumped up and grabbed a book off the closest shelf. He flipped through it, then turned it upside down. "There's nothing in this one."

Ruth found her next book to be empty, too. "It's a good thing all these books don't have seeds in them. There are too many books to go through." She looked at the spine of the book she held. "That's smart because it makes finding the seeds even more complicated. What if Fuzzy and Nana had a system to what books they put seeds in?"

"A system?"

"Yes, only books of a certain type would have seeds. To make it harder for someone to find them." Ruth quickly lined up all the opened books on the table, with their spines up. She grabbed Michael's book from his hand, putting it next to the one she had just removed from the shelf. "All these books had seeds, except these last two. Maybe there's a clue in their titles."

She read the titles out loud. "*Marvels of Nature, Science in Short Chapters, The Class Book of Nature, Experiments and Observations on*

Electricity, Walden, Leaves of Grass, The Scarlet Letter, Mark the Matchboy." Every one of them dealt with a science or nature topic. Except the last two. "I'm right. All the books that contain seeds are about science or nature. These last two are not."

"I don't know, Ruth." Arabeth said. "It kinda makes sense, though."

Ruth stared at the books. What if she was wrong? "We have no choice. We'll never get through all these books tonight. I'll put the books that have the right title on the table. You open them and take the seeds out. We'll start with the books right next to the door."

Arabeth held up both of her arms, shouting, "Wait a sec. What are we doing?" She picked up one of the containers, rattling it at them. "Look at these. They're small, made of metal, and they close tightly. If we have to take these seeds with us, why don't we just transport them in these?" She shrugged. "Right? Or not?"

Ruth looked at the pile of seed packets. The containers did offer more protection for the seeds. She picked one up and put it into one of her pinafore pockets. "I think you're right. And it will save us time opening all the containers."

Soon a large pile of containers covered the table. Lightning flashed through the dark evening sky outside the window. They had less than twenty-four hours left to create a parallel universe. And now a table full of seeds to take care of as well. She tried not to think about how tired she felt. There was so much to do!

Michael yawned wide and loud. "After we've figured out what to do with all these containers, I was wondering if we could just rest for a couple hours. I'm running out of energy."

Willie nodded. "Me, too, Michael." He looked hopefully at Ruth. "There's some beds on the second floor. Do you think we could sleep there tonight? Just for a few hours? Father knows I'm staying with you. And we're all tired."

Ruth sighed. "I don't know, Willie." She looked around the attic. "I think we should find a way to carry the containers and take them down to the biodome with us. To keep them near us. I think we should sleep there, actually."

Michael's shoulders fell. "On that floor?"

Ruth explained. "I know we couldn't get the hologram to work, but what if it does start up again? We might find out more about where to take the seeds."

Arabeth nodded. "I totally agree. Tomorrow is the day the dam breaks. We don't have much time to figure these seeds out. Maybe it was just a glitch in the hologram programming." She ran her foot along the floor. "The floor down there is flat again, no knobby roots to bother us. All we need is some blankets. If the hologram comes back, the floor should rise again and wake us up."

Willie scrunched up his mouth. "Okay, I guess we'll sleep down there. What are we gonna do with all these?"

Ruth paced around the table. "In the hologram, Fuzzy said they had to be moved. But then he disappeared. The only place I can think to look for a hiding place is at the Listening Tree." She plopped down on an old trunk sitting in front of a bookshelf. "Nana's old traveling trunk."

"Take them with us? But how?" asked Michael. He eyeballed the stack of containers. "We don't have pockets big enough for all these."

"I know. I'm thinking."

Ruth brushed dust off the trunk. "I wonder if we could fill this with the seeds and drag it down to the biodome." She jumped up, grabbing one of the leather handles on the side and began dragging it towards the table.

"Let me help you." Michael pushed on the other end. "Man, this thing is heavy. We'll never get it down those stairs."

They dusted off the trunk and propped the lid open. Ruth pulled out a white, furry object. "One of Nana's old muffs. Perhaps we can just wear the seeds."

"That's one big earmuff." Michael looked puzzled. "Where's the other one? And what do you mean, wear the seeds?"

"Not an earmuff, silly." She put one hand in each end. "It keeps your hands warm in the winter." Ruth turned the muff inside out to reveal several pockets built into it. "We can stuff these full of containers. Look for more stuff we could wear to carry them."

Arabeth handed Ruth several containers to put into the muff. "Wearing is better than dragging this old thing with us."

Michael rummaged through the trunk. "Hey, what's this? It's pretty strange." He held up a cap. "It's a hat with a lantern on top of it. Crazy."

Ruth took it from him. "It's a miner's cap. My father wears one. The lantern lets the man see in the darkness of the coal mine."

Michael took the cap back. "Cool." He took the lantern apart, holding a piece of it up to his nose. "Smells like some kind of oil. This must be where the fuel for the lantern goes." Then he paused. "Holy hair raising! People walk around with flammable liquid on their heads?"

"How else can you make a light two hundred feet down in the ground? Men need their hands to dig out the coal."

"That's just nuts." Michael put the cap on, then took it off quickly. "There's a bit of space in the tank." He rubbed his finger in the opening. "No oil. I guess I could stuff it full of containers."

They dug through the trunk and found two old jackets with large pockets, another miner's cap and two leather satchels. They stuffed containers into all of them as thunder boomed overhead, shaking the rafters of the attic.

Michael jumped at the sound. "I'm as nervous as a fly on a long-tailed cow." He sat down on a chair, putting his head in his hands. "How are we going to get all this done in time?"

Arabeth and Willie stopped and stared at Michael. Ruth was startled, too. Michael never sounded anxious. They all needed some rest. She put on one of the jackets. "Let's get the rest of these packed. We'll grab some afghans from the bedrooms and head to the biodome and sleep for a couple hours."

Michael looked over at Ruth, the anxious look on his face turning into a slight grin. "If you could see yourself," he said, a nervous quiver to his voice. He started to laugh, grabbing one of the metal tins out of his pocket and holding it up to his mouth. He spoke at it in an accent Ruth recognized from her neighbor. "Michael to Captain Ruth. We've given her all we've got, Ruth. We cannae take no more."

Ruth was stunned. "Have you lost your mind, Michael? Why are you talking to a container of seeds? And why in tarnation are you speaking like my neighbor from Scotland?" She couldn't help but giggle at his actions.

Michael chuckled. "Scottie, on *Star Trek*. He always says that. When Captain Kirk wants him to do more." He patted his cap and satchel, then pointed at her. "We cannae take any more seeds, lassie."

She looked down at herself. Her green jacket, with its pockets stuffed, made her look like a giant round squash.

"We could pass for aliens on *Star Trek*." Michael could barely speak as he bent over, holding the sides of his jacket as he looked at Willie, wearing a miner's cap. "Oh, it hurts to laugh this hard."

Ruth put her hands on her hips. She looked him over. "Haud yer wheesht, sir."

When Michael gave her a puzzled look, she said, smiling, "That means be quiet. In Gaelic."

Just then, a deafening clap of thunder sent them all jumping into the air.

Michael stopped laughing and looked worried. "We better get to the biodome." He took a deep breath. "Sorry. I make jokes when I'm nervous."

"I'm concerned, too," said Ruth. "Your joke did help me calm down."

"We are funny-looking," said Arabeth.

Willie and Michael went down to the second floor to grab some blankets. Ruth and Arabeth put on the clothing stuffed with seeds and carried the satchels to the biodome.

They stacked the clothing on top of the satchels and agreed that, after a few hours of rest, they'd take the seeds and hide them at the Listening Tree, then go to the Miller barn to see what the townspeople planned to do to save the dam.

Michael and Willie crawled under their piles of blankets and quickly began snoring softly.

Ruth rearranged her bedding several times. She looked over at Arabeth, sitting next to her on her blankets, and whispered, "Those boys are asleep already. I'm exhausted, too, but I can't stop thinking."

Arabeth pulled a blanket up over her knees. "Me, too. How far is the Miller barn from here? How long will it take to get there?"

"It's about a half mile from here. Remember the office building at the top of the dam?" Ruth shivered, thinking about the dead engineer on the floor. "About halfway to that. We can make it in a half hour." The moon rose above them. In the artificial moonlight, Ruth could see Arabeth running her fingers through her hair, staring at the tree in the center of the room. "What are you thinking about?"

"Fuzzy, in the hologram, named his lab partner, Dr. Millstone. We figure it's the Dr. Millstone at the Bristlecone Pine. Remember the dilapidated sign we saw in the desert?

"Why, yes." Ruth could see the letters clearly. M lst n I d st es Her eyes met Arabeth's. "Are you thinking what I am? Millstone Industries?"

Arabeth nodded, leaning forward. "What if Millstone Industries was started by the lab partner from Fuzzy's lab? I mean, it makes sense. This lab partner, he was angry with Fuzzy. To get revenge, he started his lab near Fuzzy's tree in the desert. I bet a haboob destroyed it, and he traced Fuzzy to Sweetwater."

Ruth thought for a minute. "Do you think he's already started creating these new life forms?" She cocked her head. "But, Arabeth, he must not be very bright. To use his own name for his industry?"

"Unless he wanted Fuzzy to know it was him and be afraid." She shook her head. "When Millstone Industries opened in Sweetwater, a new boy, so annoying, started riding my bus." She brushed at her shoulders. "He's always bothering me, like a fly that won't leave you alone. Zarek Millstone. No one has ever seen his father. He never comes to town, and no one ever goes to Zarek's house. The bus picks him up at the end of the road."

"That does sound a bit odd. We know everyone in town here."

The branches of the Listening Tree II swayed slightly in the artificial breeze of the biodome. Ruth felt like she was outside. Moonlight filtered over them. What her grandfather and Nana created was so real. They loved each other, the Listening Tree, and the world around them—so much that they built this room, and Fuzzy traveled all over the Earth, through time, to bring seeds here. To try to preserve nature. They must have felt in great danger when Dr. Millstone showed up in Sweetwater. All their work could have been lost.

"Arabeth, we have to do something. Dr. Millstone may be the one who has Fuzzy. Do you think he's coming after the seeds?"

"He needs them," said Arabeth. She squirmed down deeper into her blankets. "I know Fuzzy's your grandfather, but he's been like a grandparent to me, too. We've got to find him. And save the seeds."

Ruth put her hand on Arabeth's blanket. "I know you care about Fuzzy as much as I do. And about the Tree. We all care about that." She looked away. "It pokes me up that my father does not."

Arabeth looked at Ruth questioningly. "Pokes you up?"

Ruth rolled her eyes. "Oh, sorry. You probably don't say that anymore. Embarrasses."

"What happened when Michael followed you last night? He seemed pretty upset."

"I went home to ask my father to go to the meeting and help the townspeople. Michael heard my father yelling at me." She looked down at her blankets. "He doesn't like to be told what to do. He grabbed his bottle and walked down the street."

"His bottle?"

Ruth sighed. "My father drinks. Often. My mother suffers from melancholia. Often." Ruth rubbed her hands together. "Sometimes I get so angry with them because I have to take care of them. My nana was the only person, besides Willie, who seemed to care about me. And now she's gone." Her throat tightened and she swallowed hard. "I just wish my parents could care about something, anything, as much as I do. I wish my father could help our neighbors. Oh, how I hope he didn't go to the bar all night after he argued with me." She stopped, wiping a tear off her cheek. "I apologize for telling you all that."

Arabeth slid closer to Ruth. "No worries. I'm just thinking. I've wanted to find my real parents since I was little. To get some answers to my questions. Not that I don't love my adopted parents, but, you know, to be with my real family. You have real parents, and guess what? It seems like you're not so different from me. I mean, you're almost an orphan *with* them."

Ruth nodded. "I suppose you're right. We are both kind of the same. And we care about the same things." Then she chuckled. "We just do it in different ways."

"What do you mean?"

"Well, you always look at things in a science way. Nana and I read about the scientific method of solving problems. That's you. Making lists of what we know."

Arabeth grinned. "And you always use words, and quote people and books."

Ruth touched the necklace from Nana hanging around her neck. "But we want the same things. To be honest, Willie is my best friend and we tell each other everything. But I always wanted a sister to confide in."

Arabeth smiled. "Me, too."

Ruth held the necklace up. "Let's swear by Nana's and Fuzzy's necklaces to always be like sisters."

Arabeth grabbed her necklace, holding it up to Ruth. "Sisters it is. We won't let all your nana's and Fuzzy's work get destroyed." She smiled again. "Sometimes you drive me crazy, quoting books all the time. And I know I drive you nuts with my trying to get things done and find answers. That even makes us more like real sisters!"

Ruth gave Arabeth a big hug. "There's something else. I had the strangest sensation while I was talking with my father."

"What kind of sensation?"

"Like I was looking into a kaleidoscope, everything broken into tiny fragments. I saw my father sitting in the kitchen, looking at me. He quivered and faded in and out of sight. It was so very strange."

"How long did it last?"

"Just a few seconds, I guess. I've never seen anything like that before."

Arabeth shook her head. "Wow, I have no idea. Maybe it was nerves, because you were standing up to him?"

"Perhaps," said Ruth. She shrugged. "I know it means something, though."

They went over the list of things they needed to find out. Arabeth wanted to divide the list between the four of them and split up, but Ruth changed her mind, saying it was safer to stay together.

Finally, they nestled into their blankets, and, in a minute, Ruth heard Arabeth's breathing slow. Moonlight cast a shadow of the Listening Tree II over them. Glancing at Michael and Willie, she found herself mesmerized by the rising and falling of their blankets as they slept. Even though they seemed to be in a dangerous and impossible situation, an odd sense of peace and safety swept over her. She touched her poetry book. *Nana, my new friends mean more to me than I ever thought anyone would, except for you. We will protect each other and your work.*

A slight breeze wafted over her as she closed her eyes. They popped open as she thought she felt a hand gently brush her cheek. *No,* she told herself, *a leaf falling from the Tree.* She closed her eyes and fell into a deep sleep.

CHAPTER TWENTY-SIX
GONE

Ruth bolted upright, wide awake and filled with anxiety. They had to save the dam today, and, after last night, there were new questions about the seeds to solve. She shivered, tightening the blanket around her, as wisps of clouds moved across the artificial sky. The sunrise seemed so real—swirls of scarlet, orange, and yellow appearing at the horizon, gradually working their way through the sky. She shivered again. Something didn't feel right. What was it?

We must focus on one thing at a time, she remembered telling Arabeth last night. *First, find the seeds. Then, get to the Miller barn to find out what the townspeople plan to do about the dam.* She wrestled her way out of the tangled blankets and redid her braids, telling herself to take her own advice and calm down. She hoped the others had gotten a few good hours of rest. They were all going to need it.

In the dim light of sunrise, she saw Michael and Willie, still curled up in their blankets by the door. Turning to her right, she squinted at the spot where Arabeth slept.

She stood, wrapped in a blanket. "Arabeth?"

There was no response. Arabeth's blankets lay in a pile on the floor.

Ruth glanced around, trying not to panic. "Arabeth?" Perhaps she'd gone upstairs to look for more seeds. Or to figure out how to close the door from behind the attic bookshelf to the biodome. Ruth tried to stay calm, but her stomach churned. Why would Arabeth go searching by herself for answers when they agreed it would be best to stay together? She pressed her lips together, nudging the pile of blankets with her toe. She wondered if she should say something to Arabeth about her independent curiosity.

Ruth walked toward the door, stepping over Michael, her feet landing heavily on the narrow, steep stairway as she climbed to the attic. The darkness of the staircase closed in around her. She was almost to the attic when a noise coming from that direction made her stop. She stood in the dark, still, listening. Muffled voices drifted down the stairway. She couldn't make out what they were saying, but they sounded like they were coming from the attic. Had she heard Arabeth's voice? She wasn't sure. Who would she be talking to?

Suddenly a voice got louder. And closer. She felt certain it was Arabeth. She sat down on the step, straining to hear.

"Ouch!" Ruth rubbed her cheek, stifling a scream. What was that? Something fell from above her, smacking into her cheek, and landing on the step next to her. As she reached down to search for the object, a low grinding sound filled the stairway. The voices were gone.

Ruth hesitated, wondering what to do. She was afraid to run up the steps. What would she find? But Arabeth could be up there, and in trouble. She took a deep breath, squared her shoulders, and raced up the remaining steps and down the short hallway to the back of the bookshelf where the door to the attic had been left open last night. It was closed! They had all been too tired to figure out how to open and shut it a few hours ago. No one could get into the attic from the second-floor hallway anyway because that door was locked, and she and Arabeth had the only two lockets that could open it.

Ruth rapped on the door, now certain that she heard Arabeth talking to someone. "Arabeth? Open the door. Are you all right?" She waited. "Arabeth? Please say something."

Ruth froze in place, hoping to hear Arabeth's voice at any moment. But she didn't. She leaned against the bookshelf door, not knowing what to do. Who could be in the attic with Arabeth?

CHAPTER TWENTY-SEVEN
ARABETH

Ruth ran back down the stairway, rushing into the biodome room. "Something's happened to Arabeth." Her fingers, still clutching the object that hit her, grazed over the tender spot on her cheek. She opened her hand. In the dim light, she saw what it was. Fuzzy's locket. The one Arabeth had been wearing.

Michael sat up on his knees. "What do you mean?" Stretching out his arms, he looked over towards Arabeth's blankets. "Hey, where is she?"

"That's what I'm telling you. She wasn't in her bed so I went upstairs to look for her. I heard voices coming from the attic, then the door closed." Ruth held out her hand. "This hit me on the cheek."

Michael took the locket from her hand. "It's Fuzzy's locket. Wasn't Arabeth wearing it?"

"Exactly. There is something terribly wrong." She shook her head, twirling her braid. "Someone was in the attic with her."

"Whoa." Michael got up, holding the locket in front of him. "How'd you get this locket if the opening closed?"

"Someone threw it into the passageway right before the door shut."

"But who would be in the attic? We shut the door to the second floor, remember. The only way to open it from the hallway is with the locket. You had one locket," he frowned, pointing to his hand, "and she had this one."

"Do you think she let someone in?" asked Willie, sitting on his blanket.

Ruth walked over and sat down beside him, putting her head in her hands. "But why would she do that? And who would it be?"

Her conversation with Arabeth about wishing her father would help the townspeople flashed through her brain. She sat up straight and looked up at Michael. "Maybe it was my father coming to look for me because he decided to help? And she opened the door for him." But as soon as she spoke, her shoulders dropped. "I always think he'll change. But he never does."

"I bet Arabeth threw the locket," said Michael. "What if she did let someone in and she didn't want them to know about this room? She chucked the locket down here to us and closed the door in the bookshelf to prevent them from finding us down here." He pointed at the pile of clothing and satchels. "Or the seeds."

"Oh, my. I told her last night we should all stick together. Why did she go up there alone? We have to find her," said Ruth, grabbing him by the arm. "But how do we open the door behind the bookshelf to get into the attic? That's the only way out of the biodome."

Michael paced around the room. "I haven't got a clue." He looked at the Listening Tree II. "So you think we could rainwalk out of this room? That will take us up to the Listening Tree, then we can come back down. We can use a locket to go in through the attic door. Kinda a crazy way to get into the attic, though."

Willie sighed. "I've never rainwalked. What if I can't?" His face turned white. "I don't want to stay here by myself." He looked over at Ruth. "Please."

Michael stopped pacing. "You know, we've only rainwalked a few times ourselves, Willie. We've never tried to rainwalk with anyone else. Except that time we took Fuzzy with us, remember? When he was hurt at the Tree in the desert?" He threw up his hands. "And we know how that ended, right?"

Ruth had been thinking about the same thing. Fuzzy had been taken during that rainwalk, and they hadn't seen him since. Nor did they have any idea where he was. Willie didn't need to know about that. "That was a different circumstance, Michael. Fuzzy was injured, and Willie isn't."

"But Fuzzy is a Rainwalker. We don't know about Willie yet."

Ruth looked at Willie. "He's right. We've never tried to take someone with us like this. We have no idea what could happen. To you."

"You've always helped me, Ruthie. I trust you. Whatever you decide. But please, I don't want to stay here alone." His eyes widened. "Could we at least try to get the door behind the bookshelf opened back up before we decide to rainwalk?"

As they reached the top of the steps, the stuffy air of the hallway and the dim light made Ruth anxious. How would they get this door open?

"Michael, what if the door isn't supposed to open from this side?"

"What do you mean?" Michael paused on the top step to light the lantern.

"To protect the biodome from discovery. Only Rainwalkers would be able to leave it once they entered. Everyone else would be stuck in here." Ruth rubbed her forehead. If that were true, then they would have to take a risk with Willie.

"Right," Michael said. "Anyone else would be trapped down here. So, since we didn't find anyone stuck in here, or a dried-up skeleton, I guess no one's ever been in here but us. Unless the door *can* be opened from this side."

Michael handed Willie the light. "Hey, take the lantern. Willie, will ya? Hold it up." The light shone on the back of the door, carved into an intricate design of a tree, complete with branches of leaves and a complex root system. There didn't appear to be a doorknob or any other way to open it.

"It's beautiful, just like the walls," exclaimed Ruth. "We didn't really look at this side before."

Michael knocked on the door. "Arabeth? Are you in there? Open up, please."

No response came from the other side.

Ruth ran her hand over the carving. "So delicate." Her fingers traced the fine lines of twigs and leaves. "Oh, dear, I think I broke one." She clasped a small piece of wood in her hand. "It just came off the carving."

"Let me see that."

Ruth tried to hand Michael the small piece. "Why, it's still attached to the door."

Willie held the lantern over top of their hands.

Michael laughed. "See this? It's a small rope. Very thin and painted brown. To match the carving and the door. Move the lantern closer, Willie."

Ruth looked over Michael's shoulder. "It comes out of the door, doesn't it?"

Michael smiled in the lantern light. "It sure does. And I think I know what happens. I bet if I pull this, the door will open."

Ruth held her breath as Michael yanked on the small rope. A soft click could be heard.

Michael pushed on the door. It slowly swung open a few inches.

"It's working," shouted Willie, swinging the lantern around. "Oh, hip hoorah! No rainwalking!"

CHAPTER TWENTY-EIGHT
A MYSTERIOUS BIRD

Ruth stepped through the doorway, trying to say Arabeth's name, but her voice caught in her throat as she thought about the voices she'd heard earlier. She glanced around the attic. The coldness of her hand against her neck, holding tightly to her necklace, sent shivers down her arms.

"Arabeth?"

The table and chairs were in the same place as the night before. The books that triggered the opening of the bookshelf secret door were exactly where they'd left them. Only, no Arabeth.

Michael and Willie searched around the edges of the attic. "Nothing," said Michael as he walked over to the steps leading down to the second floor. Ruth thought she heard him suck in a deep breath.

"Ruth, come look." Michael pointed down the stairs.

Willie, standing beside him, exclaimed, "Well, damfino," as he waved for Ruth to join them.

"Why, Willie, I rarely hear you swear." The last time occurred when she'd found him stuck in the boulders. Ruth rushed across the room to find out what made him do so, and quickly saw that the door at the bottom of the attic steps, secured shut the night before, was open. Arabeth must have opened it from the inside, because no one could open it from the hallway without one of the lockets.

Willie's face flushed. "I didn't expect to find the door open."

They rushed all the way down to the first floor, searching in each room, but found nothing unusual.

Ruth opened the front door and stepped out onto the porch. Rain had fallen during the night, turning the small front yard into dark, black mud. "It doesn't look like anyone walked across the dooryard. We need to check upstairs."

Michael and Willie ran up to the second floor as she closed the front door.

"Where would she go?" Willie walked into the hallway from one of the rooms, scratching his head as Ruth reached the top of the stairway. "She doesn't know her way around our town."

Ruth frowned. "We agreed to stay together, but Arabeth gets so impatient. If she really wanted to do something, she wouldn't let the fact that she's unfamiliar with the town stop her." She felt lightheaded, not knowing what to think. "I know I heard voices. More than one, and I think I heard the word 'right'. Arabeth always says that at the end of a sentence." She leaned against the wall. "So I don't think she left by herself. I don't want to think about this, but what if someone took her?"

Willie stood beside her. "But who?"

"Maybe it was your father?" Michael asked, almost in a whisper. "Maybe he really did come here looking for you after that argument you had and found Arabeth?" He leaned against the wall beside her. "Maybe he thought she was trespassing and took her somewhere?"

She shook her head. "He took his bottle. He went to look for Mother and to the pub." *If he does anything else,* she thought, *he should go help the townspeople.*

She sat down on the bottom attic step, resting her head in her hands. "What if it was those two men? The ones we think have Fuzzy. And work for Dr. Millstone."

"Maybe they broke their way in?" asked Willie.

Ruth didn't want to think about angry men breaking a door and taking Arabeth. What would they do to her? She knew how her father could act when he was angry.

Michael examined the door. "It doesn't appear to be damaged. It definitely would be if someone broke in here from downstairs."

Goosebumps rose on Ruth's arms. "What if they knew how to unlock the attic door? Remember, we think they kidnapped Fuzzy." She pictured Arabeth and Fuzzy held captive in a dark room somewhere. "What if they tormented Fuzzy into telling them about the attic? And the seeds? And found Arabeth when they got here?"

Michael knelt by the door, inspecting the hinges on it. He peered up at her. "Ruth, you know Arabeth as well as I do. She's not afraid of anything. I mean, how often have we seen her frightened?" His eyes widened. "She's our Lieutenant Uhura, you know, the one I like on *Star Trek.*"

"You mentioned her before, but we don't have TV, remember?"

"Move over." Michael sat down on the attic step beside her. "Okay, the Starship Enterprise gets sent to a parallel universe." He stopped, then smacked his forehead. "Why didn't I think of this before? It's just like what we're trying to create. A parallel universe. Only the Enterprise gets sent there and discovers evil creatures. Uhura investigates and finds out important information on them."

He jumped up, pacing in front of Ruth and Willie. "See what I mean? Uhura helped save the crew." He stopped in front of Ruth. "Arabeth is daring, too, Ruth. She can hold her own against whoever it is. She's determined, too. She'll be fine, Ruth. She will." He dropped to the step beside Ruth. "I can't think that she won't."

Ruth turned, starting back up the attic steps. "Me neither. I just hope we find her soon."

On one of the stairs, over near the corner, she spied an object. She bent down to get a better look in the early morning light that started to filter up the steps from the window across from the attic doorway. Ruth picked it up, turning it over and over. "Look." She held it out to Michael, still sitting on the bottom step.

"Hm. That's a carpenter's pencil. How did it get in your nana's attic?" Michael's face lit up. "You know who carries a carpenter's pencil? Fuzzy!"

Ruth exclaimed, "You're right. He always has a pencil behind his ear. And it's flat, just like this one. Could it be his? Could his voice be the one I heard?"

Michael studied the pencil. "Well, it sure is possible." Holding it up in the air, he jabbed his finger at the pencil. "Holy alphabet! The letters FFG. Someone carved them into it. Right here."

Ruth took the pencil. "FFG. That could stand for Francis Ferdinand Grundle. But how would he get here?"

Michael's face darkened. "His kidnappers could have brought him here."

"Or maybe he escaped from them and came back to Nana's, hoping we'd be here."

"But, no, that can't be," said Michael. "Why wouldn't he and Arabeth just come down to the biodome?"

Ruth knew he was correct. "The only possible things are that Fuzzy was brought here by someone, Arabeth let them in, and then they were taken away."

Michael jumped in. "Or they came without Fuzzy, but brought his pencil and dropped it to let us know they have him." He stood up and started up into the attic. "I'm taking another look around to see if there's anything else."

Ruth tried not to feel overwhelmed as she went over the events of the morning. She assumed that Arabeth threw the locket behind the bookshelf for a reason. She turned the pencil over in her hand. Did Fuzzy drop the pencil as a clue, or was it someone other than him?

The attic darkened suddenly as the sky outside the attic window filled with swirling grey and black clouds. A bolt of lightning flashed. A few seconds later, thunder boomed over the house.

Willie ran down to the second floor. "Ruth, come here," he shouted up to them.

They rushed down. Willie stood with his forehead against the window. "The streets are flooding more."

Ruth could barely make out streams of water rushing down the middle of the street as she looked through the fog blanketing the world outside. The window shutters rattled, and rain pelted against the window from the wind.

Suddenly, a loud knock rang through the window glass. Ruth jumped back. "What in tarnation was that?" The knock came again.

Michael stood at the window beside her, his face pressed against the glass. "It's a bird. Bumping into the window." Crack went the window glass. "See? It's right there."

Ruth shielded her eyes with her hands to get a better look. "Gee, sure enough." A bird clung to the windowpane outside, its blue-black feathers ruffling in all directions from the wind. "Why is she not sheltering from this storm?" A sheet of rain obscured Ruth's view but she heard the bird peck again at the windowpane.

"She's not going away," said Ruth, watching the bird fighting the wind and rain to stay at the window. She opened the window. Rain blew in, instantly drenching them.

"What are you doing?" Willie wiped the rain from his face. "We're all getting wet."

"Oh, my," Ruth exclaimed as a tiny bird darted through the opening, fluttered past her, and flew up the attic stairway. "Where's she going?" She ran to the attic steps. "Here, bird, here."

The bird flew back down, flitting back and forth over their heads.

Michael brushed the top of his head as the bird swooped down at him. "It's divebombing me!"

The bird skimmed over Willie's head and started back to the attic. "That bird is hotfooting it up there."

"She wants us to follow," whispered Ruth. "I know it."

Michael started towards the steps. "Looks like we better if we don't want our heads pecked."

They ran up to the attic. The bird flew straight at them, then turned and sat on one of the bookshelves by the secret passageway, chirping loudly.

Ruth approached the bird slowly, holding out her hand. "What do you want?"

When she was inches away, the bird cocked her head, her dark black beady eye staring into Ruth's. Ruth felt warmth surge through her body. The bird had a message for them.

Ruth blinked, putting her hand to her mouth as they stared at each other. The bird blinked back, chirping softly, and then flew into the passageway behind the bookshelf. *There is danger below.*

Ruth shivered. How on Earth was she able to understand a bird? She thought about other times the Listening Tree had sent her messages: the swirling leaves when Willie's arm was stuck in the boulders, the squirrel chattering to tell them about the locket lost in the boulders. And now a bird.

Michael touched her arm. "Wait a minute. You and that bird. Something strange just happened between the two of you. What was it?"

Ruth turned. "The bird gave me a message. From the Listening Tree. I don't know how, but I understood it." Her voice quivered. "We must go to the biodome." Ruth started into the passageway.

Michael lifted his eyebrows. "Really?" He shrugged. "I guess if squirrels can tell us stuff, why not a bird? What did it say?"

Ruth stopped, looking back at them. "'There is danger below'. Hurry."

They rushed as quickly as they could down the narrow passageway to the biodome. The bird dashed in circles around the room, chattering and fluttering over top of their heads. It finally landed on a branch of the Listening Tree II and sat quietly.

Ruth looked around. "The Listening Tree in the forest thinks there is danger here." She walked around the biodome tree, running her hand across its bark. Nothing appeared to be out of place. What was it?

Michael shouted from the edge of the room. "Come here." He brushed his hand against the wall and held it up. His hand was covered with moisture.

Willie, touching the wall on the other side, exclaimed, "It's wet over here, too. Water is seeping through the walls."

CHAPTER TWENTY-NINE
WILLIE

Ruth pressed her palm against the wall, shivering immediately from the dampness. When she pulled her hand away, tiny droplets of water covered it. "The walls are weeping," she whispered.

Michael looked worried. "They weren't wet last night when we were here. I walked around and didn't see this." He paused. "We had a bad storm at home once. The ground outside got saturated with water and it came through the basement walls."

"What did you do?" asked Willie.

"We pumped the water out a basement window and away from the house. If we hadn't, the basement would have flooded. Big mess."

Ruth looked around the biodome. There were no windows. The only way out was through the door and back up the secret passageway, all the way to the attic. "There's no way to get water out of here, Michael."

He stared at her, nervously rubbing his chin. "And we just saw water coming down the street, too."

"What are you thinking, Michael? That Nana's house might flood, too?" Ruth didn't want to think about it. Nana's house? Full of water? All her books. She looked around the biodome. All her and Fuzzy's work. Flooded. And the seeds. They had to take the seeds with them now. Tears filled her eyes. "Why all this before the dam even breaks? What do we do?"

"I don't know." Michael looked up into the branches. "The bird didn't tell you that?"

Willie jumped up and down, looking through the boughs. "Where is the bird?"

They searched around the room but found nothing. Michael blew through his lips. "Darn bird. She can bring us down here to see this, but not give us a clue about what to do? I bet she flew back upstairs."

Ruth hurried back up the passageway, through the attic and down to the second-floor window just in time to see the bird land on the windowsill, turning its head to chirp at her before flying out. She closed the window as Michael and Willie appeared in the hallway. "The bird's gone."

Michael lifted up his foot. "Hey, this floor is soaked. There's been a lot of rain. We better check the first floor of the house." He ran down the steps two at a time.

As Ruth and Willie ran up beside him, he opened the front door.

Ruth felt as if all the air in her lungs was sucked out. Water filled the street, spilling onto and covering Nana's small yard. It lapped against the bottom step of Nana's porch, two inches above the ground.

She felt Willie's hand on her shoulder. "Ruthie, my father's store. We have no steps. It's at street level." His voice shook as he looked out at the water splashing against the step. "If the water is this high here, it will be coming into Father's store."

"Oh, my, Willie." Ruth could see the panic in his face.

Willie shook his head. "I have to go. I have to help him."

She grabbed his hand. "We'll figure out what to do here. Go help your father." She looked out over the street. "The rain seems to be slowing down. That will help. If you can, try to meet us later."

"Where?"

"At the Miller barn. Arabeth is somewhere—with Fuzzy, hopefully. That's where she'll head. And, I fear, if Dr. Millstone has kidnapped them both, he'd take them there as well. To sabotage the saving of the dam today."

Michael nodded. "Agreed."

Ruth touched Willie's shoulder. "Go, Willie. We'll figure out what to do about the seeds, and then go to the barn."

Willie hugged her and took off, sloshing down the street, water spraying behind him. The rain turned to a drizzle. Ruth and Michael watched him until he disappeared into the fog.

"It's rained like this before?" Michael stepped back into the foyer as Ruth shut the front door.

"Never for days at a time like the past few weeks. There's been so much rain. That's why everyone is so worried about the dam." She started back up the stairs to the second floor.

"What should we do, Ruth?" Michael stood a step down from her.

"We've got to look for Arabeth. And save the dam. If the house floods and gets swept away ...." She took a deep breath. "I don't want to think about that. We need to take as many seeds as we can while we look for Arabeth. And Fuzzy. We need to get to the Listening Tree."

Michael threw his hands up in the air. "But how do we do that?"

"We'll have to rainwalk from the tree in the biodome, carrying the seeds with us, to the Listening Tree in the forest and figure out where the seed bank is and then go to the Miller Barn. Hopefully, Arabeth will be there."

Michael nodded. "The water, coming through the walls in the

biodome, it could flood pretty quickly. Then we might not be able to rainwalk from there."

Ruth agreed. "Hiking through the woods in this storm would take longer."

Just then, a deafening clap of thunder sent them both jumping into the air.

Michael took a deep breath. "We better get to the biodome."

They raced back up to the attic, hurried through the door behind the bookshelf, closing it from the secret passageway side, and made their way down to the biodome. Ruth trembled as she descended, wondering what they'd find below.

CHAPTER THIRTY
THE FLOOD IN THE BIODOME

Ruth heard a splash as Michael stepped into the biodome. She was only two steps behind him, and, as she joined him in the room, the sensation of cold water on her feet sent chills up her legs and took her breath away.

The entire floor was covered with water. "Oh, my. It was only on the walls when we left a short while ago. The seeds!" The satchels sat in water. Ruth grabbed the miner's caps and jackets, handing one of each to Michael, then picked up one of the satchels. "Just the bottoms of the satchels are a bit wet. We got here just in time. We better put these on and hold the satchels." Michael stood, surveying the wall near the door. "Um, streams are now coming out of the walls." He took a satchel from her, hanging it over his shoulder by the strap.

Even in the dim light, Ruth could see rivulets of water running down the biodome walls.

"You know what that means? The ground outside is saturated." Michael waded along the edge of the wall. "I'd say there's an inch of water here now. But who knows how fast the water will start coming in? And if the walls can hold up." He pointed to the water in front of him. "Soil is washing off the walls already."

"Let me see," said Ruth, trying to hold her skirt out of the water as she walked to him.

She put her finger into one of the streams of water running down the wall. When she pulled it away, the tip was coated with moist dirt. Loose soil mixed with the water. When they reached the wall bottom, they spread like growing liquid brown tentacles into the pool of water covering the floor. "The wall. It's mushy."

"I know," said Michael, turning toward the Listening Tree II. "Ruth, we need to rainwalk now." Ruth knew his thoughts by the sound of his voice. The biodome would flood.

She let out a sharp cry. Nana and Fuzzy's work destroyed. She tried to breathe calmly. *Focus on how to get the seeds out of here and get to the Miller Barn. Find Arabeth, and save the dam.*

A slight rumbling rolled through the wall opposite them, behind the

Listening Tree II. They stood still, listening.

The rumbling noise ended with a slow cracking sound coming from the same direction. They waded around the Listening Tree II, water splashing ahead of them.

A large crack appeared in the middle of the wall. Clumps of soil broke off along both sides, dropping into the water on the floor, creating a muddy, swirling mess.

"Michael. I've got the heebie-jeebies." She tried to keep her voice from shaking. The packets of seeds in the pockets of her jacket seemed to tremble. Would the biodome be destroyed? Had Fuzzy thought about this and taken precautions the hologram didn't explain?

"The hologram didn't tell us how to rainwalk out of here." Michael looked down at the floor. "We know we have to be on a root. But what if the roots have to be 3D for us to do that? We don't know how to activate them."

"I know." Another chunk of soil fell from the wall. "We'll have to try with them flat in the floor."

"Are we gonna wear the seeds everywhere, though? What are we gonna do with them?"

"We'll figure that out later." Ruth fiddled with her skirt, trying to keep it out of the rising water on the floor. "The water's getting deeper. Come on. Remember, we need to be holding our amulets and thinking of the location we want to go to: The Listening Tree in the forest."

Michael struggled to get to his pants pocket. He pulled out his tree carving. "Can you see a root through the water?" He bent over as far as his jacket would let him, looking around. "Step slowly. Walking makes the water murky and then we have to wait for it to calm down. There's a root right there."

Ruth waded towards him, trying to get to her poetry book in her pinafore pocket while holding up her skirt and wearing the large puffed-out jacket and satchel. "I can't get to my book."

"I'll help you." Michael held up her skirt and jacket as she reached in and took out her book.

"Thank you," she said. As she took her skirt from him, her hand rested on his. Her heart fluttered and her cheeks felt warm. More chunks of dirt fell from the wall, lightly splashing them with muddy water.

"We're quite the team, aren't we?" Michael said, red-faced and in an awkward voice. "We're gonna be all right."

"Yes, we are." She forced a smile, then looked through the water. "The root is right there. We'll stand on it. Together. Are you ready?" She held tightly to her book and skirt with one hand and looped her other arm through Michael's. Her eyes filled with tears. Would all this be lost? Nana's house? Her chair in the parlor? The attic, her books? Would she ever see any of it again?

She felt Michael squeeze her arm with his. "Let's go."

She closed her eyes and filled her mind with images of the Listening Tree. She was glad to have the comfort of Michael's arm on hers as she faintly heard another section of the wall crumple before everything turned black.

CHAPTER THIRTY-ONE
THE SEED BANK

Ruth's eyes popped open as she dropped out of the Listening Tree onto the damp ground. A few raindrops splashed onto her hair and forehead. She looked up through the branches at the dark clouds, waiting for the secure feeling the Listening Tree always gave her. But something was wrong. She shuddered, goosebumps rising on her arms. Was she shivering from the dampness? No, this felt different. Something or someone nearby was experiencing an overwhelming sense of dread. She put down the satchel of seeds and glanced around, resting her hand on the Listening Tree. As soon as her fingers touched the Tree's bark, the feeling of dismay seeped through them, soaking deep into her heart. It was the Listening Tree's terror she felt.

Michael sat next to her, shaking his head. "I'll never get used to rainwalking." He brushed wet dirt and leaves from his pants, patting the bulky pockets of his jacket as he stood. He picked up the satchel laying on the ground and looked inside. "Phew. I thought it opened. We don't wanna lose these now." He froze, leaving the satchel hanging open. "Something's wrong here," he whispered. Ruth watched his face, flushed from rainwalking, turn white. He closed the satchel and stepped to the Tree, touching the bark. "The Tree is afraid." His eyes widened as he said, "I've never felt fear from the Tree before, have you?"

"No," Ruth said. "We must hurry." The rain turned to a drizzle, but the sky still looked menacing, full of swirling black and grey clouds. "That's a dark sky for morning. I'm not sure what we do now." Her voice quivered as a gust of wind blew through her damp clothes. A shiver rippled through her.

"I'm shivering, too," said Michael. "And not just from the cold." He jumped up and down. "Moving helps."

Ruth rose and began shifting from one foot to the other. "The Tree must sense the danger of the dam breaking soon. Or perhaps what's happening to Arabeth and Fuzzy." She rubbed her arms, trying to warm them up. "Let's get to the barn and see what the townspeople have collected to strengthen it. I do hope Willie is there. And Arabeth. I know that's where she'll go if she can." She took out one of the seed containers from the jacket and walked around the Tree. "Where can we hide these?"

A nagging question poked its way into her thoughts. Fuzzy knew the dam would break; that's why they were recruited to save it. Surely, he'd thought about the possibility that the biodome could flood. And the house as well. He must have had a place ready for the seeds if that should happen. It only made sense for that place to be at the Listening Tree.

They examined the Listening Tree for cavities to put the seeds in, but only found a few small holes capable of holding several acorns.

Michael scrunched up his mouth, sucking through his teeth. "Nothing large enough." Craning his neck, he looked up into the branches. "I can try to climb and look higher." He took off the jacket and jumped up, his arms raised, struggling to grab the lowest branch. "Not even close." He dropped to the ground, sighing. "I've got no clue what to do."

A sudden gust of wind blew a few of the remaining dried leaves off the Listening Tree. They swirled around Ruth and Michael, whirling over top of their heads, and funneling like a tornado towards the boulders behind the ancient oak.

A memory flashed across Ruth's mind. When Willie's arm was stuck in the boulders, the leaves did the same thing, and showed her what to do. She followed the tornado of leaves into the passageway between the boulders. "Come on, Michael. We found Fuzzy's locket here, remember?" she said, turning to him. He grabbed his jacket and satchel, following closely behind her.

"Yep, I do," he said. Two squirrels ran along the top of the boulders. "The squirrels are back, too."

Ruth stopped. "Why did Fuzzy drop his locket? We thought he dropped it to let us know he was alive and here." She raised her eyebrows. "But now that we know about the seeds and the biodome, I wonder if maybe he brought his kidnappers here to keep them away from the biodome." She touched the locket around her neck. "Or, maybe the seeds can be hidden here and he dropped it as a clue."

"Could be." Michael walked along the boulders. "The hologram disappeared before he could tell us enough." He rubbed his hand across the rock. "This stone is solid. You'd have to dig underneath to hide anything."

Ruth moved down the path between the boulders, inspecting them the same way. Some of the rocks had cracks in them, but too small for the containers. Were they wasting time here? She stood still, thinking about the dam, and noticed a small round section of cracks in the opposite boulder. She moved closer, running her fingers along the crevices. The cracks made a pattern that looked familiar, a design she knew immediately.

"Michael, come quick. I might have found something." She took out her own book, flipping through it until she came to the pages where she saved the fragment of aged paper. She held it up beside the design in the rock.

"Look! The same design as on the paper from my nana." She held up her locket. "The same design on the lockets. It must mean something."

Michael looked at them both. "You're right, but what?"

She thought about all the secrets they'd discovered so far. Several of them involved inserting something, like the hat pin, or the acorn in the biodome. Several of them involved figuring out a system, like the books in the attic and the note from Fuzzy.

"Look for anything unusual, like a small hole. I want to study this design." Ruth leaned against the boulders behind her.

Michael looked closer. "There's no holes. Maybe this design means nothing, and we should just carry all the seeds." He glanced up at the sky. "And get going!"

Ruth didn't look up. "No, it has meaning. Water doesn't just carve the same design on Nana's paper into a rock, Michael." She gasped. "Look. The tree's branches have leaves on them, all facing in one direction. See?" She held the paper up for him. "But look at these five leaves. What do you notice?"

Michael squinted, studying the paper. "They're facing the other direction?" He turned to the cracks in the boulder. "Hmm. Same here." He appeared to be lost in thought for a moment. "The placement of those leaves and the number. It's like a hand." He tried putting one finger on each leaf. "It doesn't work. My hand's too big." He motioned to Ruth. "Try cupping your hand until your fingers will fit, one on each leaf."

Ruth put her fingers on the leaves. "Nothing seems to be happening." She shrugged, just as the leaves beneath her fingers quivered slightly. "Wait. The leaves. It seems impossible, because it's rock, but I think they're moving."

They watched as the design section of the boulder rose out of the rock.

"It's turning," said Ruth as her hand was moved to the right by the twisting design. Her heart raced as she wondered what they'd find.

The circular design stopped turning and now sat inches above the rest of the boulder. "Whoa. Can you take it out?" asked Michael.

Ruth grabbed it with both hands, gently lifting it away from the boulder. "Now it feels like it's stuck. Did you hear that click?" A low cracking sound came from the rock surrounding the design, about three feet away all the way around. Ruth dropped her grip and backed away as the rock around the design began to swing away from them.

Michael stood beside her, blowing out a breath. "No way. A door. In a rock."

A blast of cold air swept over them as the rock door swung into the boulder.

They stared into the dark opening. "We need some light, but we can't go back and get a lantern." Ruth touched the edges of the opening, taking a hesitant step into the darkness. As she crossed the threshold, dim lights began to shine above her. "Oh, my." She reached behind her, grabbing for Michael.

As they stepped further into the chamber, the lights on the ceiling brightened, illuminating metal drawers lining the rock's interior from the ground up. The chamber appeared to be long, extending for as far as they could see into the blackness.

"Holy hollow. What is this place?" Michael walked ahead of Ruth, lights coming on as he went further into the chamber. As he returned, the lights behind him went off. "Now that's cool. Too bad Arabeth isn't here. She'd be able to explain it." He walked over to Ruth, looking at the drawers near her.

"They have the same design that's on the paper." Ruth touched the design on one of the drawers with her fingers on the leaves, and the drawer opened to reveal similar containers stored inside. She took one out. "It has the same acorn design with the little hole in it."

"Yeah, but we didn't bring the hat pin." Michael took the container from her, examining it. "This looks exactly like the ones we have. They must contain more seeds."

Ruth slid the container back into its slot in the drawer. "I know this is what Fuzzy wanted us to find. We put the seeds in here. There's space for them."

"There must be a gazillion seeds in this place. Why here, though?"

Ruth had a theory. "Perhaps the books in the attic hold them until they can be brought here to be stored. They'd be safer here. Then all of them could be sent to the future when we accomplish creating a parallel universe, saving the dam and the Tree. And the seeds."

Michael nodded. "Yeah, I guess. We won't know until we find Fuzzy and ask him."

Ruth started to put the containers from her jacket pocket into the open drawer. "Come on, we need to hurry." She opened several drawers for them to use.

Michael put the last of his seeds into a drawer, closing it. He held up the empty satchel. "Um, what do we do with these? And these jackets?"

Ruth hadn't thought about that. "I guess we could leave them in here. We certainly don't want to leave them outside. What if Millstone's men find them? They might start looking around here and discover this."

Michael put his hands in the jacket pockets. "Now that it is empty, I wouldn't mind wearing this. It's keeping me warmer."

Ruth nodded. "You're right. Let's keep the jackets but leave the satchels." She opened several drawers. "Maybe we can put them in an empty drawer?" She found two drawers with enough space each for a satchel.

After stashing them, Ruth started towards the door. "How do we shut this rock door when we leave? You're strong, but I don't think you can push that shut."

Michael walked up beside her. The lights inside the chamber began to dim. He looked at the edge of the door. "Unreal. No sign of a latch or anything. Just smooth rock. And we can't see the inside of the door because it's up against the boulder. Something has to trigger it closing. Maybe all the lights turning off?" Michael walked out into the passageway between the boulders. "Come out. Let's see if it shuts."

As Michael moved out, the lights turned off and, slowly, the rock door began to slide back into place. It clicked and the design twisted back into its flush position against the rock.

Ruth shook her head. "You can't even see where the door is."

Michael ran his hand over the rock. "I think it's right here, but no way to tell. That's crazy!"

Ruth wondered why Fuzzy felt the need to put all the seeds here. Did this mean the biodome and Nana's house were truly lost? She pushed that thought to the back of her mind as she headed to the Listening Tree. "Let's hurry and get to the barn."

She rushed out from between the boulders, turning to Michael, a few steps behind her. "I do hope we find Arabeth there."

A weird expression swept across Michael's face as he pointed repeatedly at the Listening Tree behind her. Ruth turned.

A boy she'd never seen before stared up at the Tree, his hands on his head.

He looked at them, his eyes darting between them. "Whoa. That was a rush." He dropped his hands and took a step toward them. "Did I hear you say Arabeth?"

CHAPTER THIRTY-TWO
ZAREK

Ruth stared at the boy. His rumpled black hair tinted with red on the ends, and his style of clothing reminded her of Arabeth. "Who are you? Do you know Arabeth?"

"I should be asking you those questions." He glanced around. "Where am I?"

Michael stood with his arms crossed over his chest, holding up his tree carving. "We know Arabeth. She's missing." He looked at the boy suspiciously. "You're dressed like her." He nodded towards the Listening Tree. "Did you rainwalk here from 2035? Do you know where Arabeth is?"

The boy slumped, putting his hand to his forehead. "Wait a minute. Rainwalk? What are you talking about? And how would I know where Arabeth is? She only rode the bus one day." He looked at Michael. "Man, you can put that thing away, okay? Like, I don't even know where I am and I have no clue where Arabeth is. But we need to find her. She's in danger."

"How do you know?" asked Michael, dropping his arms cautiously to his sides, but keeping his carving visible. "Who are you?"

When the boy mentioned the bus, Ruth thought about the conversation Arabeth and she had in the biodome. She struggled to remember the name of the boy, the one Arabeth thought might be the son of Martin Millstone, Fuzzy's old lab partner. Suddenly, it came to her. "Zarek?"

The boy jumped back. "How do you know my name? What is going on here? Wherever here is." He looked frightened and yet ready to fight the next person who came near him. "I need to find Arabeth."

Ruth wondered how much she should explain. Arabeth didn't seem to like this person very much. And she wondered why he had the same last name as Martin Millstone. But he sounded genuinely concerned about her. "I'm Ruth and this is Michael. Arabeth mentioned you to me. She was here with us. But we've lost her, and we're trying to find her, too. This is Sweetwater in 1896 and you probably got here through The Listening Tree. Do you know what kind of danger—"

Zarek interrupted, turning to stare at the tree. "The Listening Tree? That Arabeth is always talking about?"

Ruth and Michael nodded.

Zarek raised his eyebrows, "Yeah, I came through the Tree, all right. What a rush! Wait, 1896?" He looked at Ruth. "Did you all get here the same way? Arabeth, too?"

"I'm from 1896," said Ruth. "But I've been through the Tree like you. That's how Michael and Arabeth got here."

Michael added, "I'm from 1966." He held up his wood carving. "I wasn't sure about you. Like are you friendly or not?" He shrugged. "I'm still not too sure." He waved the carving. "It's small, but I would protect us with it if I needed to. It's actually my amulet for rainwalking. What's yours?"

"Amulet? Don't know what you are talking about. I drank some fluid of my father's and I ended up here."

"A liquid?" asked Ruth.

"Yeah, some concoction I guess he's been working on in his lab. Look, I followed him down there when I heard him talking about capturing Arabeth and my science teacher, Fuzzy." At the mention of a laboratory and Fuzzy's name, Ruth looked at Michael and then at Zarek. Arabeth had been right. "Your father, is he Doctor Martin Millstone?"

Zarek frowned. "Yep, the one and only, right? Doctor Martin Millstone. He's got something against my science teacher, and he's been doing all kinds of secret stuff in his lab. So I asked him about it, and he got really angry and stormed off. I spied on him in his lab, talking to a hologram on his Skincom about capturing Arabeth and Fuzzy. Then I saw him drink this fluid and disappear into a small tree he grows in his lab." He tapped his head. "Rainwalking. Now I remember. I've heard my father talking about that before. Something about genetics and needing blood samples."

"The tube," exclaimed Michael. "When the two men came at Fuzzy and stuck something into his arm, remember, Ruth?"

"They took a blood sample from him. But why blood?"

Zarek explained, "To analyze and find the genes for this thing you call rainwalking. Then duplicate them in the lab, and use that to enable anybody to rainwalk. They disappeared into the tree, and I followed them."

"Why would you do that?" Michael frowned.

"I don't want anything bad to happen to Arabeth, right? Or Fuzzy." Zarek bit his lips. "We have to find them. My father is up to something. If Arabeth is here, he might be here, too. And maybe Fuzzy. I'll help you find them."

"How long ago did your father drink the fluid?" Ruth asked.

138

Zarek looked at his Skincom. "If this is accurate, about an hour ago."

"So, Doctor Millstone has been here for an hour? Arabeth's been gone for much longer than that." Who had been in the attic with her? "Let's get to the barn, and hope Arabeth somehow got there. Willie's supposed to meet us there, too." Ruth started off into the woods with Michael and Zarek following. She turned to glance at them every few feet, not quite sure how sincere Zarek was about helping them.

The canopies of the forest trees sheltered them from the steady rainfall as they made their way to the Miller barn. "No wonder the Tree is fearful," said Ruth. "We've never had rain like this. And she might sense Doctor Millstone is here."

They came out of the woods into the clearing where the Miller barn stood on a small hill. Hay bulged out from the openings between the weathered gray wooden boards it was constructed from. Rain dripped off the roof, creating muddy streams around the foundation. Neither Arabeth nor Willie were outside the barn waiting for them, as Ruth hoped.

Michael said, "Lots of footprints leading up to the front, Ruth. Have the townspeople been here already?"

Zarek walked toward the front of the barn, looking at the ground. "These footprints here are really scrambled together. Like people were having a group hug or something." He took a few more steps. "Come here, quick."

Ruth and Michael ran up beside him. Leading toward the barn were two scrapes in the mud. "Oh, dear! Someone was being dragged, wouldn't you say?" Ruth raced up to the large double doors and rattled the handles. "They're locked from the inside. We can get through the bottom."

She led the others around the side of the barn to the back. "This is the door to the animal pens on the bottom level." She pulled up the latch and pushed the door open. In the center, between all the pens, a steep wooden ladder led to a door cut in the ceiling. "This goes to the main level."

Ruth climbed up the ladder. Someone had been dragged to the barn. Was it Arabeth? She shuddered. Zarek had confirmed that Dr. Millstone probably was here, in 1896, putting their mission to save the dam and the seeds in danger. She took a deep breath and pushed up on the door.

CHAPTER THIRTY-THREE
THE BARN

Dust and hay fell on top of her. She choked, spitting hay out of her mouth. Holding the door up with one hand, she turned her face to the side, rubbing dust out of her eyes. Michael stood several rungs below her, while Zarek waited on the ground, one foot on the bottom rung.

"Be careful," Michael sputtered in between coughs.

Ruth heard a whimpering sound, coming from the right side of the barn. She shoved the door with both hands until it fell open. She climbed out onto the barn floor, rushing toward the sound.

Dim light filtered between the slats of the barn sides. She followed the moans to a large pile of wood stacked against a post. "Arabeth!"

Arabeth sat on the floor, leaning on a wooden plank balanced precariously against the pile. Nana's headscarf was tied across her mouth. Her hands and feet were bound with baler twine. Ruth quickly undid the scarf. "Oh, Arabeth. What happened?" She struggled to undo the knotted twine around Arabeth's wrists.

Arabeth shook her head, coughing and sputtering. "Two men. They came to the attic when I got ... Michael!"

Michael squatted down, working on undoing the twine around her feet. "Jeez, Arabeth, are we glad to see you! Who did this? It must be painful. I'm trying to get it off as fast as I can."

"Where's Willie?" asked Arabeth, grimacing as Ruth and Michael yanked on the twine.

"He had to go help his father. The rain has been torrential. He said he'll come here when he can." Ruth pulled on a strand of twine at Arabeth's wrist. "Sorry. I'm almost done. The dam will soon be overwhelmed. Even the Tree is afraid. We have to hurry."

Arabeth looked beyond Ruth, her mouth hanging open. Ruth knew Arabeth wasn't paying attention.

"Zarek?" Arabeth's voice cracked. "How? What are you doing here?"

Zarek lingered in the background, behind Michael. "I followed my father. You and Fuzzy are in danger." Zarek sucked air through his teeth. "I want to help you."

Arabeth rolled her eyes and looked puzzled. "Help me? Followed your father?" Her eyes widened. "He is *the* Doctor Millstone, isn't he?" She rubbed her wrists. "The two men talked to him through their Skincoms. He told them he's bringing Fuzzy here."

Michael finished untying her feet, and she grabbed her ankles, rubbing them. "Thanks, Michael." She stood up, gripping Ruth's arm. "I shouldn't have gone up to the attic alone to look for more seeds. I'm sorry."

Ruth frowned. "I was angry at first. Promise you won't go off by yourself again." Arabeth nodded. "I'm glad we found you. Were the two men the ones from at the Tree in the desert in 2035?"

Arabeth cast a sidelong glance at Zarek before answering. "Yes. When I got to the attic, Fuzzy's voice came from the second-floor hallway, asking me to open the door. I did, but he wasn't there, just the two men, playing a recording of him. They shoved me back up the stairs into the attic." Arabeth put her hand on her chest. "Listen, we don't have much time. They showed me Fuzzy's pencil and his glasses. They said they'd harm him if I didn't tell them where the seeds were. I lied and told them the seeds were here, in the barn, as I worked my way over in front of the secret passageway to the biodome so I could close it. I said I'd bring them here and I threw my locket behind me into the passageway and leaned on the door to close it. I didn't want them to get it and use it."

"Smart thinking, as always," said Zarek. "Have you seen Fuzzy?"

"No." Arabeth said in a disgusted tone to Zarek. She turned to Ruth. "Did you find the pencil? I bumped the guy so he dropped it."

"We did." Ruth sighed. "We hoped Fuzzy was with you."

Zarek paced behind Michael. "My father talks about seeds." He paused. "He wants the genetic material in them."

Arabeth looked at Zarek apprehensively and nodded. "He does." She frowned. "Right now, we're all in danger."

Michael scratched his head. "Because we found you?"

Arabeth's voice rose. "Yes. They went ballistic when they found no seeds here. Doctor Millstone told them to tie me up, figuring you would come here. That's why the bottom door was left unblocked. It's a trap. They'll have all of us in one place." She paused. "Quick, did you find the seed bank?"

"We did," said Ruth. "It's in the—"

Arabeth interrupted loudly, casting a sideways glance at Zarek. "It's okay. Don't tell me right now." She stretched her legs. "So, we were right. Fuzzy and Nana kept the seeds at the house until they could be moved to a more secure place. Keeping them in several locations spreads them out so Millstone wouldn't find all of them at once."

A loud pounding on the main doors of the barn startled all of them. "Ruth? Michael?" Ruth recognized Willie's voice and ran to the door. She lifted the bar off the bolt and slid it over to the side. Willie rushed in, breathing hard as the wind grabbed the double doors, banging them against the barn, blowing leaves inside. Michael ran out, snatched the barn doors, and slammed them shut, putting the bar back into place while Ruth led Willie to a bale of hay. He patted Arabeth on the shoulder as he passed her. "They found you!"

Ruth sat him down. "How is your father's store?"

Willie shivered. In a low, soft voice, he said, "Not good, Ruthie. Water is running into buildings from the streets." His eyes filled with tears. "We moved most of his merchandise upstairs. The storm is the worst ever, Ruth. The railroad track is out, too." He hugged himself tightly, shaking. "No one has heard from the Sweetwater Resort Association. Neighbors saw streams of water coming through the retaining wall of the dam yesterday. People are headed there later this morning, after they protect their homes."

Michael sighed. "How much time do we have?" He smacked his forehead. "Why didn't I pay more attention in school? We probably talked about all this."

Arabeth punched at her Skincom. "October 14, 1896. The rain picks up in the early afternoon hours, it says." She looked up. "It's eleven now. The dam breaks at five this afternoon."

Michael rested his head in his hands. "Six hours?"

Silence filled the room. Six hours wasn't much time to begin with, and even less when Ruth thought about the fact that they really had no idea what to do yet.

"Wait a minute," said Willie, gawking at Zarek. "Who are you?"

Arabeth, rubbing her ankles, didn't look up as she spoke. "That's Zarek. He came here from 2035." She looked at Zarek. "Did you come to help? Or to spy for your father?"

"His father?" Willie asked.

Zarek put his head down. "My father is Doctor Millstone. And I came to help."

Arabeth gazed up at him. "Why would you do that?"

"My father used me."

Ruth asked, "What do you mean?"

Zarek's answer filled Ruth with sadness. "He's never paid attention to me. Hiring nannies all the time. We moved to Sweetwater and, bam, he's interested in what I do and where I am. And wanting me to find out stuff." He looked at Arabeth, his eyes glassy. "Specifically, about you, Fuzzy, and the Listening Tree."

Arabeth jumped up. "So that's why you bugged me all the time in school? And on the bus?" She scrunched up her mouth. "You were spying on us. And you still might be."

"Don't you get it? I had no idea it was all a set-up for this moment." As Zarek spoke, he appeared to be struggling to keep his voice sharp and stern. "I," he said, "started to ask him questions about his work. Now I know he wants those seeds. And the dam to break. And the Tree to be destroyed." He kicked his toe into the floor. "I didn't want to hurt you or Fuzzy. Or the Tree. Can't you believe me?"

Arabeth sneered. "Well, sorry, but no. You'll have to prove it somehow. Right now, we need to get away from this barn."

Ruth peeked out through the cracks in the wall of the barn while they talked. Fog drifted through the clearing, shrouding everything in murky whiteness. Zarek seemed pretty sincere. She wanted to trust him. But she also understood that Arabeth had reason to be hesitant.

Rain started to fall again as the sky darkened, making it look more like dusk outside than late morning. The woods surrounding the clearing looked gloomy and foreboding. Through the mist and fog, Ruth thought she saw something moving at the edge of the woods.

She panicked and turned, waving. "Michael, Arabeth, look right there."

Michael rushed up beside her. "There's three people moving along the edge of the woods. One of them looks injured."

Arabeth shivered, whispering, "It's them. One of the men walks with a limp. Just like that."

Zarek stepped up beside her, moving Michael out of the way. His voice caught in his throat. "My father's here." He rested his head on the barn wall, his body deflating like the bellows Ruth used to keep the fire going in the woodstove. "Get ready. Nothing good ever happens when he's around. He always gets what he wants."

Ruth felt as if a thousand needles pricked her heart. She knew how Zarek felt. It was the same way she did when she longed for her father to behave differently. She turned to him. "I believe you want to help us. We'll figure something out." She ran to the main doors of the barn. "We can't leave this way without them seeing us. Thank goodness Willie made it and these are locked from the inside."

Arabeth pointed to the open door in the barn floor. "That's how they got in here."

Willie dashed over and slammed it shut. "It'd be easy for them to push it open."

Michael walked around the edge of the barn. "We need something heavy over that door."

"Right here, Michael," shouted Zarek, yanking on an object on the other side of the barn. "This thing, whatever it is."

"A manure spreader. That'll do the trick," said Michael as he grabbed the other edge. They lugged the heavy metal spreader across the barn and heaved it on top of the door in the floor.

Zarek collapsed onto the floor beside it, panting. "There's no way they can get up here with that over the top of the door." He glanced over at Arabeth, who stood watching him. "Do you believe I'm trying to help you now?"

Arabeth shrugged. "That helped."

Ruth ran back to the barn wall and peered out the crack at the shadows. "Oh, Lord. The two men are coming to the barn." Her heart pounded in her chest as they all froze, silent and motionless, watching the spreader and the door beneath it.

CHAPTER THIRTY-FOUR
DOCTOR MILLSTONE

No one spoke as they watched the spreader banging on the floor, interspersed with angry voices drifting up from below. Michael gazed intently at it. Ruth wondered if he thought he could will it to hold the door shut.

Everything went quiet. Ruth looked out as lightning flashed across the sky. "They ran back to Zarek's father," she told the others, who were still standing near the manure spreader.

Michael bent down, examining the wood underneath it. "But now what? How do we get out of here?"

Ruth watched Dr. Millstone gesturing wildly at his two men. He held his arm out and the air beside him quivered as if being heated. An image appeared near Dr. Millstone, twice as large as the men beside it.

Arabeth moved beside Ruth. "A hologram."

Ruth gasped. "Oh, my." The blurry image showed a man in a chair with a strap around his chest and arms, his hands tied in front of him. "That's Fuzzy." What kind of place was she looking at? Behind him, metal cabinets, equipment, and shelves of glass bottles filled the room.

"Holy captive!" Michael exclaimed. "Zarek, is that your father's lab?"

Zarek's voice was low. "Sure is."

Behind her captive grandfather, Ruth thought she saw the crown of an oak tree. "Look! Behind Fuzzy. Is that a tree? How can a tree grow in a room full of metal?"

Zarek answered, "It's growing in a special pot." He reached into his pocket and held out a small vial. "We disappeared into it. I grabbed an extra vial of the solution before I followed them. But Fuzzy wasn't in the room then."

Ruth wondered why Dr. Millstone would have a tree in his lab. "It must be from an acorn of the Listening Tree. So he can have his own to learn how to rainwalk."

Arabeth looked bewildered. "That tree is big enough to be five years old. But you just moved to Sweetwater last year, Zarek. Had you been to it before?"

Zarek shook his head. "Not that I remember. Why?"

Ruth interrupted them. "Fuzzy's shaking his head, like he heard what Millstone said."

"This is a real-time hologram, not a recording like the other ones you've seen. That's Fuzzy right now, in Millstone's lab," explained Arabeth.

"We can see him and he can hear and see what's happening here?" asked Ruth. "Even though he's in a different time?"

Arabeth nodded.

Michael said, "We see him, but we can't help him."

Zarek motioned to Arabeth. "Do you see what my father just picked up?"

Arabeth inhaled deeply. "A flame thrower. Used to start backfires to burn up combustible material during forest fires." Panic rose in her voice. "They're going to set fire to the barn."

"But why?" asked Willie, his face ghostly white.

"If they threaten to burn up the barn, with Arabeth in it, maybe Fuzzy will tell them where the seeds are." Michael raised his eyebrows questioningly at Arabeth.

"It's all of us now. When they came back, a heavy object was across the door. I'm strong, but I couldn't do that alone. They know you're all in here with me."

Ruth added, "And burning the barn destroys anything in here that could be used to help fix the dam."

She watched as Dr. Millstone gestured wildly between Fuzzy and the barn, holding the flame thrower up in front of the hologram. Fuzzy's head shook frantically.

"And we're blocked in," said Michael. "Either we leave and get caught, or we burn."

Zarek whispered, "My father doesn't know I'm here, but that might not make any difference."

Ruth looked up as the barn swallows above them abruptly began darting from rafter to rafter. Did they sense the danger outside? She knew animals sensed stormy weather before she did. Birds in the Listening Tree often disappeared before a thunderstorm. Suddenly, she had an idea. She reached into her pinafore pocket, pulling out her poetry book. "We send Fuzzy this fragment of paper from Nana, the one with the design on it."

"But, Ruth, that's just a hologram out there." Arabeth shook her head. "We can't give it to him."

"I know," responded Ruth. She held up the fragment. "Fuzzy told us we are all connected—the Tree, the animals, and the Rainwalkers. We've gotten messages from animals to us. Why would that bond only

146

work in one direction?" She walked around. "The birds must be as upset by this as we are." She whispered, "Come, bird. We need your help."

The birds swooped over top of them for a few seconds. When they returned to the rafters, one of them remained, landing on her hand. Ruth looked at the bird for a sign of recognition. Its feathers ruffled and it blinked, chirping loudly. Ruth understood what it said. *You need my help?*

"Fuzzy must see this," she said softly, waving the piece of paper. "Hurry." The swallow cocked her head to one side, then snatched the paper out of Ruth's fingers and darted up to the rafters. A moment later, the flock of swallows fluttered out a hole at the top of the barn.

Everyone gathered at an opening to watch. The birds swooped down over the two men and Dr. Millstone, who covered their heads with their arms.

Ruth kept her eyes only on her bird. It flew in front of the hologram, swooping back up over Dr. Millstone's head and back down. Millstone appeared to be following the path of her bird.

"Oh, no," she whispered.

He reached out as the bird flew towards his head, grabbing it by the body. The bird struggled, pecking at his hand. Millstone let the bird go, grabbing at the paper as it fell.

"No," screamed Ruth. The wind tore the fragment from his hand, casting it up into the air and out of sight.

"The paper. It was too fragile." She grasped her head in her hands. "We don't even know if Fuzzy saw it. And if Millstone did, does he know what it means?"

A loud shriek filled the air. Ruth looked out as Millstone shouted up at the barn, waving his arms. He screamed at the hologram of Fuzzy and motioned for his men to approach the barn. Her blood went cold. "They're coming! They're going to set fire to the barn."

Ruth thought back to the last time they'd encountered Martin's men. At the boulders when the men tried to kidnap her. She'd been afraid but, with the Tree's help, she'd been able to knock the two men out with pheromones. She looked at her fingers. Should she try again? She was afraid for her life, like she was then. Was fear what triggered the power? Would it even work this far away from the Tree?

She pulled out her poetry book with the leaf amulet inside and climbed up a pile of hay bales to a large crack. Holding the book out in front of her, she aimed it out the gap, toward the two men approaching the barn as she imagined herself at the Listening Tree. *Help us, please.* A surge of strength and power passed through her as the poetry book glowed from the inside. A strong smell of ammonia and sulfur emanated from her fingertips. It wafted out the opening, spreading towards the two men.

They bent over, coughing, their bodies shaking, just like before. They dropped the flame thrower and stumbled off into the woods.

Michael and Willie shouted at the same time, "Try it on Millstone."

Ruth looked at Zarek. Should she? He glanced at her, and then, staring at Arabeth, nodded.

Ruth aimed her fingers and the book at Dr. Millstone as he bellowed at the two men. She waited for him to collapse, but nothing happened. Instead, he grabbed the flame thrower and faced the barn.

Ruth screamed, "I can't stop him." Her heart pounded in her chest. Her body and mind were exhausted from trying as she braced herself for the barn to catch on fire.

Michael scrambled up beside her. He held his tree carving out in front of him, shouting, "No, you don't, Millstone. I'm not ready to die yet."

Flashes of light streamed from Michael's fingertips, flowing out through the opening. A loud crack filled the air outside. High above Dr. Millstone, a large, forked bough snapped off from a tree and crashed downward, knocking aside other branches on its way to the ground. It landed over top of Martin, trapping him beneath a mound of broken boughs. The hologram of Fuzzy fizzled and disappeared.

CHAPTER THIRTY-FIVE
FIRE

Michael stood stiff and straight, his face white as a sheet, staring at his tree carving. "Holy smokes," he yelped, gazing at his hands. "What did I just do?"

Ruth touched his carving. "You knocked out Millstone. By using your amulet. What happened?"

"I thought he would burn us all up. You couldn't stop him, Ruth. I had to do something. A voice inside me said, "Use your amulet", so I grabbed my tree and aimed it at that branch." He pointed to the one on the ground where Millstone lay, motionless. "All I could think about was sawing through that branch above him. I asked the Listening Tree to help me. Before I knew it, I felt this power surging down my arm and out my fingertips, and the branch was cut free from the tree." He stopped for a second to take a breath. "I wanted to be a world class woodcarver, but this is crazy!"

Ruth and Michael climbed down from the pile. Zarek grabbed Michael's hand, inspecting it. "Wow. Bet my father doesn't know you all can do that. That'll be the next thing he'll want to figure out how to do himself." He looked out at the woods, rubbing his forehead. Ruth thought she heard him say, "If he's still alive."

Ruth wondered what Zarek thought, seeing his father knocked down. She thought about her father—what was he doing? Was he in danger? As much as she was angry with him for the way he treated her, she wasn't sure how she'd feel if he was hurt badly or killed. "I think your father is just stunned, Zarek. I don't think our powers are deadly."

Zarek didn't respond.

"I used my power once before on the two men. They acted sick and disoriented and staggered away just like now. We never saw them after that, so I have no idea how long it lasts. Oh, my. What if we can really hurt someone? Or even …?" She wanted to protect them all and the Tree, but the idea of being able to seriously hurt someone, perhaps even kill them, she wanted no part of that.

Michael rubbed his arm. "I had to stop him, Zarek. Your father's very powerful."

Zarek gave him a weak nod.

Arabeth held her acorn necklace out. "I don't know what power this amulet gives me." She bit her lip. "But I'm with you all. Millstone is powerful, we have to combat him with something, but to be able to ...."

Zarek looked at Ruth, his eyes pleading. "I want to go over and see how he is."

Ruth knew they all needed to know the condition of Zarek's father. She turned to Arabeth. "Let's get out of here. We don't know where the two men went. Let's go to the resort office. If Doctor Millstone is knocked out and Zarek can get his Skincom before we go, do you think one of you can activate the hologram of Fuzzy when we get there? We can perhaps try to communicate with him. Maybe he can tell us what to do."

Arabeth looked apprehensive. "Zarek can get the Skincom, but he has to give it to me. We can tell Fuzzy about moving the seeds and find out where he is."

Zarek shrugged and looked up at the ceiling. "What's it gonna take for you to trust me?"

"Wait, should we tie Millstone up?" asked Willie.

"There's no time," Ruth responded. "We'll take a chance."

They opened the front doors to the barn and crept slowly towards Dr. Millstone. Zarek reached the pile of branches first. Motioning for the rest of them to stay behind him, he moved a few branches aside and leaned over his father. "His chest is moving, but he's out cold."

Zarek turned back to his father. Ruth couldn't see what he was doing, but a moment later, he held up his father's Skincom. He started to back away, but his foot stuck in between two boughs and he tumbled backwards, losing his grip on the Skincom, which landed on Millstone's chest. One of the boughs at his feet shot up into the air and smacked his father's face.

"What the..." Millstone struggled to raise himself. "Zarek!"

Zarek tried to crawl off the pile of branches. "Dad, listen. Don't go through with this."

Ruth could see the look of total confusion on Millstone's face as he shouted, "How did you ... what are you doing?" He picked up his Skincom. "What were you going to do with this, heh? Where are my men?" He reached out to grab Zarek, who scrambled away.

"Dad, please!" Zarek looked back at Ruth and the others just as the two men emerged from the woods on the other side of the broken pile.

"There they are! Get them, all of them," shouted Millstone, pointing at Ruth. The two men moved unsteadily and slowly around the pile. "Make your choice, son. Me or them?"

Ruth was overcome with sadness for Zarek, having to make such a tough decision. He hesitated for a moment, and she thought he might go with his father. But then he turned and dashed towards her.

"Run," she screamed and led the way down the overgrown trail to the resort office.

She heard a whooshing sound behind her and they all stopped and turned. A ball of fire exploded into the air. Through the woods, Ruth watched as the bottom level of the barn exploded with fire leaping up its sides. Dark black smoke billowed out, filling the air with the smell of burning wood and hay.

CHAPTER THIRTY-SIX
THE RESORT OFFICE

"He did it," cried Willie.

"Shh," whispered Ruth. They needed to run, but everyone froze in place. Smoke drifted into the woods. She held her breath, trying not to cough.

Michael stood beside her, holding his head. "Holy smokes."

The fire engulfed the barn like a wild, angry animal, chewing one section into blackened burnt pieces and spitting them onto the ground, and moving rapidly onto the next. Silhouetted against the blazing building stood Millstone and his men. Watching.

Ruth jumped as part of the roof fell inward, her heart pounding and stirring her back into action. Dr. Millstone's threats were real. "His men will be after us. Run."

As they raced down the path, she wondered what Zarek was thinking. "Are you all right?" she asked him as they climbed over a bough blocking the path.

Zarek didn't respond immediately. "He's angry now. At me and this whole mess. He'll take his men and go back to our time period and confront Fuzzy." His voice fell. "I've never really done anything against him like this before. But I had to."

Michael, Willie and Arabeth scrambled over the branch.

"You did a brave thing. For us," said Arabeth. "Trying to take his Skincom."

Willie nodded. "You are a bricky fella, Zarek."

Zarek cast him a forlorn look. "I don't feel made of bricks right now. I let you down by losing the Skincom. And now my father—"

Michael held Zarek's arm. "You stood up to him. That takes courage." He glanced back down the path. "Now the supplies are destroyed."

Zarek was silent for a moment. "Remember, he doesn't want us to save the dam. I told you. He gets what he wants. At any price."

"Maybe there'll be something at the resort office we can use at the dam."

Off in the distance, lightning streaked across the sky. A few seconds later, loud thunder crashed overhead and rain began to fall again.

Ruth shivered. What they had to accomplish seemed impossible. Nana appeared in her thoughts, reciting one of her favorite quotes from *Alice in Wonderland*. "Why, sometimes I've believed as many as six impossible things before breakfast."

She thought of all the impossible things that happened recently. Rainwalking, the power given her by the Tree and her amulet, having friends from different time periods. Losing Nana, gaining a grandfather. Many impossible things. Saving the dam would just have to be another one. They had to figure out what to do. But first, they needed to keep moving.

They raced down the dirt path leading from the barn through the woods. Tree limbs skreiched against each other as the wind blew through the forest. The smell of burning wood and smoke lessened. She watched for shadows and listened for the sound of anyone in the forest near them. Where were Millstone and his men?

They reached the short turn-off for the resort office fifteen minutes later and dashed down it. As they rounded the building to the front door, Ruth trembled at the memory of what they'd discovered there the last time.

Michael pushed the door open, peering into the darkness inside. Putting his hand out, he said, "Wait here. I'll find a lantern and check it out first." He disappeared into the building.

Ruth huddled with the others underneath the overhang of the roof, escaping the rain. Leaning against the building, she wished she was at the Listening Tree, feeling the safety and comfort it gave her.

The door opened and Michael held out a small flickering lantern. "Come on, get in here. There's another lantern we can light."

She stepped into the building. With only one lantern, the main room was filled with eerie shadows cast by the upended furniture and objects scattered around the room. Michael shuddered beside her. She knew he was thinking about the dead engineer they'd found there only three days before.

Arabeth held up a lantern.

Ruth could still picture the man's body on the floor. "Did anyone ever find out what happened about the engineer?"

Willie stepped over a pile of papers on the floor. "Father said the Sweetwater Resort Association never found anyone responsible, but everyone thinks they killed him over the blueprints. Because he tried to warn them about the danger from the changes they made to the dam."

Lightning flashed across a small window near Ruth."We need to find one of those changes. And correct it."

Willie continued, "Father also said the constable, Mr. Miller, came up here to find the blueprints as evidence that the dam was not built to standards. He searched, but he never found them."

Michael walked toward the side of the room. "We looked at the blueprints. They were on this table." He set the lantern on the table. "Before we left, I rolled them up, and put them back in the paper tube, remember? Then I stuck them back here." He searched behind the table. "They're gone."

Zarek jumped in. "Someone stole them?"

Arabeth handed Ruth her lantern. "We learned in school that they were never found. So maybe they *were* stolen." Her eyes flashed and she waved her arm in front of herself. "Duh, guys. I took pictures of the blueprints, remember?" Her Skincom glowed.

"You did," said Michael excitedly. "We forgot about that." He looked at the spot on the floor where the engineer had died. "Some things, I can't forget."

Arabeth punched at her Skincom, and a hologram of the blueprints appeared over her wrist.

The five of them huddled around her to look. After a moment, Michael said, "Can you blow it up bigger? We didn't really study it the first time."

Arabeth pressed on her Skincom and the hologram enlarged several times. The lake, drawn in blue, was on one side of the dam. A road across the top of the dam was labeled CREST ROADWAY and a path along the right side of the dam was labeled SPILLWAY.

Michael pointed at the right side of the dam. "The spillway is too high. We know that."

Arabeth chimed in. "The top of the dam and the spillway should *not* be the same height."

"Right," said Michael and Zarek together.

"There's not much we can do about that now," added Michael. "It's too late."

Willie grabbed Ruth's arm. "Father said something else. The members of the resort association like to fish, so they put screens out in front of the spillway to keep fish from going over."

Zarek shook his head. "Screens will keep debris in, too, and plug the spillway. The screens are probably blocked."

"Fuzzy told us all we had to do was change one thing about the dam, enough to create a parallel universe where the Tree is stronger. But he was kidnapped before he could tell us what that one thing was." Ruth crossed the room to the door. "Remember what the Mother Guardian said at the meeting? We can save our world. We have to find a way to do that." She opened the door. "I think we need —"

"— to clean the screens at the spillway!" Arabeth finished Ruth's sentence.

Ruth blinked and the room fractured, as if she were looking through a kaleidoscope. The same as when she confronted her father. She knew it meant something. But what?

CHAPTER THIRTY-SEVEN
FATHER

Just as she was about to step outside, Ruth heard rustling in the woods, to her left, in the direction of the path to the dam. Her heart beat loudly and blood rushed to her head. Was it Dr. Millstone? His men?

She turned back to the others. "I hear noises on the path. Someone's out there."

Willie walked up behind her. "I'll go with you."

"We'll all go," said Arabeth. "We're sticking together from now on, remember?"

They snuck along the front of the building to the corner to look.

A large group of people scrambled through the woods on the main path to the dam. Even though it was mid-afternoon, some of them carried lanterns. They hurried passed the turn-off without hesitating. Her heart leapt. It wasn't Dr. Millstone or his men. Ruth felt an instant sense of relief sweep over her.

"It's people from town, heading to the dam." At the end of the turn-off, people continued to rush by, talking as they went, pushing wheelbarrows and carrying picks and shovels. Halfway down the path, Ruth stopped and turned. "Oh, dear. We can't all go out there right now. It isn't the right time to try to explain the rest of you. We'll have to split up. We need to find out what's happening. Willie, come with me. The rest of you, go back to the resort office. Look for anything we might use at the dam. We'll be right back. Promise."

She and Willie walked slowly toward the path to the dam. Ruth stopped, shocked by a voice she heard.

She grabbed Willie's hand and darted out onto the path. "Father? Is that you?"

He whirled around, a startled expression on his face. "Ruth? What in tarnation are you doing out here?"

As surprised as he looked, she knew her face must reveal her shock at seeing him. "Father. What are you doing?"

"I will ask the questions. You didn't come back to the house after our argument." He stared at her, as if waiting for an answer. He never waited for her to answer, usually continuing to rant and rave.

She squeezed Willie's hand. What was wrong with her father? "I didn't return because ... because you left to go to the bar. Right after that, Willie showed up. We went up to the Tree, then we decided to come up here to help with the dam."

She braced herself for him to yell and berate her about being at the Tree, but, instead, he moved to look at Willie and then back to her. "Well, girl, you do not know everything I do. If you're helping, then follow me. Some are already at the dam, clearing away brush at the spillway and patching holes in the sides. Lightning must have struck the Miller barn. It's completely burnt. We stopped there. Otherwise, we'd have been here sooner."

She took a deep breath, dropped Willie's hand, and asked, "Father, are you actually—"

"No questions, Ruth. There's no time. You and Willie follow us."

Ruth stood still, her mouth hanging open, not knowing what to think. Her stomach fluttered. He must be helping. She wondered what happened to make him change his mind.

"Close your mouth, girl, and get moving." He started down the path. "I have to catch up to Mister Decker."

Ruth stared after him for a moment, then turned to go back to the resort office and figure out what to do with the others. Hidden in the shadows at the end of the turn-off were her friends.

"Holy craziness, Ruth. That was your father. What's he doing here?" Michael asked. "Are you all right?"

She wiped away a tear, filling her lungs with air to keep from sobbing. "It's hard for me to imagine, but he's helping. I don't know why. He wants us to follow him." She looked at Michael, Arabeth and Zarek. "No one can see you all. Since it's foggy and dark and people are busy, perhaps if we stay to the back, no one will notice."

Willie stepped ahead on the path. "Should you and I try to catch up with your father, Ruth?"

Ruth looked at the others. "Yes. We should work on cleaning the screens on the spillway."

Michael waved his arm in front of Zarek and Arabeth. "That's what we just talked about doing. We'd better go back and get the lanterns. It's getting pretty dark. We'll meet you at the spillway."

"We just take this trail, right?" asked Arabeth.

Ruth nodded. She looked down the path toward the dam. She wanted to smile. Her father was one of them. Another impossible thing had happened. "We'd better hurry, Willie, and catch up."

CHAPTER THIRTY-EIGHT
THE DAM

Ruth and Willie sprinted down the path. They didn't have far to go. She knew Arabeth, Michael, and Zarek wouldn't get lost because this was the only pathway to the dam through the woods.

When Ruth reached the group, she didn't see her father.

"Willie, I wonder where Father went," she said.

A man in front of her turned around. "Ruth, is that you? And Willie?"

"Yes, Doc Brown, it is." She rushed up beside him. "What are you planning to do?" Doc didn't know that there was less than four hours before the dam broke. How could she impress upon him the urgency of the situation?

"A group is already at the dam. Joseph Johnson came back to us with word that the crest and spillway are covered with debris. One group's working on the debris while another heads down the face of the dam to try to plug major leaks."

He stopped, glancing back and forth between them. "This is dangerous work. Why are you here?"

Ruth replied, "We know, Doc Brown. But boys go into the mine all the time, and that's dangerous, too. You know, we don't have much—I mean, we need to do something now."

"We can help. Really, we can," added Willie.

Doc Brown patted Willie on the shoulder and hurried down the path as he spoke. "I know. Be careful, though." Ruth and Willie raced to stay with him. "And by God, your father is here, Ruth. How glad we all are. He's the strongest man in the mine. You know what he did in the Great Mine Collapse of 1882?"

"No." Ruth frowned as she struggled to keep up with the doctor. That was the year before she was born. Perhaps that was when her father's dad died in the mine.

The doctor stopped again, putting his hand on Ruth's shoulder. "When this is over, Ruth, you ask him. He was a great man. And still could be if he'd stop—"

An urgent voice from the front shouted through the darkness. "Doc

Brown, quick. We need your help."

The doctor hurried off, his lantern swinging from side to side as he pushed his way through the group. Ruth and Willie followed behind him.

The crowd surrounded a man lying on the ground. Lantern light showed his face, contorted in pain, as he groaned loudly. His right leg bent away from his body at an odd angle.

"Oh, my," Willie choked out. "I don't feel well."

Ruth grabbed him, turning them both away. "Don't look."

The doctor knelt down. "How did this happen?"

One of Ruth's neighbors shouted, "He tried to move a tree limb off the dam crest. A branch attached to it swung back and crushed his leg into another limb."

Someone else shouted, "Where's Samuel Weaver?" They were asking for her father! "Get him on the crest. He'll know how to remove the debris. After what he did in the mine that time!" Now Ruth understood why Mr. Decker had begged her to convince him to help. Her father knew what to do!

A frantic voice up ahead answered. "Doc, he ran ahead when he saw Charles' leg. He should be there by now."

Doc Brown pointed at the men kneeling beside the injured person. "You two, help me carry him back to town. Hurry." He turned to Ruth. "Tell your father to take charge. We need someone who knows what they're doing. We don't need anyone else injured. Now go."

Ruth and Willie scrambled past. They raced along the edge of the path, their feet splashing in the soaked ground, their clothes soaked from brushing up against bushes and trees.

The stormy sky darkened as they ran. Several lanterns blazed along the crest and spillway even though it was late afternoon. Ruth thought she recognized some of her neighbors perched precariously along the face of the dam, furiously patching small leaks with mud, hay, twigs, and wooden boards. Where was her father?

She turned to Willie. "Look for Michael, Arabeth, and Zarek. On the spillway. I have to find Father."

He nodded, rushing away.

Fog began to roll in as Ruth reached the crest, where a line of people occupied the center of the roadway across it. Ruth shoved past a man throwing branches into the woods. She slipped and slid on the wet, slick leaves and mud, getting bumped and jostled by branches brushing against her face and arms as people passed debris from person to person.

In the middle of the crest stood her father, his back to her. His clothes, soaked and covered with mud, stuck to his body. His matted hair sprouted twigs and leaves poking out in all directions. In front of him, a huge pile of fallen tree limbs, some of them half as big around as she was, filled the roadway across the crest of the dam.

"Father," she shouted. He whirled around, his face caked with dirt, the whites of his eyes the only light-colored thing on him as he shouted directions to the people around him.

As he focused on her, a startled look swept across his face. "Ruth, what are you doing out here?" he yelled. He turned, pointing at a tangled mass on the pile of tree limbs, hollering, "James, watch out for that, it could shift easily."

She didn't need to tell him that Doc Brown said to put him in charge. He already was.

She'd never seen her father behaving in this fashion before.

He took her by the arm, shouting, "Ruth, get off this crest, now!" He steered her toward the end. "It's too dangerous! Go help somewhere else."

She felt overwhelmed with emotion. Her father, helping, caring about her. She grabbed him, hugging him to her for a second, and then made her way off the crest.

"Ruth, over here." Zarek and Willie stood by the edge of the woods, near the spillway. She hurried over, struggling to compose herself before she saw them. "Father is on the crest. Where are Michael and Arabeth?"

Willie pointed. "Out there. Zarek's been lugging debris off the spillway while they clean the screens."

Through the rain, she recognized Nana's scarf. Arabeth knelt, pulling twigs and mud from a screen along one side of the spillway with Michael on the opposite side, doing the same thing. Once again, the world in front of her appeared fractured as if she were looking at it through a kaleidoscope. She shook her head to clear her vision, but the image continued for a few seconds more. She couldn't imagine what it meant, or why it was happening.

"Did you see that?" she asked. "Did everything look strange to you?"

Willie looked surprised. "Strange? No. Why?"

Zarek swiped wet hair away from his face. "What do you mean?"

"Like wavy, like looking through a kaleidoscope?"

"Isn't that a toy?" His eyebrows went up. "Maybe you're just tired." He looked back into the woods, nervously rubbing his Skincom. "I bet my father and his men are nearby. Maybe I should stay here and keep an eye out for them."

Willie shook his head immediately. "Nope. I can stay. I'll hide by a tree and watch for them." He held up his empty sleeve. "I can help here better than out there. But what do we do if they're here?"

Ruth's insides knotted with fear. She had no idea what to do if Millstone showed up. Beside her, Zarek fiddled with his Skincom, glancing toward the woods. *He's worried, too*, she thought. He'd chosen them over his father. "If you see them, do you have that whistle your father gave you?"

Willie pulled the whistle out, hanging on a chain around his neck, from under his shirt. "I do." His hand shook. Ruth knew he was afraid.

"Willie, this is so brave of you. Blow it if you see them, and hide. We'll have to figure out what to do after that."

Willie nodded and ran toward the dark woods behind them.

"Let's go, Zarek. We've got to help Michael and Arabeth."

The six-foot wide path across the top of the spillway still had debris scattered across it. Ruth almost lost her footing stepping over a branch. She kept her eyes down as she picked her way slowly towards Michael. She didn't dare turn around to check on Zarek for fear she might misstep and slide off.

Glancing up quickly, she saw Michael a few feet ahead. He pointed to the edge near her. "There's one there, Ruth." She knelt down and began pulling at the jumbled mass of leaves, grass and twigs intertwined through the screen. No water could flow through something that tightly packed. The spillway couldn't function properly at all. They were right. What they were doing was key to saving the dam. Only the engineer knew about the screens in her 1896 because the blueprints were lost. In a few minutes, Ruth accumulated a muddy mound beside her.

Zarek pushed a small rickety wheelbarrow up beside the pile. "I got the biggest branches off, and I found this over by the woods. I'll get the piles from all of you." He stomped by and returned after picking up Michael's and Arabeth's. She threw her mess on top and stood up.

"I'm going to help them," she said as Zarek started toward the woods. "Come back. I think we'll have more."

She headed back toward Michael. A squirrel scurried in front of her, sitting back on his haunches and barking loudly. Ruth tried to step around him, but he moved, blocking her path.

"Now? What do you want?" she asked, bending down close. He extended his front paws, holding out an acorn. Ruth tried to scoot him away, but he wouldn't budge. "Am I supposed to take that? Now?" She grabbed the acorn and the squirrel skittered off towards Zarek. Ruth shoved the acorn in her pinafore pocket next to her poetry book. *Is it a message from the Listening Tree?* She didn't have time to decipher it because a loud commotion broke out behind her.

"Ruth!" Zarek yelled. She whirled around to find him digging his heels into the mud, still holding onto the wheelbarrow, as a man struggled to drag him backwards towards the woods. Millstone's men were there.

Ruth screamed, "Michael, Arabeth! They have Zarek." She lost her footing as she moved toward Zarek and thumped onto her knees.

She hadn't heard Willie's whistle. "Something's happened to Willie, too," she yelled, struggling to her feet. Had the other man captured him? She glanced back toward Michael and Arabeth as lightning flashed, illuminating them making their way to her. "I've got to find out."

"Ruth, watch out. Behind you!" A clap of thunder crashed above them.

She whirled around. Zarek was gone. Panic coursed through her body as Dr. Millstone made his way toward her. Ruth's throat tightened. She couldn't swallow. She was trapped. "Help!"

Michael shouted, "I'm coming!" as Millstone reached for her. She took a step away, but he seized her roughly, holding his body in an odd fashion. Was he pulling something behind him?

"You can't save the dam and create a parallel universe. It's too late. Look." He moved to the side. Millstone held Fuzzy by the arm. "Ironic, isn't it? I'm holding him captive with vines from your Listening Tree." He laughed sharply as Ruth noticed the same brown plants that climbed up the Tree bound Fuzzy's hands together tightly. A gag covered his mouth. "He'll tell me where the seeds are, now that I've got all of you."

Ruth jumped as something brushed the back of her leg. She caught a glimpse of Michael kneeling beside her, his tree carving in his hand. Michael's fingertips glowed as flashes of light swept past her, and the smell of fresh sawdust wafted over her. The vines around Fuzzy's hands split open and fell to the ground.

Millstone dropped his hold on Ruth. "No!" He struggled to keep his grip on Fuzzy, who squirmed out of his grasp and fell.

Michael rushed forward, snatched Fuzzy up from the ground, and clambered toward the woods. "Come on, Ruth!" She was almost past Millstone when she felt a rough yank on the back of her dress.

"You're coming with me," Millstone screamed.

Ruth twisted and turned, trying to escape, but his grip only tightened as Michael yelled for her from the woods. What could she do? Her pheromone power had proved useless against Millstone.

A strange greenish light emanated through the rain from Arabeth's direction. It swirled along the ground toward Millstone, enveloping his legs in a misty yellowish-green cloud. The air smelled sweet, like rock candy.

He looked down. "What is hap…en…ing?" The colored cloud evaporated as twigs and branches beneath him began to sprout new growth, vining and twirling over top of his feet. He wiggled frantically, attempting to free himself, but he was already bound tightly.

Ruth struggled to get away from Millstone, but her feet felt cemented to the ground. A wave of nausea overwhelmed her as she realized the vines that gripped his feet had grown over hers, too.

A loud rumbling sound rang through the air from the ground beneath her. It vibrated throughout her body. Mud along the edges of the spillway began sliding off in places.

Arabeth grabbed her arm, shouting, "The spillway's breaking apart. I've got you."

A loud cracking sound reverberated around Ruth as the ground beneath her began to slip away. "No," Arabeth screamed, pulling her towards the woods as Millstone pitched forward, dragging Ruth with him. Arabeth's grip slipped to Ruth's hand, tightening and trying to pull her away from Millstone and the spillway.

Abruptly, the tugging stopped. Ruth felt herself fall, mud and branches surrounding her, all spiraling downward as if in a slow-motion tornado. Everything went black.

CHAPTER THIRTY-NINE
IN THE WATER

Water rushed everywhere, above and below, tossing Ruth about violently. She remembered falling and hitting something hard. The water. She must have blacked out for a second when she hit.

Ruth struggled against the water's force. Her lungs were empty; she needed air or she would perish. Her limbs felt simultaneously frozen from the frigid water and burning hot from the exertion of trying to move upward. Every movement took so much energy. With great effort, she shoved herself skyward.

As soon as Ruth's head emerged into the air, she opened her mouth, gulping. White foam swirled around her as she fought to keep her head above the surface. Waves splashed over her, causing her to cough and sputter.

The flowing water carried her along so swiftly, Ruth couldn't get her bearings. She caught glimpses of the forest along the bank as she swept past, more branches and mud from the land alongside it being pulled into the raging water. Then she remembered. *I fell from the spillway!*

Ruth almost had her lungs full when she saw a large boulder jetting out into the water. She tried to move away from it, but the raging water bumped her against it, driving her under the surface again. She tossed and twisted about, bouncing off tree branches, rocks, and debris.

Her pinafore and dress swirled upward and wrapped around her body. *Do I still have my amulet and my poetry book? The necklaces and the acorn?* An uncontrollable shiver rattled over her, shaking even her bones. *Did we save the dam?*

In an instant, the last ounce of strength drained from her body. Ruth couldn't fight the cold or the water any longer. Her arms drifted to her sides, pushing her dress down little by little, her hand resting on her pinafore pocket. Instinctively, her fingers closed around her poetry book with her leaf amulet inside. This couldn't be the end. She'd never know if they'd succeeded.

Ruth's eyes closed and Nana appeared, sitting in her parlor chair, clutching the locket Ruth now wore around her neck. Fuzzy was there, too, holding Nana's hand. "You saved the Tree," they whispered. "We love you."

The dreamlike scene played in front of Ruth as she floated, detached from her body, as if watching a picture show. Or perhaps a hologram from Arabeth's time. She smiled. She'd wanted a new life. And she'd made one: standing up to her parents, finding a grandfather, befriending Rainwalkers from the future. Things that seemed unattainable or unimaginable before were now part of her life.

Willie, her best friend, walked into the scene from Nana's kitchen. He smiled. "Soon, I'll know if I'm a Rainwalker, too," he said. Her heart pounded. She wanted that for him more than anything. She knew Arabeth and Michael would, too. They were all part of her life now.

The front door of Nana's house opened and in walked her father. And her mother. They sat on the loveseat together. "We love you, Ruth," they whispered. "Your words saved us. And the Tree."

My words? She saw herself sitting at the Listening Tree the day she found her amulet. The trail eaten through it that said "Words are seeds." A parable Nana told her once came to mind. How some words land on rock and never grow and some land on soil and sprout into new ideas. Her parents always seemed like rock to her. She feared challenging them, telling them how she really felt. She thought they didn't care and didn't listen, particularly her father. They were like stone—her words fell on them but didn't make a dent. Perhaps all this time, she'd had it wrong.

The Mother Guardian stepped out from behind the Listening Tree, smiling warmly. Ruth gasped. She thought the Mother Guardian had perished in the earthquake at the Bristlecone Pine.

"Oh, I did," whispered the Mother Guardian. "I could not survive without the Tree to which I was connected. A new Mother Guardian must now be found. Francis will lead the search. He needs your strength to help him."

The Mother Guardian turned to mist and the Listening Tree image disappeared.

Ruth shivered. Had all the important people in her life appeared because she was now dead? Her cold fingers weakly squeezed the poetry book. She could feel it. She must still be alive.

Ruth's hand felt the acorn the squirrel at the spillway had given her beside her poetry book. The mighty oak, like the Listening Tree, makes acorns, a sign of strength, her Nana had said. She thought about the many acorns they'd encountered in their quest to save the Tree and how those acorns led them, always, to the right place, to a puzzle she, Michael, and Arabeth had solved. To the hologram in the biodome. To the seeds hidden in the books in the attic. To Fuzzy's locket at the boulders.

Oh, if only this acorn would help me find the strength to stay alive! To see my family and friends again.

Michael, Arabeth, Willie and Zarek appeared before her. She could hear them calling her name.

"Ruth. Ruth."

She held the acorn in her hand. She would not die now. Fuzzy needed her, and so did the others. Her mother, her father. She had important things to say and do for the future. She was a Rainwalker! With all her power, she thrust herself upward.

Emerging from the water, gasping for air, her lungs burning for oxygen, Ruth saw the same boulder she'd just hit. Why, she realized, her dream couldn't have lasted more than a few seconds. She thrashed her arms and legs about, and the water swept her around the boulder toward a large tree limb hanging out over the swirling water ahead of her. "Grab me," the tree seemed to be saying. "You have the strength." She aimed herself toward the overhanging limb. Directly in front of her, two branches reached out in a Y, reminding her of open arms waiting to embrace her.

Ruth reached the Y and threw her arms up over it, clutching the acorn in her hand, and wedged herself into the forked area between the two branches. The force of the water swept her legs under the limb, almost pulling her off and away. She squeezed the acorn and a surge of strength flooded through her. Yanking herself upward, Ruth flopped face down across the tree, swinging her legs up onto it.

The sharp edges of the tree's bark poked Ruth's cheeks as she pressed her face against it, sobbing with relief at something solid underneath her. Through her tears, she gazed down at the raging water, rushing beneath the tree limb, spraying her with mist. She inhaled the tree's musky smell, filling her lungs with air and its sweet scent. She relaxed. She could rest now. She was alive.

She closed her eyes, tears streaming down her face, joining the water on the bark.

Something scratched at Ruth's hand. She opened her eyes to find a squirrel, chattering at her. She looked at the water rushing toward them and screamed. A giant mass of branches, mud, and debris was headed straight for her.

CHAPTER FORTY
FOUND

Ruth felt paralyzed, staring at the swiftly moving pile. Far away, she heard a voice.

"Ruth! Give me your hand. Now! Please!"

She raised her head, trying to focus on a shape in front of her. "Michael," she whispered and stuck out her hand.

He grabbed it and pulled her forward. "Hang on!"

Her knees scraped on the bark as he yanked her off the tree limb. They fell backwards onto the muddy ground. Only few seconds passed before the mound of debris slammed into the tree limb, heaping up along its side, until the whole pile slowly fell over the top and was carried downstream.

Ruth clung to Michael's arm. He pulled her up, shouting, "Get away from the bank."

Arabeth grabbed her other arm and they helped her into the woods, propping against a tree. Ruth laid her head against it, every beat of her heart thundering through her body. Several raindrops fell onto her cheek from the leaves above her. She wiped them away and looked at Michael and Arabeth, kneeling beside her. "You saved me. I could have been crushed. Or fallen off." She looked around the woods. "Where are we?"

"Rest," said Michael. "You went over the spillway. The top of it broke in the middle. Arabeth grabbed you, but she couldn't hold on."

Ruth closed her eyes for a moment, still disoriented. "I remember," she whispered, opening them again.

Michael rubbed tears from his eyes. "I—I mean we—were so scared," he said, glancing at Arabeth. "We saw you go over. We thought you were dead."

Ruth shivered from the cold as she thought back to those moments. "Millstone was holding me. I tried to get away, but I couldn't move my feet. What happened to him?" She glanced around. "Where are Zarek, and Willie, and Fuzzy? Where's my father? And my mother?" Ruth rubbed her arms, raising her head off the tree. "Did you see it, when we cleaned the screens? The world as if we were looking through a kaleidoscope?"

Arabeth looked at Michael. "I did. The same effect you described when you confronted your father. Very bizarre. There has to be a scientific explanation."

Michael bit his lip. "I don't know anything about a kaleidoscope, but I saw something pretty psychedelic. Like the world through a broken mirror. Only I didn't see myself, I saw the world in front of me in many images."

Arabeth blew out through her lips. "That's it! We all saw the same thing."

Ruth shivered and hugged her legs to her chest, wrapping her dress over them. Her voice quaked. "But Willie and Zarek didn't. Only we Rainwalkers. Could we have been looking into the parallel universe? As we created it?" The thought of being successful filled her with warmth, only to be replaced by the chill of worry over what happened to everyone else.

Arabeth moved beside her, putting her arm around Ruth's shoulders and pulling her close. "I want to believe that. We've got to find out, but first we need to get you warmed up." She pointed towards the rushing water. "Do you have any idea where we are, Ruth? Does this look familiar enough that you can get us back to town?"

Ruth studied their surroundings. She and Willie had been here before. "I think we're at the turn, where the spillway meets the river. If we follow it, we'll come out in town." She tried to stand up. "I'll be all right if you help me for a bit." Her legs were wobbly, but she knew they had to move. She'd find the strength somehow. "We've got to get to town. And find everyone."

CHAPTER FORTY-ONE
NANA'S HOUSE

They followed the river, staying back from the angry waves lapping at its banks, and emerged from the woods onto a street. Water rushed down it, turning yards into lakes and flooding porches on houses at street level. Ruth noticed that no homes had been washed away, and breathed a sigh of relief. The rain turned to a drizzle, and the sky brightened to a dull gray. She hoped the storm was over.

But she wondered what she'd find at her house or Nana's. Hers sat slightly uphill, but Nana's was right at street level. The biodome surely was gone, and the attic had several leaks. Ruth wanted to get home quickly as the three of them joined the people wading through the muddy water. Some carried household items, but others strode aimlessly about as they yelled for neighbors or loved ones.

Ruth rushed up to a woman carrying a small child. "Have you heard anything about the dam?"

"The spillway broke. Which saved the dam," the woman said, stroking the hair of her crying baby. "People think they saw someone go over it, though."

"What about the crest? My father was out there." Ruth held her breath as the woman answered.

"Oh, my dear. I heard several people were injured at the top. Doc Brown is at the Weavers right now. I sure pray that isn't your father."

That was her father! Despite her weak legs, Ruth ran as best she could in the deep water, hoping Michael and Arabeth followed. As she approached her house, she could see that lights shone through the kitchen window and upstairs. She raced up the back steps, water lapping at the bottom step to the kitchen door and slammed the door open.

The kitchen was empty. She raced through to the parlor. Empty as well.

Ruth ran up the steps and into her parents' bedroom. Her father lay on the bed, covered with quilts, his head wrapped in white bandages, and one arm strapped to a board. Her mother sat in a chair beside him, talking to Doc Brown.

"Father. Mother," she cried, and ran to them. Her mother rose and grabbed her, holding her tight.

"Oh, my Ruth! We've been so worried. Doc Brown said people thought you went over the spillway. We feared you were gone." Her mother rubbed Ruth's cheek. "But you're here. Oh!" She buried her head in Ruth's neck. "You're shaking." She grabbed an afghan from a chair and wrapped it around Ruth's shoulders.

Her father looked up at her from the bed, his face bruised and one eye swollen shut. "Ruth," he whispered, "I did the best I could." He brushed his hand across her cheek. Ruth grabbed it and held it on her face.

"The town of Sweetwater owes you, Samuel Weaver." Mr. Decker stood in the bedroom doorway. "You cleared off the crest. Without debris for the water to collect on and pull the crest apart, the dam held." He walked into the room and over to the bed. "And we owe your daughter, too." He nodded to Ruth. "We thought you were swept away."

"People told me," said her father, his chest heaving for breath every few words, "people told me … as they carried me down … some kids … cleaned off the spillway. The fog." He paused, closing his eyes, then opening them. "No one was sure who they were. Was it you and Willie?"

Ruth nodded just as Willie rushed into the room, racing over to Doc Brown. "How's my father?" Willie asked, breathing hard. Ruth's heart leapt. She hadn't seen Willie since he disappeared at the spillway.

Doc Brown smiled. "He's fine, Willie. He could use your help now, though, I'm sure. Parts of the store flooded."

Willie dashed around the bed to her. "You're fine and I'm fine, Ruthie. I'll explain later. I've got to see Father." He rushed out of the room just as Arabeth and Michael appeared in the doorway, followed by Zarek and Fuzzy. The sight of all of them filled Ruth with relief. Everyone was okay. Now that she knew Father was all right and the dam was saved, she could think about the others. She had so many questions.

Doc Brown looked over from the bed. "Who are these people?" He held out his hand to stop them from entering any further. "What are they doing here?"

Ruth's mother ran to Fuzzy. Ruth knew they hadn't seen each other since the day he brought the note to her. They embraced. Doc Brown looked puzzled. Her mother turned. "This is my father, Francis Grundle. He just arrived in town the other day."

Fuzzy nodded to Doc Brown and looked at her father. "Thank you, Samuel. Lizzie explained everything to you?"

Her father answered, his voice weak. "Yes. We can talk tonight. After I rest."

Ruth raced around the bed. "You're fine, Grandfather? You're not hurt?" She grabbed both of his hands, remembering the vines that held him captive.

Fuzzy smiled. "I'm fine, thanks to all of these young people."

"And who *are* all these young people?" asked Mr. Decker. "I don't believe I've seen them around town before." Doc Brown nodded in agreement.

A slight twinkle flashed through Fuzzy's eyes. "Why, these are three wonderful orphans I met on the train coming in the other day."

Ruth stood by Michael. "This is Michael, Arabeth, and Zarek. Along with Willie, we all worked on the spillway."

Fuzzy put his arm around Ruth's mother and her. "Nana would be proud." Ruth's mother smiled.

Her father took a deep breath, wincing as he tried to sit up. "I never thought I'd say this, but your words, Ruth, to me and your mother, made us think ... how we've been these past years." He fell back on to the pillow. "Things will be different."

Ruth's mother walked over to Samuel and patted his hand. "We should go out and let him rest, right?" The doctor nodded. "We can talk in the parlor."

Ruth kissed her father on the cheek and took her mother's hand as they walked down the stairs.

CHAPTER FORTY-TWO
A PARALLEL UNIVERSE CREATED

In the parlor, Ruth's mother sat her on the couch, and covered her with several afghans. She showed Mr. Decker and Doc Brown out, then ran upstairs and brought down some dry clothing for all of them.

After they were all dressed in dry clothing and covered with afghans, Ruth's mother went into the kitchen to make hot tea. Ruth snuggled into the comfort of the afghans and her parents' love. She sighed deeply. Only a few hours ago, she'd wondered if she would see her family ever again. "I've got so many questions. What happened at the spillway?"

Arabeth fiddled with the fringe on her blanket. "I found my secret power, Ruth. I made the branches below Millstone sprout new growth and grow over his feet. I tried to tie him to the ground so you could escape." Her shoulders sank. "But things went wrong. The new growth grew over the top of ...," Arabeth choked back a sob, "of your feet, too, Ruth. And the spillway broke right then." She buried her face in her hands. "I tried to pull you away, but you were stuck. Just like Millstone. I didn't mean for that to happen."

Ruth touched her shoulder. "Arabeth, please don't feel bad. You just saved my life. What happened to him?"

Michael's voice lowered. "We don't know yet." He glanced at Zarek.

"Look, it's okay. You did what you had to do. My father's mean." Zarek scratched his head. "And very tricky. He found a way to survive that fall, I bet." He shot a glance at Arabeth. "Besides, I chose to go with you all, not him."

Arabeth looked away. "You did." She smiled softly at Zarek.

Ruth knew Zarek's decision had been a difficult one. "I survived the fall. If he's alive, someone will find him." She pulled an afghan tighter around her shoulders. "What happened to you and Willie and Fuzzy?"

Zarek leaned forward. "When my father fell, the two men just ran off. I haven't seen them since. Willie and I stayed with Fuzzy—"

Ruth turned to Fuzzy. "We were so worried."

Fuzzy smiled. "Millstone held me captive for quite a while. But I never doubted you all would figure out what to do."

"How did you two find me, anyway?" Ruth asked Arabeth.

"After I lost my grip on you, I crawled to the side. Zarek was there with Fuzzy and Willie, so Michael and I raced alongside the spillway, trying to find you. We saw your head bobbing up and down. The water was moving so fast, we couldn't keep up and we lost sight of you."

Michael added, "But, luckily, there was a bend."

Arabeth continued, tears welling in her eyes. "I saw you there, hanging on that limb."

"We shouted for you," Michael said. "Then we saw the pile of debris heading for you."

Ruth whispered, "The tree called my name, too. Earlier. I swear. And the acorn, it helped me find my strength." She gave them a weak smile. She picked up her poetry book on the seat beside her. "I think I know why my poetry book never got wet. Or dirty. This fabric on the cover. It's from the future, isn't it Grandfather?" Now she knew why she had her own copy of the poetry book. Nana's would have been ruined.

Before he could respond, Michael shouted, "Hagfish fabric, right?" He winked at Arabeth as Fuzzy agreed.

"The Tree is connected to us, no matter what we're doing." Ruth's weariness turned into anticipation and excitement. "So, were we successful? Did we create a new timeline and save the Tree?"

Fuzzy looked around. "Why, of course. Where do you think you are?"

Ruth and the others looked around the room. "This is it? We're in the parallel universe now?"

"Do you have any idea, Ruth, when it started to form?" Fuzzy's eyes twinkled. "Your words started it. There were clues."

Clues? Ruth thought about the strange kaleidoscope effect. The first time occurred when she confronted her father in the kitchen. "When Father and I had an argument in the kitchen, I saw the world differently." She fiddled with one of her braids, frowning. "Was that the beginning of the parallel universe?" Suddenly, it became clear to her. "Father didn't help in the original 1896, did he?"

Fuzzy shook his head. "No, he didn't. The crest of the dam was filled with debris. No one helped to remove it. So when the water rose high enough, the debris started washing off, pulling parts of the dam with it, leading to a total collapse."

Ruth jumped up. "My amulet says,'Words are seeds'. And Father said my words made him and Mother think. So,Father helping at the dam started the new universe?"

"Absolutely," exclaimed Fuzzy. "You stood up to him, and changed him and the universe, Ruth. For the better."

Ruth's mother walked into the room, carrying a tray of tea cups and the kettle, smiling. She poured a cup and handed it to Fuzzy. "After what you said to me in Nana's bedroom, I spoke with him. That's the night you had an argument with him. I left, and Samuel came and found me. We talked. You made me see how wrong we've been as parents."

Michael jumped in. "There's more, though. The screens never got cleaned in the original, did they? Because the blueprints weren't found!"

"That's why Michael and I saw the same kaleidoscope effect on the spillway," Arabeth exclaimed.

"Exactly," said Fuzzy. "Those actions helped create the parallel universe. Where the Tree is stronger and the dam is saved from the poor decisions made by the entrepreneurs."

Ruth took out the leaf she'd found with 'Words are seeds' eaten in it by an insect. "Nana told me a parable, about words falling on stone and not growing. Or falling onto soil and sprouting new thoughts." She looked at her mother. "I'm so glad you and Father are like soil."

CHAPTER FORTY-THREE
THE NEXT ADVENTURE

The next day, Ruth sat beside Willie, their backs resting against the Listening Tree, staring up at its canopy, just like they'd done since they were young. "Thanks, Willie, for watching over the seed bank and looking in the attic for more seeds while we go to 1966."

Willie gazed up through the Tree's branches. "It's too bad the biodome got destroyed in the flood. It would have been fun to go down there once in a while. And you may have found all the seeds anyway." He shrugged. "I do wish I could come with you. To the future." He struck at the dirt with his foot. "But Father needs help at the store. He's going to be real busy since the townspeople put him in charge of investigating the Sweetwater Resort Association and their responsibility for the design of the dam." His face lit up. "Besides, I'll be thirteen in one week. Then I'll know if I can rainwalk and I can join you!"

Ruth put her arm around him. "You will." Willie was her best friend. She couldn't imagine the future without him as a Rainwalker. "You're keeping an eye on the Listening Tree. Like we said we always would." She sighed. "It's hard to believe how much our lives have changed in less than a week."

Arabeth and Michael walked over from the passageway between the boulders. Arabeth sat down by Ruth and began fiddling with her Skincom. "No kidding."

Michael brushed his hands together and leaned against the Tree. "Everything looks secure in the seed bank. Arabeth was able to open it. Millstone hasn't been found yet, has he?"

Willie shrugged. "Not that I've heard. Maybe Fuzzy and Zarek will have more information when they get here this morning."

Arabeth stood. "I've changed my mind about Zarek. I didn't trust him or like him. But he told me last night he hopes he can make his dad see how things could be different. Just like you did with your father. That is, if his father is still alive." She bent down by the Listening Tree's roots. "The flood washed this part out. Look how rutted they are." She reached above her. "And the branches on this side are all broken. This looks bad enough. What would the Tree be like if we hadn't saved it from even more damage?"

The bark near Ruth shimmered, the smell of fresh rain wafting over them. Ruth rolled out of the way just as Fuzzy stepped out of the Tree.

"Oh, helium," he exclaimed, crossing his arms as he studied the tree. "We didn't mean to drop in on top of you." He pulled Ruth to her feet.

Arabeth paced in front of him. "Did you find Doctor Millstone? And where is Zarek? Is he coming back?"

The bark on the Tree glistened and shimmered again. Zarek stepped out of the Tree, tapping the side of his head. "That was a rough trip." He grinned when he saw them.

Michael smirked. "Feeling a bit fuzzy, Zarek?" He and Zarek chuckled, as Fuzzy twitched his eyebrows.

Arabeth's lips formed a straight line. "Let's be serious, right? Did you find your father?"

Zarek bit his fingernail. "No. He's not in 2035. Neither are the two men that were here with him. No one's found a body here, have they?" Ruth and Willie shook their heads. "He's alive then. I know it. We just don't know where."

Ruth turned to Fuzzy. "When Mother gave me your note, after Nana died and we found the two lockets, she said a scientist in your lab was after something you found. That scientist is Martin Millstone, isn't he?"

"Right, Ruth. He was a young geneticist in my lab in the 1990s. He discovered the existence of Rainwalkers and spent years figuring out the genetics behind our abilities. Now he wants to use that information for his own genetic research company, Millstone Industries. To create a new world."

Arabeth clapped. "Millstone Industries. The dilapidated sign in the desert."

Fuzzy nodded. "Yes. He first set up a lab in the desert near my experimental Tree there. But that lab was destroyed by a massive haboob. Then he found out I was in Sweetwater and moved his lab here in an effort to sabotage me."

Ruth asked, "But why did you become a science teacher in Sweetwater, Grandfather? Why didn't you hide somewhere?"

"I wanted to be near the Listening Tree while your nana was dying. It comforted me to go there every day. And the Society of Rainwalkers needs each Mother Tree's guardian to be near the tree they're connected to in these perilous times when we're trying to create parallel universes and save the Earth." He patted the Listening Tree. "There's power in connections, you know. Connections with nature and with each other." He took Ruth's hand. "Things don't change, we do. Remember who said that?"

"Thoreau. Nana loved that quote." Suddenly, she wanted to see Nana. Maybe he did, too. "Is it possible we could go back in time and see Nana? Before we go to 1966?"

Fuzzy touched her cheek. "No, my dear, once a parallel universe is created, the old universe is no longer accessible. And we can only move forward in this one, not backward." He wiped a tear from his face. "We have our memories of her." He patted the locket on Ruth's neck and cleared his throat.

"You mean I can't come back here? To my home and my family when we're done?" Ruth looked at Michael and Arabeth, who looked shocked as well. She wasn't sure she wanted to go if she couldn't return. She'd just discovered her family.

"Oh, no." said Fuzzy, putting his arm around her. "You can return to this 1896, certainly. You just can't go back in time from here. The same for the rest of you when we get to your time." The three of them breathed sighs of relief.

Ruth opened her poetry book and brought out a fragment of paper. "Nana gave me this. The day she died." She handed it to Fuzzy.

E and F
Psithurism and Petrichor 1845

He took it. "Ah, 1845. The year we got married. She always said she could smell rain— petrichor—and hear the sound of the wind blowing through leaves—psithurism—when I was about to arrive. They became code words for entrance to the biodome, too."

Zarek turned to Ruth. "Speaking of connections, I talked to Fuzzy about this." He shot a quick glance at Arabeth. "I think I can help you all with my father, make him see the good of working together to save the Earth, not try to conquer it. I'm not giving up on that."

"But how will you help?" asked Ruth.

"I can use the serum to travel with you. I took all that my father made so he can't use it. And I destroyed the computer disc the formula was on. He'd have to get another blood sample from one of you and remake the formula. That'll take time."

Fuzzy paced in front of them, pulling a pencil out from behind his ear and gesturing with it. "That's another reason we must get going to 1966. Before he can try to sabotage us again. And the window connecting this universe to a new 1966 is only open for a limited amount of time before it closes for good."

"Hey, what about me?" asked Willie. "Can I use the serum?"

Fuzzy winked at him. "No need to worry, Willie. I think in one week you'll be just fine."

Zarek put his hand on Willie's shoulder. "And I'm going to stay until you're thirteen. I want to make sure my father isn't here to try to destroy things. I can help you at the store. I am an orphan from the train, remember?" He winked.

"Why, sure, you can help." Willie looked ready to burst with excitement. "Father's always glad to help out an orphan!"

Ruth turned to Fuzzy. "You will go with us, right?"

Fuzzy pulled on his beard. "I'll take you to 1966. But we must replace the Mother Guardian, and we can't seem to find the Guardian of the next oldest Tree on Earth." He scrunched up his lips. "I'll hurry and find him, and then join you. You'll have to be on guard for Millstone, though."

The Mother Guardian had told Ruth Fuzzy would need her strength. Did she mean about finding the new Mother Guardian or being on guard for Millstone?

Footsteps crunched on leaves in the woods nearby. Ruth's mother held Samuel's arm, helping him walk toward the Tree.

"Father! Mother!" Ruth ran to them, her father's arm in a sling.

Her mother took her hand, then turned to Fuzzy, who stood by the Listening Tree. "It's been great to spend some time with you, Father, after all those years you had to stay away. But I know it's time for you all to go."

Fuzzy nodded. "Yes, it is." He turned to Ruth's father. "Samuel, I'm glad I was able to tell you about myself and your daughter. She'll need your support when she comes back from her travels."

Her father smiled. "We'll be here. Where do you go now?"

"Michael, are you ready to get back to 1966?" Fuzzy asked.

"Holy time travel, you bet," Michael exclaimed.

Ruth looked up at the Listening Tree. "It is beautiful, isn't it? And to imagine trees like it around the world. In danger."

Willie asked, "How will we know how you are?"

Ruth turned to Willie, Zarek, and her parents. "Nana said the Trees know." She patted the Tree. "The Listening Tree will help, right, Grandfather? Come here anytime. The Tree will let you know how we are."

A gentle breeze blew through the Listening Tree, sending a cascade of leaves swirling through the air above them, as they said good-bye.

"Amulets ready, everyone?" Fuzzy asked.

Ruth took out her poetry book with the Listening Tree leaf in it and lined up on a root behind the others. She thought of Nana and knew she'd be proud of what they'd accomplished.

Then, in the moment before they rainwalked, she wondered what unimaginable things to believe and do were waiting for her in the future.

About the Author

Kathryn Randall's interest in science and writing began in elementary school. In third grade, she collected rocks, leaves, and seeds, and wrote her first story about life in an anthill. In seventh grade, her biochemist neighbor, witnessing her love for science, gifted her a chromatography column. Kathryn instantly fell in love with experiments and uncovering how our world works. With this love of the scientific process, Kathryn chose a career encouraging curiosity and research among young people.

While developing her writing skills, Kathryn completed three university degrees, worked in academic and industry research labs, raised two daughters, taught middle school science, became a nature storyteller, owned a greenhouse and a small farm, produced maple syrup, conducted forest restoration research in Panama, worked for a nonprofit environmental organization and trained as an art therapist. Across all these adventures, she hoped to one day write stories for young people, inspiring them to be curious about our natural world.

She is thrilled with the publication of *The Listening Tree*, her debut middle grade novel. Kathryn and her husband recently moved to WI from their small farm in PA. When she is not writing, she volunteers at a local nature center, spends time with her grandchildren and bakes anything with cinnamon crumble topping.